Book One in the *I Wish* Series

ELIZABETH LANGSTON

SPENCER
HILL
PRESS

Spencer Hill Press

Contact: Spencer Hill Press, PO Box 247, Contoocook, NH 03229, USA

Please visit our website at www.spencerhillpress.com

First Edition: November 2014.
Elizabeth Langston
I Wish : a novel / by Elizabeth Langston – 1st ed.
p. cm.
Summary:
A genie grants a month of wishes to a struggling teenage girl.

The author acknowledges the copyrighted or trademarked status and trademark owners of the following wordmarks mentioned in this fiction: Advanced Placement (AP), Barbie, Eagle Scout, Ford Focus, Gatorade, Godiva, *Gone with the Wind*, Google, iPad, JELL-O, McDonald's, Mustang, Pez, *National Geographic*, *The Twilight Zone*, *The Washington Post*, Wikipedia

Cover design by Lisa Amowitz
Interior layout by Marie Romero
Image credit: Svetlana Prikhnenko

ISBN 978-1-939392-23-7 (paperback)
ISBN 978-1-939392-24-4 (e-book)

Printed in the United States of America

To the original Lacey—
thank you for daring to take a different path

Also by Elizabeth Langston

The *Whisper Falls* Series
(Spencer Hill Press)
Whisper Falls
A Whisper in Time
Whispers from the Past

1

Innocent and Ordinary

I skipped the pep rally that day. No one would notice, and I could use the extra hour.

Apparently, a lot of my classmates had the same idea. There was a traffic jam at the side door, dozens of us streaming out, smiling silently as we headed off on our separate paths. My route home took me through the senior parking lot, down a shaded alley, and along the town square—each step changing the school-me into the home-me.

I rounded the corner onto our street and leveled a critical eye on our house, a grumpy old pile of bricks baking on an overgrown yard. *Mowing* needed to move higher on my to-do list. I thumped up the front steps, across the wooden porch, and in through the door.

It was dim and cool in the foyer, way cooler than we could afford. Yet for a brief moment, I closed my eyes and let myself enjoy it.

Okay, enough. I reached for the thermostat as I shouted, "Mom?"

There was no response. I hesitated, wondering whether I should hunt her down, when I saw that the door leading to the attic—and my bedroom—stood ajar.

Strange. I charged up the narrow staircase.

When I entered my room, I could tell she'd been in here. Maybe it was a sixth sense, or a lingering whiff of her unwashed body. Either way, I knew.

I also knew why.

Rushing to my desk, I yanked the top drawer open. Empty. This morning, it had held an envelope full of twenty-dollar bills. Now, nothing.

My heart rocketed into overdrive. "Mom?" I took the stairs two at a time and skidded to a halt in the doorway of the kitchen. "Where's my money?"

She sat at the end of the table, hands wrapped around a mug of coffee, hair clinging to her cheeks in dark, greasy strands. "Gone."

"Did you take it?"

"Yes."

"All of it?"

"Yes. I gave it to Henry."

Wow. "You gave Henry *my* three hundred dollars?"

"Yes."

Okay, deep breath. An eight-year-old boy didn't need that kind of cash. She must be confused again. "Why?"

"So he can play soccer."

I repeated the sentence silently, one word at a time, waiting for the concept to sink in. Soccer? "Henry knows we can't afford to waste that much money on a game."

"He didn't ask. The coach did." She hunched lower over the table. "The team wants Henry back. He was one of their stars last year."

"You could've said no."

"I didn't want to. He loves to play."

I swallowed hard against the panic scalding my throat. After nearly a year of her uncontrolled stupidity, I should be used to it by now. But no. "Mom. I haven't paid the electric bill or bought groceries this week. Do you understand?"

"Yes."

I slumped against the doorframe for support. Had she looked at our bank statements recently?

Of course not. In the ten months since my stepfather's death, it had become a habit for her to leave everything to me. "Mom, I don't think you realize how much trouble we're in."

"We'll manage." She tightened the belt on her bathrobe.

"We're not managing now." I pressed fists to my eyes, fighting back the feeling of being overwhelmed. "Who can I contact to get the money back?"

"The fee is non-refundable." Her voice had thickened. "We have to find a way to let him do this, Lacey. He's good."

"He won't be if he's starving." I gripped the doorframe, my fingernails scraping off flecks of paint, and tried really hard to pretend that I didn't want to slap her. If I didn't raise two hundred dollars by tomorrow, we'd have the power to the house turned off, a horrible thought with September temperatures in the nineties. "What do you want me to sell this time?"

She wrapped her arms around her waist and laid her head on the table. "What's left?"

"Great Grandma's silver. Your sewing machine."

"No, neither one of those," she said, tears squeezing from closed eyes. "What else?"

"Aunt Myra's candlesticks."

"I never liked Aunt Myra," she whispered.

I stared at her still form. Depression hovered around her like a fog. "Don't worry. I'll take care of it." And I would somehow, just like she'd counted on. I grabbed the car keys, rummaged in the closet for the candlesticks, and headed out the door.

When I pulled into the flea-market parking lot, the Carolina sun had already driven away most of the shoppers. I hurried past the clothing stalls and the tacky reproduction furniture and walked straight to my destination. Madame

Noir's Collectibles sweltered in its prime location at the intersection of the two main aisles.

"Hi, Madame."

"Lacey Linden, it's good to see you." She sat in an extra-wide lawn chair under a huge umbrella, too fat to budge often from her spot, which didn't matter because people came to her. "What have you got for me today, sugar?"

Much as I hated the reason that I was here, haggling with Madame was always fun. I held out the brass candlesticks.

Her gaze flicked over them. "Hmmph." She lifted first one, then the other, weighing them in her hands. "Business is slow."

She was trying to psych me out. It wasn't going to work. I forced myself not to smile. "You won't have any trouble selling these." Madame had several "special clients," a mysterious group of people who never came to the flea market yet always had plenty of money for the antiques she found for them there. It was good for me; her special clients had bought enough stuff from my house to keep the creditors away for months.

Madame took a sip from her glass of sweet tea and grunted. "I don't know."

I said nothing. It was best to leave her alone until she made up her mind.

"There's a basket of stuff in my station wagon, sugar. Do me a favor and fetch it."

It was a ploy to get me out of the way while she considered a price. Cool. The more she thought, the more I'd get. "Sure."

I circled the stall to where Madame had parked her car. It looked sort of like a hearse—big, black, and muddy with rusted tire wells. When I opened the back door, the smell of stale fries and ripe banana peel puffed out. Holding my breath, I ducked into the car, hoisted a huge wicker basket, and kicked the door shut. "Are you going to unload this stuff now?" I asked.

"No, sugar. You can."

I set the basket on the display table and considered her latest discoveries. On top were two silver handheld mirrors, the kind of collectibles Madame sold in bulk. The third object resembled a squarish shoebox made of inlaid wood. I placed the badly scratched box on the table, released the catch, and lifted the hinged lid. Half of the inside held a small compartment, lined in golden velvet. The other half? A miniature winter scene.

Wow.

Chills whispered along my spine. A tiny Victorian couple skated across a frozen lake framed by inch-high, snow-dusted evergreens. Snowdrifts formed along a cobblestone street which curved past shops and a church. "What is this thing?" I asked.

"It's a music box." Her eyes narrowed speculatively.

I'd never owned a music box before—had never wanted to—but I couldn't help coveting this one. Unable to contain my curiosity, I twisted the key at the back and listened to a few bars of "Silent Night, Holy Night."

It was perfection.

A long-forgotten memory tickled in a corner of my brain. My dad and I had traveled somewhere up north for Christmas. Michigan or Massachusetts—I couldn't remember any more. It'd been incredibly cold. He'd bundled me up and taken me out to a frozen pond—just the two of us.

The tall, handsome Marine laces up my little-girl skates and helps me onto the ice. "Are you ready, princess?"

"Yes, Daddy," I say, clutching at him with mittened hands. "Don't let go."

"I won't let you fall. I promise." He skates backwards, pulling me along. And it's so much fun that I forget to be afraid. We circle around and around, until we laugh so hard that we have to stop—

"Yoo hoo, Lacey!" Madame's drawl brought me rudely back to the present. "What do you think? Are you going to buy something for a change?"

"Not a chance." I adored it, but no way could I let her know. "It's too beat up." Disinterest, feigned or not, played a role in any negotiation.

"Are you sure? I could let you have it for thirty bucks."

That was thirty more than I had. "I don't think so." I closed the lid and turned my back on the box. "What will you give me for the candlesticks?"

"One hundred fifty."

I gritted my teeth to keep my expression neutral. That wasn't close enough to what they were worth. "Two hundred."

"One seventy."

Maybe the utility company would take one hundred seventy dollars as a down payment and I could owe them the rest, something they were used to from us. It was just hard to know when they'd run out of patience.

The music box tinkled two more notes.

I turned and looked down at it. Was it trying to remind me of its presence? Did it want me to take it home?

I needed to get a grip. A music box did not communicate with the random humans who stopped by to admire it. No matter how perfect it was.

Oh, who was I fooling? For the past year, I'd only thought about our *needs*. It had been so long since I'd allowed myself to want anything that I'd forgotten how it felt, and I wanted the box. Badly. I couldn't leave it behind. Before I could think through the words, I blurted, "One hundred seventy-five and throw in the music box."

"Deal."

Even though it was Friday night, my mother had gone to bed early, claiming to be worn out by her day of doing nothing. When I got home from my shift at the bookstore around nine, she was snoring lightly. I shut her door with a quiet click.

"Lacey?" my brother called from his room.

I stopped and looked in. "Hey, little man. Do you need something?"

He sat cross-legged on his bed, wearing his father's Carolina Panthers football jersey instead of pajamas. "Do you mind that I joined the soccer team again?"

"I'm not thrilled about it."

Henry's face fell. "Sorry."

"I'm sorry too. I hate to say 'no' so much, but we don't have the money for extras. Okay?"

He nodded, his lower lip trembling. "Mom said you'd figure it out."

She had more confidence than I did, but I couldn't let Henry know that. "Mom's right. I will." I stepped farther into the room and gave him a good imitation of a smile. It was impossible to stay upset with Henry around. "Do you know what you can do to pay me back?"

His eyes grew big. "What?"

When he looked at me like that, half-scared and half-hopeful, my heart just melted. "Be the best player on the team."

He blinked. "That's easy. I already am."

"Uh-huh. And the most modest." I kissed him on the top of his head and left, turning off his lamp as I went.

Restlessly, I wandered into the kitchen and stared out the back window, my gaze landing on the detached one-car garage. It sat in the shadows, a lonely, padlocked hulk. My stepfather had converted it into an art studio, a place where he'd coaxed masterpieces from bits of wood.

When I'd returned from the flea market that afternoon, I'd stored the music box in the studio out of desperation. It made more sense than bringing it into the house, especially since I didn't want to explain to my mom why I got it when I didn't understand that myself.

The box awaited me now, its appeal stronger than my reluctance to spend any time in Josh's studio. I left the house, inserted an old brass key into the padlock, and stepped inside. After flicking on the light switch, I latched the door behind me and then crossed the space, my clogs clomping loudly on the dusty concrete floor.

My new treasure sat on the rough worktable, its flaws clearly visible in the stark pool of light cast by a single bulb. In spite of the gunk and gouges on the lid, this music box would be a thing of beauty once restored. I'd be able to sell it for a good profit. If I could bear to give it away.

Parking my butt on a stool, I dabbed oil soap on a rag and scrubbed the dirtiest spot.

It quivered. At least I thought it did. I stopped and watched.

Nothing moved. Must've been my imagination.

I lifted the lid. The box quivered harder. I slid off the stool and backed up a step. Was there something inside the box?

While I debated the possibilities, a wisp of smoke curled from the steeple of the tiny church.

Fire? I looked frantically for the extinguisher. By the time I'd grabbed it, the smoke had billowed and swirled into a tall column—thick, fast, and dense. It rotated its way to the edge of the worktable where, as suddenly as it had come, the smoke cleared.

In its place stood a guy. A hot guy. Amazingly hot, like one of those unsmiling male models on the cover of a teen magazine.

Adrenaline shuddered through me. Had I really just seen…?

No. Not possible. He must've come in some other way while I was paying attention to the smoke. Not that it mattered how he got in there. I was still alone with him.

I brandished the extinguisher like a baseball bat and demanded with fake courage, "Who are you? What do you want?"

He fixed an unblinking green stare on me, his hands clasped behind his back. "My name is Grant, and I don't want anything." He inclined his head. "I'm here to serve you."

His claim, uttered quietly in a delicious British accent, momentarily distracted me from my fear. "*Serve* me?"

"Indeed. You're perfectly safe. I am at your disposal."

Not the approach I would've expected from the average home intruder. This guy seemed more intent on being arrogant than violent. But maybe that's how he got his victims to let down their guard. "How did you get in here?"

"Perhaps we might continue this conversation after you've lowered your weapon."

"Not a chance. Tell me how you got through a locked door."

"*You* brought me in."

"Really? I don't remember that at all."

He gestured toward the worktable. "Did you purchase the music box this afternoon and bring it home?"

Weird. How'd he know that? "Yeah."

"I live inside the church."

"Uh-huh." Grant was at least six feet tall. The church was the size of a blueberry. "It seems small for you."

His lips twitched. "I manage."

Arrogant *and* crazy. "Are you on drugs or something?"

"Is that how I come across to you?"

"No, you come across like a jerk." I lowered the extinguisher. It was heavy and, besides, he looked as if he could take me with or without the weapon. "Let's try this again. What exactly are you?"

"My official title is 'Benevolent Supernatural Being.'"

"Right." I took a not-so-subtle step behind the worktable, determined to keep something sturdy between us. "Do you have any identification?"

"Naturally." A card, about the size of a driver's license, appeared between his fingers. He set it on the worktable and pushed it toward me. I waited until he'd backed away to grab it.

Somebody had spent some major money on this card. It had his photo, name, and title, plus a website for his organization. "You belong to a league?"

"Indeed."

There was a sparkly watermark-type seal in one corner. When I brushed it with my thumb, it gave me a faint jolt of static electricity. I dropped the card on the tabletop and pushed it back. "Okay, let's pretend for a moment that you're for real. What does a Benevolent Supernatural Being do?"

"Whatever you wish." He bowed.

"You're joking."

"I'm afraid not." His voice was clipped. "Mistress, it would speed matters along if you would proceed with telling me today's wish."

Mistress?

Okay, I was hallucinating. Yes, that had to be it. Malnutrition had finally won.

No longer trusting my legs to hold me up, I lowered myself onto a stool and considered the facts. Smoke. Big guy. Little church. "Are you a genie?"

"If it helps you abandon your skepticism, 'genie' works."

Why couldn't he just give a simple answer? "You don't look like a genie."

"Palazzo pants and sequined vests don't cut it in the United States."

This from a guy wearing sweats in the middle of a North Carolina heat wave. "On TV, genies live in lamps."

"Some do. I prefer a more livable space." He watched me with studied calm. "If you're done with the interview, I'd like to get down to business."

Oh, yeah, somebody definitely had an attitude. "What business?"

"The wish?"

I frowned at the music box. It looked so innocent and ordinary. Yet it had attracted my attention—and it came with a genie. Which meant...no. What was I thinking? He had to have broken in. I glanced at the window and it was latched, the lock rusted shut. Of course. I shook my head. "Sorry, but I can't believe any of this."

"Do you think it's a prank?"

"No."

"Are you prone to insanity?"

My gaze snapped back to his. That got closer to the truth than I liked. "I hope not," I said through stiff lips.

His eyes narrowed. "Perhaps you would like me to offer proof."

"Yeah, you could give that a shot."

"Very well. Tell me an object in your bedroom, and I'll summon it."

My mind raced around my room, considering objects and then discarding them before settling on a few select items in the top drawer of my dresser. "My *favorite* piece of jewelry."

There was a faint curl of his lip. Something clinked on the table in front of me. I glanced down and there it was—my dad's class ring.

"Convinced now, Mistress?"

Wow. I snatched up the ring and jammed it into my pocket. That trick was hard to reason away. "You cannot call me *Mistress*," I mumbled as I tried to ignore the chills streaming down my body.

"Certainly. Whatever you think best." He inclined his head again. "Your first wish?"

As incredible as this conversation was, it would be amazing if it turned out to be real. It would mean so much to my family—to me—if we could get even a few of the things we needed. "How many wishes do I get? Three?"

He shook his head. "One per day for the next month."

"Thirty?"

"Indeed."

"Why so many?"

He gave a half-smile. "Recent policy changes."

Thirty wishes! "All I have to do is ask for something, and you'll give it to me?"

"Within guidelines, yes."

What should I ask for first? There were so many things to choose from. Clothes for Henry. Food coming from somewhere besides a can. Appliances doing what they were supposed to. And I could add a gazillion other items to a wish list if I gave it some thought.

Under the circumstances, it was probably best to start with something simple yet flexible. Like cash. "I wish for three hundred dollars."

"Your wish is not within guidelines."

It felt like I'd been body-slammed. "And why is that?"

"I cannot break any laws. Robbing a bank is out of the question."

"You can't blink and make the money appear?" Like he had with my dad's ring.

"No."

How naïve could I be? For an instant, I'd allowed myself to believe in miracles, like Grant the Benevolent Supernatural Being was an answer to a prayer I couldn't recall praying.

A hot fullness clogged my throat and stung my eyes. I had to get out of there before I lost it in front of this jerk. I slid off the stool, grabbed a flashlight, and crossed to the studio door.

"Mistress?"

I hesitated, a hand on the doorknob. "What?" The word came out on a croak.

"Are you retiring for the night?"

"Yes."

"What about today's wish?"

The guy was relentless. I had to say something or he wouldn't let up. "I wish that you would leave."

There was a puff of blue smoke. A faint hiss. And he was gone.

Status Report #1
Friday's Wish: Pass

Dear Boss,

I was discovered today.

This assignment is unexpected. Haven't I reached my quota of self-centered American teens yet?

My new mistress has significant attitude issues. She burned her first wish when I refused to give her cash.

I am disappointed. I thought this would be the last assignment before my promotion. I don't see how this case will be challenging enough to earn the qualifications I lack.

Naturally, I will strive to do my best.

Humbly submitted,
Grant

2

A Whisper of Reluctance

*I*t was a lovely dream, all shimmery and golden, full of sequined vests and British male models.

The "Lacey, wake up" didn't fit at all. I groaned and rolled over.

"Please, Lacey? We've gotta go."

I opened one eye. One very angry eye. A little boy, visible from the neck up, peered anxiously at me from a few inches away. "It's Saturday morning, Henry. Are you bleeding?"

"No."

"Do you want to be?"

"No." He giggled.

The second eyelid fluttered open reluctantly. "What do you want?"

"My soccer practice starts in ten minutes."

I groaned louder and wiggled deeper into my soft, cozy bed. "Can't Mom take you?"

His smile died. "Her tummy hurts again."

"Of course it does." I hated soccer. I hated that my brother was playing soccer. I hated that, because of soccer, the Linden-Jones house would go meatless for the rest of September. Yet here I was, about to drive my brother to soccer practice. There was no justice. "Okay, little man. Let me throw on some shorts, and I'll meet you at the car."

We were late. Only six minutes, but Henry acted like we'd missed an audience with the Queen. "Coach is going to make me run an extra lap."

"Sorry."

"You don't sound sorry." He got out of the car and gestured at me. "Come on. You're supposed to sign me in."

"Right." Henry had left off that part of the deal—where I had to get out of the car looking like crap. I shut off the engine, slammed the door behind me, and followed him to where a group of little boys clustered in a circle around a much taller guy. They fell silent as we approached.

Henry hung his head. "My sister overslept."

"I did not…" My voice trailed away when I got a good glimpse of the coach standing in the group's center. Eli Harper—the gorgeous, injured star of our high school's soccer team. "Hey."

"Hey." He smiled in surprise. "You're Henry's sister?"

"Yeah." I pasted on an answering smile. Under normal circumstances, I wouldn't mind running into Eli. These circumstances were not normal. I couldn't have looked worse had I tried. Sloppy T-shirt over shorts. Ratty slippers. No makeup. And tangled brown hair that desperately needed a brushing.

"Great." He limped closer, a clipboard in hand. "He has to be signed in and out for each practice."

"Sure," I said, taking the pen he offered and scribbling my name.

Henry darted over, eying the huge coffee stain on my shirt before frowning up at me. "You know each other?"

"Yes." I hated that I looked so bad I'd embarrassed Henry, but he could've warned me. "Eli and I take English together."

"Whatever." Henry pointed at the clipboard. "If you're done now, you can leave."

I handed back the pen and turned to go.

"Practice ends at ten," Eli said, shifting his weight off the leg that was encased in a big black knee brace. "Does Henry need a ride home?"

"No, thanks." This time, my smile was genuine. I'd been in a lot of classes with Eli since he'd moved to Magnolia Grove our freshman year. Eli Harper was one of those guys that seemed to make everything better when he walked in a room. He was nicer than the average popular guy, really smart, and super confident—in a good way. I still missed the three hundred bucks, but it did make me feel better to know that my brother would be spending time with someone like Eli. "I can pick him up."

"Okay. See you." He backed up a couple of steps before returning to the team.

"Right." I watched Eli join his players and then caught the eye of my brother, who gestured for me to vanish.

When I got home, I paused outside the back window and stared in. My mother sat motionless at the kitchen table, her head cradled on one arm, the other extended toward her ever-present coffee mug. This was going to be another of her bad days.

It was hard to pinpoint when I'd given up hope that she would pull herself together—that me being in charge would be a temporary thing. But too many months had passed with nothing changing, except somewhere along the way I'd stopped feeling sympathy for her. Or anger. It was easier to not feel anything where my mother was concerned because then I could never be let down.

Right after my stepfather's accident, I tried to get her professional help. We'd shown up at a free clinic all hopeful and eager, until the social workers began to direct their questions at Henry and me.

"How are you two kids doing? Is there a responsible adult living in the household?"

"We're fine," I'd said. "Thank you for asking."

We left and never went back.

I didn't want to be around my mother when she was like this, so I detoured to the studio. I might as well see if my hallucination had stuck around.

It was already getting stuffy inside. I left the door ajar and switched on the ceiling fan. The air began to circulate.

In the center of the worktable waited the music box, illuminated by a sunbeam. I called out, "Grant?"

No wisps. No quivers. Just an inanimate object doing what inanimate objects do. Nothing.

I concentrated. How could I get my imagination to conjure him up again?

Scrubbing did the trick last night. Presumably it would work again today. I scrubbed.

The tornado swirled and then evaporated, leaving a sleepy Grant standing before me, sweatpants on but nothing else.

Wow. My reaction was real enough. I could hardly tear my gaze away from his upper body. Obviously, Benevolent Supernatural Beings worked out in their off-hours. He looked so good it was distracting. "Could you put a shirt on?"

"You didn't give me much warning." He crossed his arms over his chest. "Do you know what time it is?"

"I do."

"And?"

"It's eight-thirty."

He growled in the back of his throat. "Might we have this conversation later?"

"No, we might not." I held back a smile. Genies liked to sleep in? That was adorable.

"Very well, Mistress. May I at least dress properly?"

"Please."

Once Grant had disappeared, I locked my gaze on the music box, uncertain what to do but totally certain what *not* to do—which was look around. I hadn't entered the studio during daylight hours in nearly a year. Not since the day my stepfather died.

I didn't want to see his things. Didn't want to know which of his projects had been completed and which had not. Every jar of paint or stiffened brush had a memory attached. Josh's laughter seemed to shimmer in the sunlight streaming through the windows.

As if drawn by a magnet, my gaze flicked to the makeshift desk in the corner and skittered away. Too late. The image was already burned on my brain. Debris cluttered the rough plywood top. Scraps of paper lay scattered about, with numbers scrawled in my stepfather's handwriting. Tacked up on a corkboard were photos of Henry, photos of me, and a childish drawing of red tulips in a purple pot, inscribed "To Josh, Love Lacey" in precise block letters.

I turned around and stood in the doorway, my back to the studio.

"Mistress?"

I glanced over my shoulder. He was close enough for me to catch a whiff of pine-scented soap. His dark hair was still wet from the shower, and his face was freshly shaved. Too bad he was wearing those dorky white sweats for the second day in a row. "What?"

He released a noisy breath. "Have you looked long enough yet?"

What a jerk. "I'm curious, Grant. Is this your first gig?"

"No, I've worked in this position for nearly two years. Why?"

"If you're this hostile all the time, it's a wonder you're still in the business."

"Hostile?" He gave a confused shake of the head.

I pressed on before he could say more. "I need to know your guidelines."

There was a long pause. I could see the urge to debate flickering in his eyes for a brief moment before he looked away. He snapped his fingers and a scroll appeared. "Here you are, Mistress."

I straightened, took the parchment paper, and unrolled it. At the top, in flowing calligraphy, was written:

The League of Benevolent Supernatural Beings Guidelines for Wishes

"Why do BSBs have a league?"

"We must. You'd be shocked at how abusive some human masters can be."

"No, I wouldn't." I continued to read.

Wishes must comply with the laws of God, the laws of nature, and the laws of the country in which the master or mistress resides.

Wishes must be completed on the same day requested.

Wishes may not be repeated.

Wishes must be humanly possible.

The rules surprised me, especially the last one. "Humanly possible? As in *no* magic?"

"None."

"The scroll appeared out of nowhere."

"I can't use magic for *your* wishes. I can use it for my own."

"Nice." I allowed the scroll to curl up and then tapped it against my chin. The things my family needed most would cost a lot of money, which I did not have and Grant would not counterfeit. In fact, the rules disqualified just about every wish I'd thought of since last night. "What are you good at?"

He sighed heavily. "Whatever you require."

"You know how to do everything humanly possible?"

"I am an expert at many things, and what I don't know already, I can learn."

I stepped back into the studio, my brain humming. It could be cool to have someone around who was able to do whatever I wanted, like a multi-talented handyman, except Grant was the kind who disappeared in a puff of smoke. Since everything in the house was either broken or wearing out, it would be hard to know where to start.

I handed him the scroll. It dissolved into a lavender mist the instant his fingers touched it, which was fun to watch but also reminded me how bad my luck was. Why couldn't I have found a league-less genie?

Someday I'd want to know more about his so-called powers. But not now. It was time to give him something to do. *Within guidelines.* Something I couldn't—or wouldn't—do myself. "I wish you would clean up the studio."

"The space we're standing in?"

"Yes."

He scowled. "That's all?"

"Why? Is my wish beneath you?"

His lips pressed together. He wanted to speak but something held him back.

"Go ahead, Grant. You can be honest."

"I've rarely received a wish so pedestrian that I felt the need to check my understanding."

"Sorry to be a disappointment." It was time to get out of here. I headed for the door.

"Pardon me, Mistress, but would you care to provide more explicit instructions?"

Sure, I would. Like, maybe we should leave the desk exactly the way Josh left it. Or maybe we should forget about sweeping away the dusty footprints from his boots. And those wads of paper that had missed the garbage can? They could stay right where they were.

"Whatever you decide is okay with me." I resisted the urge to look around the studio one final time. It would be perfect when I returned. Grant seemed like the kind of guy who didn't make mistakes.

But I couldn't help feeling a twinge of sadness, a whisper of reluctance to have the place change, as if cleaning it up would scrub away the last remnants of Josh. I could only hope my mother didn't come out here any time soon, because I didn't want to deal with her tears. Although, now that I thought about it, tears might be a nice change from her more typical ghost-hood.

I hung onto the doorframe, facing away from Grant, facing away from the room. "We need to find something else for you to call me."

"What do you suggest?"

"Lacey."

"I'm not permitted to call my mistress by her given name. It compromises the proper level of detachment."

Predictable, but I'd come prepared. "How about 'Boss?'"

"I already have a boss. What about 'Madam?'"

"'Madam' is as bad as 'Mistress.'" Seeking inspiration, I surveyed the yard. The grass needed mowing. The bushes needed trimming.

Okay, focus. Another term for person-in-charge. "How about 'Chief?'"

A long pause. "Chief works."

Status Report #2
Saturday's Wish: Garage Cleaning

Dear Boss,

I cleaned a garage. It contained a jumbled mess, heavily coated by a layer of dust. Evidently, my mistress hasn't bothered to clean the space for several months. I don't understand the point in doing so now, unless it was her attempt to test my resolve.

In addition to being rude and argumentative, my mistress has squandered one wish and displayed an acute lack of imagination with the second. Indeed, she spent more time discussing how she wants to be addressed than on her expectations for the garage.

I cannot believe that Lacey Linden and I are a good match. Why did you send me?

Humbly submitted,
Grant

3

Exact Opposite

I put off checking on the studio until Sunday morning.
Even so, I hesitated outside the door, frowning at my toenails, bracing myself. I should've given Grant more specific instructions. What if he'd screwed up? What if he'd thrown out important reminders of Josh?

I twisted the knob.

It was like stepping back in time. Everything had been organized into its appropriate places. Blocks of wood had been stacked on shelves in neat rows. Tools and paintbrushes no longer littered the countertops. The floor had been swept. And the mustiness was gone. I'd forgotten the way it used to smell in here—like orange and turpentine—as if I could peer around the table and find my stepfather crouching on the floor, buffing one of his carvings.

"What do you think, Chief?"

I blew out a relieved breath. It was all good. The cleaning hadn't stripped us of Josh. It had just dusted away the sadness.

"It's amazing," I said and looked around to find Grant reclining against the desk. "Thank you."

He gave a curt nod.

"Did it take very long?"

"Yes." He pushed away from the desk. "Let me show you what I uncovered. I wasn't sure what to do with them."

I joined him at the worktable where a dozen long, narrow strips of wood lay in a pile. The sight made my heart squeeze. "It's the raw material for picture frames. My stepfather was an artist, only he couldn't make a living with his carvings, so he built picture frames for steadier income."

There was a hitch in Grant's breathing, and it seemed as if he wanted to ask a question. Yet he held back, just as he had yesterday. We had to get past this. "If you and I are going to be working together for the next month, you have to get over the fake subservient thing, and just ask me what you need to know. If I don't want to answer, I won't. Okay?"

"Yes."

"So what's the question?"

"Where is your stepfather?"

I should have been used to this one, but it never got easier. I looked away. "He died last November."

Beside me, the genie stiffened. "My sympathies."

I nodded as I counted the strips. There was a decent amount of wood here. Josh must've had big plans. Funny, I hadn't noticed this among his receipts. I spun around and looked at the shelves on the rear wall. The correct supplies were available. Nails. Glue. And all the right tools. "Do you know how to make frames?"

"Not at present, but I can learn." His narrowed gaze made a methodical sweep of the supplies, as if he was cataloging the various items for future reference. "I'll search online if you'll show me where your computer is."

The laptop had been one of the first things I'd sold. It covered our groceries for a couple of months. "We don't own a computer."

"Indeed?" His gaze snapped to mine. "I thought American teens viewed them as a requirement."

"Not this one."

He frowned. "How do you complete your school assignments?"

"I go to the library." I studied the woodpile, estimating the volume. It held enough raw material to build forty or more frames. Five-by-sevens would yield the highest profit margin. "If *you* make the frames, am *I* allowed to sell them?"

"As long as frame-selling is legal in this state, I don't see why not."

I did some quick calculations and did a mental happy dance at the amount. There would be enough to pay off the utility bill, buy some decent groceries, and have a little left over to apply to our credit card debt. "What is your cut?"

"I don't get a cut. I'm here—"

"Yeah, yeah. To serve." The grudging way he said it made it sound like the exact opposite. "I wish to turn this pile of wood into picture frames."

He turned to face me, arms crossed over his chest, an eyebrow raised in question. "Is there anything else I need to know?"

"Such as?"

"Do the frames need to be painted or stained?"

"No." Wow, this was great. He was inviting me to think bigger, and I would. I knew who I might be able to sell them to, and she liked to stain her own. But that didn't mean that the frames had to be plain. "Carved would be nice, though," I said with a challenging smile, "if you can figure that out."

There was no change in the marble-smooth beauty of his face. "I will."

Status Report #3
Sunday's Wish: Crafting Frames

Dear Boss,

Forgive me. It was inappropriate to question your decision to assign me here. I accept that your wisdom is superior to mine. Of course, I shall take your suggestions. Until my judgment skills mature, I shall rely on my patience instead.

Today's request allowed me to exercise more creativity. It was a pleasure, although it appears that Chief intends to sell the frames for profit.

Why didn't you mention her stepfather's death? Are there other surprises in store for me? I can't be as effective if I don't know what I'm facing.

Humbly submitted,
Grant

4

Living on the Edge

Magnolia Grove High School looked like an old brick prison minus the barbed-wire fence, which made the inside completely unexpected. Five years ago, they'd gutted the building and started over. Now it was clean and cool and bristling with technology. We had the best facilities money could buy.

The faculty? Not so much.

Our school administration had a frightening tendency to hire anyone with a pulse and a college degree. The poster child was my teacher in AP U.S. History. Mr. Jarrett was not much older than we were, convinced of his own hotness, and unapologetically mean. He amused himself by verbally abusing students, and he was careful to choose kids who had plenty to be teased about and little likelihood of fighting back.

He'd made a mistake with the new girl in our APUSH class.

"Excuse me," he said, stopping before her desk. "Electronic devices aren't allowed during class."

"Mine is." She looked up from her iPad. "Didn't you get the memo?"

Some of the braver students snickered.

"No, I didn't get the memo."

"You will." The snorts of laughter grew louder, masking her next words from all but me and the teacher. "I have a lot of accommodations. One of them is using a tablet," she said with a patient smile.

She had accommodations? I shot her a curious look. Those were given to people with learning disabilities, weren't they? Yet she was openly admitting to them *and* taking an AP class? That was interesting.

Mr. Jarrett's lips pinched, a sure sign that he was annoyed. He waited until the noise died down before saying, "When you showed up on Friday, I mentioned a group project. Are you on a team yet, Poodle?"

Her eyes narrowed. "What did you call me?"

"Poodle."

With her black curly hair and long nose, she did look vaguely poodle-like. Yet only Mr. Jarrett would be mean enough to point it out.

"My name is Kimberley Rey."

There seemed to be a collective holding of breath as we all tried to gauge how well Mr. Jarrett was reacting to this unprecedented resistance.

"All right, Kimberley Rey, have you found partners for the group project?"

"I don't remember."

The whole class lost it, except me. Since I was sitting next to her, I could tell she was either dead serious or a wonderful actress.

Mr. Jarrett attempted to regain control, but the laughter drowned out whatever he was saying. He walked back to his desk, picked up his gavel, and slammed it hard. The noise stopped.

His blazing eyes scanned the room. "Does anyone 'remember' if Poodle is on their project team?"

Twenty-five pairs of eyes stared back innocently. Kimberley frowned intently at her iPad as her fingers flew

Elizabeth Langston

across its surface. The only indication that she might've heard him was the faint flush to her cheeks.

"Well, class? Anyone?" His tone implied that he understood why nobody wanted her.

It was sickening to watch him publicly humiliate Kimberley, even if she didn't acknowledge it. From the looks on my classmates' faces, he'd succeeded in stamping a bull's-eye on her back for the rest of the semester. I couldn't sit there and just let it happen, so I raised my hand. "She's my partner."

Mr. Jarrett lowered his chin to peer at me over his fashionable-but-wrong-for-him glasses. "I didn't know you had functional vocal cords, Lacey, but you managed a three-word sentence with eloquence. Who else is on your team?"

Creep. "Just me and Kimberley."

"Lucky you. I can't wait to see what the two of you come up with." He flopped onto his chair, opened the lid on his laptop, and became instantly absorbed in something that didn't involve his students. My classmates traded glances, relieved to have today's dose of evil out of the way.

Kimberley smiled at me over the top of her tablet. "Thank you for rescuing me."

"No problem." So she *had* been paying attention.

"Were we in first grade together?"

"Yeah." I was wondering if she would remember me. She'd missed a lot of school back then, but on the days that she did show up, she'd mostly hung out with me and another friend, Sara Tucker. The three of us had eaten lunch together, gone to the same birthday parties, sung in the same choir. When Kimberley hadn't returned for second grade, we assumed that she'd moved away.

"I thought I recognized your name." Kimberley gestured toward the teacher. "Will he act like that all the time?"

"'Fraid so."

"That's too bad." She smiled smugly. "For him."

She sounded so confident, it made me laugh. I flipped open my folder and pulled out the rubric on the group project. "Daily Life in the American Colonies." The kind of lame thing we did in fourth grade. And eighth grade. Most high-school teachers would've come up with something more original.

Mr. Jarrett jumped to his feet to start his lecture. I tuned him out and spent the rest of the period doodling random colonial ideas. Tobacco plants. Muskets. An outhouse with a surprised eyeball staring through a knothole.

After class ended, Kimberley caught up with me. "Have you decided what you want to do for the project?"

"Not yet."

"When's it due?"

"In two weeks."

"Then we should get started."

Why did she sound so anxious? Two weeks was plenty of time. "Our library has more stuff on Colonial America than any other period in history. This'll be the easiest project we have all semester." I crossed the hall to my next classroom.

"I prefer to get things out of the way early." She followed me. "What do you think about doing a demo?"

"Demos are fine." Maybe I should show her my doodles. An outhouse demo would be memorable. Or tobacco. Or muskets.

"Can you meet after school today?"

"No, sorry. I'm busy." I had to sell the new frames this afternoon. And besides, there was no reason to be in such a hurry. "How about Thursday night after I get off work?"

"Let me add that to my calendar." She pulled out her tablet, leaned against the doorframe, and tapped. "What time?"

"Seven."

"What kind of job do you have?"

"I work at The Reading Corner." I hesitated, completely aware that my AP English classmates buzzed with irritation in the hall around us. "Kimberley, you're blocking the doorway into English."

Without looking up, she said, "I'm almost done."

Eli was at the front of the crowd. He shifted his weight onto his good leg, then glanced from her to me. "Hey, Lacey. Will Henry be able to make practice this afternoon?"

"Sure." This was the first I'd heard of it. I'd have to hope my mom was having a good day. It would be great if she could take him and let me sell the frames.

"Okay," Kimberley announced as she closed her tablet case and stepped away from the door.

Eli nodded at her and then at me. "Good. Maybe I'll see you at practice." He stepped past Kimberley, a stream of students following him into the classroom.

"Who is that guy?" She craned her neck to watch Eli take his seat. "He's hot."

Yes, he was. "Eli Harper."

"Eli Harper," she repeated. "Does one of his parents work at Piedmont College?"

"His mom's an English professor there."

"Yeah, I think I may have met Eli at a faculty party." Her face scrunched. "I thought his mom was black."

"She is. Eli is bi-racial. His father is white." I glanced at the clock. "Aren't you worried about being late to your next class?"

"Not particularly." She cocked her head, studying me with an odd thoroughness. "Is Eli taken?"

"Not that I've heard."

"Are you interested in him?"

That was an unexpected question. If she'd asked it three years ago, I would've said yes. I'd had a crush on him, like every other girl in our class. But then a popular girl had snapped him up, and they'd stayed together until she dumped him this past summer. Now, my only interest in Eli was to be assigned to projects with him—because he was great to have on a team. "Nope, not interested. Are you?"

"I might be." She stuffed a business card into my hand and turned to leave as the bell rang. "Here's my email address and phone number. Call me about Thursday."

Mom drove Henry to soccer practice, which fit in perfectly with my plans. I didn't have far to go either, since the shop I was targeting, The Magnolia Gallery of Art, was only a few blocks away.

Location was one of the few advantages of our home. When we moved into the house four years ago, Josh had claimed it was the perfect investment, near the center of Magnolia Grove yet within easy biking range of Piedmont College. I had been loudly skeptical, afraid that—even after he fixed it up—we'd be stuck in a house we couldn't afford. Our little college town lay in a mostly agricultural part of North Carolina. The real estate market wasn't all that great.

Josh had remained optimistic, though, and given the recent influx of new professors, he'd been proven right. Our neighborhood had become popular for its sturdy houses with big yards and huge magnolia trees. Unfortunately, since Josh hadn't finished the remodeling, the house wasn't ready to sell.

I filled an old wagon with the picture frames and dragged it five blocks to the gallery. After picking up a few examples of Grant's handiwork, I entered the shop. It was dim and cool inside. I paused to get used to the change in light.

"May I help you?"

I turned in the direction of the voice. It belonged to Sara Tucker, my best friend since first grade. At least, we had been until our friendship fell apart last fall. We'd had a huge fight over the fact that she was dating a world-class jerk. She wouldn't give him up, and I couldn't stand to be around the person she'd become because of him.

Sara attended my stepfather's funeral, but we'd barely spoken since. She was still dating Gryphon, and I was too busy dealing with survival to want to get mixed up in that mess.

At least she was being polite today. Maybe that was a good sign. I smiled hesitantly. "Hey, Sara. Is Mrs. Bork here?"

Sara straightened a stack of prints in the sales rack, avoiding my gaze. "She's in the workroom."

"May I speak to her?"

"Just a moment." She disappeared through a door in the rear wall.

It only took a few seconds before the gallery owner hurried out, wiping her hands on a stained apron. "Why, Lacey, what have you brought me?" She pushed her glasses high on her nose and peered at the wooden frames I'd placed on the counter. "My, my. Beautiful work." She lifted one and inspected it. "The carving is exquisite. How many do you have?"

"Forty."

"What dimensions?"

"Mostly five-by-sevens, but a few eight-by-tens."

While Mrs. Bork studied the frames, Sara reappeared and made her way slowly around the perimeter of the shop. Curious, I watched as she stopped at the front door and peered out.

What had her attention? My wagon?

"I'll take the entire stock, Lacey. How much do you want for them?"

With a startled jerk, I faced the gallery owner, reminded of my reason for being here. "Whatever you think is fair."

"Excellent." Mrs. Bork called out, "Sara, can you bring in the rest of the frames?"

"Yes, ma'am." She glanced over her shoulder and, for a brief moment, her puzzled gaze met mine. With a tiny shake of her head, my former best friend pushed through the door, the chimes announcing her exit.

"Which do you prefer?" Mrs. Bork's voice rang loudly in my ears.

"What? I'm sorry. Could you repeat that?"

The older woman patted my arm, her eyes warm with sympathy. "It'll be all right. Don't give up on her. She'll come around. Now, cash or check, dear?"

While Mrs. Bork played with the cash register, I watched Sara unload the frames from the wagon and haul them to the rear of the store. She made four trips in all, never once making eye contact with me.

I wouldn't let Sara's attitude get to me, because something wonderful had come out of the visit to the art gallery. Mrs. Bork paid a very fair price—much fairer than I would've asked for, which was the point of not asking her.

It was such a tiny victory, but I had to celebrate anyway. I rushed home to share the news. "Grant?" I yelled from the entrance to the studio.

He appeared in an instant. "Yes?"

"Thanks." I held up the wad of bills.

There was no change in his expression, as if I hadn't spoken. Not sure why, but his reaction was disappointing. I folded the money and slipped it into my pocket. It might mean nothing to him, but it meant everything to me. "Are you interested in a cookie?"

My rush home had included a detour to Cooper's Convenience Mart on the town square to splurge on their closeout nail polish. Midnight Shimmer for one dollar. When I got to the checkout counter, they had day-old chocolate chip cookies for sale, Henry's favorite and mine. Couldn't resist them either.

"No, thank you, Chief. I don't care for any."

Good. More cookies for us. "Can you even eat human food? Or do you just eat BSB food?"

"I can eat both, but I prefer my own. My senses are more acute than yours, so the human diet tends to be a bit intense for me."

"Do you drink coffee?"

"Occasionally."

"Follow me."

When we entered the house, it was empty and quiet. The smell of burnt coffee wafted from a pot on the stove. I filled two mugs with the inky liquid and handed one to Grant. "My family is gone this afternoon. Do you want to take a tour while the coast is clear?"

"Yes, thank you."

I gestured around us. "This is the kitchen." It looked like it had come straight out of a black-and-white movie. Checkerboard floor. Clean white cabinets. Really ancient and really cool, except for the appliances. They were older than me and way more stubborn.

"Indeed." He frowned at his mug, walked to the sink, poured half of it out, filled it with water, and fell in step behind me.

Our next stop was the living room, with its bay window and brick fireplace. Across the foyer, the formal dining room waited, jammed with gloomy furniture. Down the back hallway, the two bedrooms sat behind closed doors, the messy room belonging to my mother and the clean one to Henry.

Grant scanned the hallway, a confused crease to his brow. "Where do you sleep?"

"In the attic." I opened the narrow door in the wall behind me, led him up the steep stairs, and paused with him at the top to survey my room. There was my twin bed covered by a snow-white quilt and blood-red pillows. The wooden desk, a rug covering half of the hardwood floor, and my antique dresser were solid black. Behind the bed, Josh had covered an entire wall in whiteboard paint, so that I could draw and doodle from ceiling to floor. My room might be small, but it was perfect for me.

If only it weren't roasting in the afternoon heat. I crossed the room to switch on a floor fan and then turned to watch him. It had been months since anyone besides my family had been up here. I was curious to see his reaction.

Grant took his time studying the space before wandering over to the keepsake shelf above my desk, and its collection of toy cars.

"This space feels more like a haven than an ordinary bedroom."

"Thank you," I said, warmed by the compliment. I'd worked hard to get my refuge exactly right.

"That purple Mustang is a classic. How long did it take you to acquire this collection?"

Wow. Next to Dad's class ring, the toy cars were my favorite legacy from him. It was interesting that Grant had noticed. "I got them from my dad." I walked back to the stairs. "Vehicle maintenance was his job in the Marine Corps. He could fix anything that moved."

When we returned to the kitchen, I half-sat on a cabinet while Grant stood before me, hands cradling his coffee mug.

"It's a fine house," he said.

I surveyed the room, half-proud, half-resentful. "We really can't afford to live here. I'm trying to talk my mom into selling, but she won't hear of it. She says, 'My husband loved this house. We'll stay. End of discussion.'"

I hadn't given up, though. If I could catch her in a lucid moment, when rational thought was in charge rather than emotion, I was going to change her mind. Not that I was in a hurry. The house wasn't sellable in its present condition. That's where the genie came in. Grant had better be as good as he said, because he was about to start some major home improvements.

Since my BSB provided free labor but wouldn't conjure up the supplies, I had to pick projects we could pay for out of limited funds. With the cash I got from Mrs. Bork, I'd decided to put aside three hundred dollars—two hundred to fix up the house and one hundred for emergencies. The rest of the frame-sale money would be applied to our credit card debt and monthly bills.

With the renovation budget so small, I had to have a plan. A solid, detailed plan. And I wanted *Mr. Perfectly Skilled* to help me figure out how to squeeze the most out of my money. I fumbled in a drawer of the cabinet for paper and pen and then gestured toward the kitchen table. "Have a seat."

He took a sip of his coffee and grimaced. "Perhaps you could give me my next task."

"I *wish* you would sit down and help me with my wish list."

He closed his eyes briefly and sighed. "Do you realize you've just used up today's wish?"

"Of course I realize it." As if I would be stupid enough to casually use the word "wish" around him. "I'm going to make a list of everything we need to do. Then you and I will organize it. So have a seat."

"Certainly, Chief." He perched on the edge of his chair and stared stonily.

I picked up the pen and frowned at the blank page. Here came the hard part. I had way too many things that needed to be done to this place. So, as much as I might love to indulge a little, I had to reserve most of my wishes for projects that made our home function properly or appeal to prospective buyers.

It took us about an hour, but we completed a master plan. Twenty-six wishes, scheduled in order from most urgent to least, with cost estimates for supplies. I was excited by how much we had crammed in.

Grant, however, had this whole dark look going. "Landscape the yard? Stain the deck? They're mostly home repairs."

"True. Is there a problem?"

"Could you not hire a handyman to do these tasks?"

"I don't have to. I have you."

"I know that, but your list wastes my talents. I'm capable of more."

Okay. I'd admit to being curious. "Such as?"

He rose, paced the length of the kitchen, and then whipped around to give me a frustrated stare. "I could give you a photo shoot and create a portfolio for launching a modeling career."

I choked on a laugh. Was he serious? "Not interested."

"College essays will be due soon. I could assist you."

"I'm a decent writer, so no." Besides, my current plans included early graduation, a gap semester, and then community college—none of which needed essays. Even my dream college didn't require much of one. Not that I allowed myself to think of William & Mary as my dream school anymore. The distance was too impossibly far.

"I could give you ballroom dancing lessons."

His words evoked an image of me twirling in his arms as he patiently, expertly taught me how to waltz. Now that was something I would love to try. "You can teach that in one day?"

"You use a separate wish for each dance you want to learn."

Multiple wishes just to learn how to dance? As lovely as that sounded, it was completely out of the question. I shivered with regret. "Nice, but no thanks. We need to stay focused on this wish list."

"You might use your imagination. A complete renovation of the kitchen, perhaps." He crossed to the pantry and flung open the door. "For instance, you could..." He froze.

Something about his stillness got to me. "What's wrong?"

"The pantry is practically bare." The words were mild, but the tone was fierce.

Crap. I hadn't meant for him to find out so soon. "And your point?"

"Is this all you have? Pasta, bread, and canned fruit?"

"Welcome to my world." I tried to smile and failed.

He spun around to face me. "I don't understand."

"Neither do I." And I wasn't just being a smartass. I really didn't understand how my stepfather could've been so irresponsible with our future. Not that anyone expected to die young, but Josh had taken living on the edge to an extreme. He'd been all about having fun and creating his art. It wasn't until after his funeral that I discovered what a mess he'd left us in. "My stepfather left no life insurance, no savings, and an insane balance on his credit cards." It would be years before I'd get his debts paid off.

"What about your mother?"

"She's too hollow to work." Mom had battled depression for years; Josh's death had only made it much, much worse.

"Indeed?" Grant strode over to the refrigerator and wrenched open the door. "Only coffee and milk?"

"My mom can't function without a caffeine hit."

"What else do you eat?"

"We have a vegetable garden."

He closed the door with a soft *click* and turned, his body crackling with anger. "Why haven't you said something?"

"It's not exactly my favorite topic." Keeping it a secret had become second nature. No one at school knew. The neighbors weren't asking, and I hadn't volunteered the information to anyone. *We're broke and hungry* wasn't something that I liked bringing up in casual conversation. "If you're really a supernatural being, why can't you read minds?"

"We *can*, but we don't. It raises privacy issues."

Right, as if my dad's ring was a guess. "Too bad you can't Google information like humans."

His lips thinned. "We can, actually. My boss failed to suggest it."

Grant was mad at his boss, but he was taking it out on me. It was more than I could bear. I popped out of my chair and drew so close to him our noses were mere inches apart. "Now you know my reality. The house is falling apart around us. We eat salad and spaghetti 'til we're sick of it. My brother is outgrowing all his clothes. And my mother is a total case of arrested development. It would be really nice if you would lose the attitude and help me."

"Got it."

"Good." I took a step back, surprised and kind of pleased by my own boldness. "My family will be home soon. I'd like you to change clothes before they get here."

"Do you anticipate introducing us?"

Where had this guy learned to speak? At Buckingham Palace? "No, but it's a possibility and you look like an idiot in those sweats."

"They aren't sweats. My clothing is a…uniform of sorts."

"You'd look better in jeans."

"I don't have any."

"Can't you snap your fingers?"

"For my wishes. Not yours." His smile appeared out of nowhere. "I have no wish to change."

A smile from Grant? He should do that more often. It was breathtaking.

Okay, time to refocus. "If I gave you some regular clothes, would you wear them?"

His face softened thoughtfully. "I would."

I led him down the hall to my mother's room, and then reached under her bed for a suitcase full of men's clothing. All likely to be about the right size.

"Permit me." He dumped the contents of the suitcase onto the bed. Items fell out into neatly sorted piles. Loose buttons had tightened, frayed hems had mended, holes had been patched. "Your stepfather's things?"

"They are." I laid a hand on the stack of shirts and drank in the memory of spicy cologne. "If my mother notices you wearing Josh's clothes, she'll fall apart," I said around the lump in my throat.

"I'll disguise them, Chief." Grant pulled out jeans, shirts, and sneakers.

"Here's a tie."

"I don't do ties." He gathered the clothes into his arms. "I have what I need to keep from embarrassing you."

I hadn't meant to insult him. "Sorry."

"No need to be. I'm here to serve." He bowed his head and faded away.

I perched on the edge of the bed, staring into the empty space where seconds ago he had been, and wondered how I was going to survive a month of Grant.

Status Report #4
Monday's Wish: Schedule and Budget

Dear Boss,

I owe Chief an apology. Why didn't you prepare me for this assignment?

Chief is remarkably adept at hiding her family's circumstances. I have lived in this household for three days and never suspected the depths of their difficulties. No doubt her close friends are unaware of the family's financial straits.

You chide me for my tendency to jump to conclusions, yet with this assignment, you allowed me to misjudge my new mistress. Today's conversation with Chief was awkward and avoidable. I hope that it doesn't set the tone for the remainder of our time together.

She's asked me to dress as her equal. I don't think it's necessary, but I've chosen to concede the point.

Humbly submitted,
Grant

5

Curves and Circles

I didn't sleep well last night, and it wasn't just the lack of air conditioning in my attic bedroom. My brain wouldn't let go of the possibility that my master plan, instead of being perfect, was missing something essential.

Mr. Jarrett's lecture on Native Americans didn't make a dent in my obsessive worry over getting the wish list right. Nor could Ms. Dewan, my favorite teacher ever, get me engaged with *The Canterbury Tales*.

She did, however, capture my attention at the end of the class period.

"Lacey and Eli, could you drop by my desk for a moment?" she called over the thunder of thirty pairs of shoes trying to cram through the same door.

There was a slight hitch in Eli's stride as he stepped out of the flow of students and headed for her desk. I joined him seconds later.

Ms. Dewan rummaged in a huge purse while we waited.

"Here we are." Ms. Dewan slapped two brochures on her desk and pushed them across to us. "I want you both to enter an essay contest."

I picked mine up, flipped it open, and skimmed. The 38th Annual Persuasive Essay Competition. Sponsored by the Association of Writing Educators. AWE.

The grand prize made me blink. A one-thousand-dollar scholarship to the college of my choice. Really impressive. Not that I needed it. My college fund was one of the few things in my life that was fine the way it was.

"Thanks, Ms. Dewan," Eli said, "but I don't plan to major in English."

"It doesn't matter what your major will be. I just want one of my students to win, and the two of you are the best."

Her best writers? Rare praise from Ms. Dewan. I breathed in those words and let myself savor them for a moment. "Thank you," I said with a smile.

"So you'll do it?"

Okay, back to the real world. "I'm not sure." I was uncomfortable at having to dodge her question, especially in front of Eli, but there was no time in my week to add anything else. "I'm pretty busy right now."

The corners of her mouth twitched upward. "Each finalist wins a two-hundred-dollar grant for his or her teacher."

That almost made me want to win for her—although being a national finalist might be a stretch. "What's the prompt?"

She tapped my brochure. "It's in the box at the bottom."

I read the prompt and sagged. Really? AWE couldn't have picked something moderately intriguing?

"Is there a problem?"

"Yes."

"What is it?"

"The topic is lame."

Eli nodded. "It's not controversial. It'll be hard to come up with unique arguments."

Ms. Dewan picked up the sheet and read aloud. "'Should a credit in English Literature be required for high-school graduation?'"

"Of course," he said.

I shifted to see him better. "Of course what?"

"High school seniors should be required to take English Lit."

For the length of a breath, I debated whether to ignore his completely wrong-headed and unsupported position on the prompt. But I just couldn't. "There's no 'of course' to it."

His glare was arrogant. "Why not?"

"High-school students wouldn't take English Lit if they didn't have to. It's not useful."

"Not useful? Do you know how hard it is to go a single day without hearing a quotation from classic literature?"

"Then teach us the important quotes and move on. Why make us listen to everything else?"

"What about Shakespeare?"

"What about him?" I loved Shakespeare, especially his sonnets, but not a semester's worth.

"I don't think anyone should graduate from high school without studying Shakespeare."

"And I don't see any long-term value in dissecting *Macbeth.*"

"There is value in the process, even for people who are more used to farm reports than four-act plays."

Score. "Spoken like the son of an English professor."

"Which happens to be what I am." He stared at me as if I were some kind of exotic insect. "What would you require in senior English instead?"

"We could learn how to take apart a contract. Maybe there could be a unit on how to tell the difference between good content and bad content on the internet." I was making this up as I went. Hopefully I would remember the good parts later for what could be a winning essay.

When Ms. Dewan laughed, we both jerked. Guess I wasn't the only one who'd forgotten she was there.

"Uncontroversial? Lame?" She smiled. "If your papers are anywhere near as good as this discussion has been, I'm already looking forward to them." She shooed us away. "They're due to me on the second of October. Don't forget."

When I got home from school, our Ford Focus sat sparkling in the driveway. Grant reclined against the bumper, looking smug, which I would overlook since Car Repair Day meant I had transportation I trusted. "How'd your day go?" I asked.

"I've been rather busy."

He showed no signs of annoyance. Cool. Maybe this wish had actually pleased him.

I looked toward the windows of the house. There was no visible movement inside. "Did my mom see you?"

"I really couldn't say."

He pushed up from the bumper and stretched, a sight which probably gave heart palpitations to the nosy neighbor across the street.

"Chief, you should warn your mother about me."

I hadn't come up with a description she would buy. An Eagle Scout looking for a project? A criminal with community service to work off? Since I hadn't settled on an explanation yet, avoidance of the issue seemed as good a coping strategy as any. "I'll wait until she brings you up."

A noisy sigh. "Won't I scare her?"

"Everything scares my mother." I circled the Ford. The tires were getting bald, which would have to remain a problem since I didn't have the funds to replace them. But the rest of the car looked amazing. Waxed and buffed. Vacuumed and scrubbed. Duct tape discreetly placed at effective intervals to hold the vehicle together. I couldn't stop smiling.

"I think you should introduce us," Grant said as he trailed me. "Just a thought."

"I'll get around to it." I popped the hood and whistled. Everything looked shiny and new, from the fresh green coolant in the overflow reservoir to the clean oil on the dipstick. He'd done a remarkable job. "This looks great. Thanks."

He nodded. "I've had practice. Auto repair is requested often."

"I bet." I listened as the hood fell into place with a satisfying *thunk*. Our car hadn't looked this good in years, and I was itching to take it out. I could pretend it was a Mustang. Same manufacturer. Yeah.

"You should see a ten-percent improvement in your MPG." He tossed the keys to me.

I caught them. "Want to go for a ride?" I smiled hopefully, oddly anxious for him to come with me.

"Where are we going?" He slid onto the passenger seat and buckled up.

"To buy gas."

We drove around the town square (twice—because the car took the corners really well now) and through several quiet neighborhoods to the outskirts of town, passing a couple of convenience marts along the way. I could feel Grant's curious gaze on me, but I didn't explain. He'd find out soon enough.

I pulled into a full-service gas station, the kind with repair bays and vending machines burping out glass bottles of soda. The station was owned by a friend of my father's. Allyn Taylor was the closest thing I had to a godparent. It felt good coming here, 'cause he was always glad to see me.

Mr. Taylor walked out with a huge smile of welcome. "Hi, darlin'," he said in his sleepy drawl. Leaning down to peer in the car, he studied Grant for a few hard seconds, then returned his attention to me. "I don't believe I've seen your friend around."

"This is Grant, and we're not exactly friends."

Mr. Taylor frowned. "Is he one of your classmates?"

"No, he doesn't go to…" Flustered, I stopped, wondering how to keep this vague. "Grant's working for me."

"Working?" Mr. Taylor narrowed his eyes at my BSB. "Is that so?"

"Yes, sir," Grant said.

"Uh-huh. What kind of work?"

"Home repair." Grant's voice was crisp and professional.

"What kinds of repairs?"

I needed to end the interrogation now. "Painting and stuff," I said as I opened the coin box and fished around for dollars. "Mr. Taylor, you *are* going to take my money today. Right?"

"Sure, darlin'." Straightening, he patted the top of my car and reached for the pump. "How much can I get for you?"

"Eight dollars' worth, please."

He chuckled. "That's not going to get you very far."

"I don't have far to go."

The numbers on the pump whirred past the eight-dollar mark and still kept going. An extra two gallons later, he stopped. Mr. Taylor and I had an understanding. As long as he didn't refuse my money, I overlooked how much he put in.

I drove away with a few more miles in the tank and a couple of free drinks.

Grant twisted the cap off his bottle, held it up to his nose, and sniffed suspiciously. He took a sip and cringed. "The proprietor regarded me with suspicion. Is he related to you?"

"Not by blood." I slowed for a traffic light and flipped on my shades. And if those shades made it more difficult to read my expression, well, fine. Conversations about either of my fathers were uncomfortable, but I figured that I ought to share something with Grant after he helped me with the car. "My dad's name was Eric Linden. He and my mom and Mr. Taylor all graduated from Magnolia Grove High the same year."

"Your father served in the Marine Corps?"

I gave a sharp nod.

"Where is he now?"

Hard swallow. "He was killed in a training accident."

Grant's voice was solemn. "How old were you?"

"I was in kindergarten." The principal and a policeman had shown up at the schoolroom door and spoken to my teacher. Although I didn't understand what was going on, I could tell from their expressions that something bad had happened. It sucked the sound from the room. Or maybe that had been my imagination.

"My sympathies."

I nodded away his response. Even though Dad died twelve years ago, I still didn't like to talk about it. The events of that day and the weeks following were burned like scars into my being—which was why, when I thought about my dad, I focused on the good memories.

We drove around for several blocks before Grant spoke again. "Does Eric Linden have any family in town?"

"They moved to Florida." My grandparents didn't get along with my mother. Even if they had been healthy, they wouldn't come up here to visit. And I couldn't afford to go down there.

"Can they assist you?"

"No." I hoped that Grant wouldn't ask why, because I wasn't going to answer. How could I explain the Linden family history? I loved Grampa and Nana, but it was hard to forgive all the mean things they said about my mom.

Yeah, I couldn't let them know what was going on now. They would offer to send a little money, but in exchange I'd have to listen to nonstop criticisms of my mother and Josh. It wasn't worth it. I wasn't that desperate yet.

After turning onto a side street, I cut through an older neighborhood and headed straight for the town square. "I'm working a shift at the bookstore. Do you want me to drop you off at home first?"

"No. I'll manage." He hesitated before taking another sip of his peach-kiwi iced tea, screwed the top back on, and slipped the bottle into a cupholder. "How many AP classes do you take?"

I frowned at the unexpected question. "You know about AP classes?"

"I've been working the American circuit for a while. How many?"

"English Lit and US History." Those two classes, plus pre-calc, were all I needed to earn my high-school diploma. If all went well this semester, I'd be able to graduate early.

"You're carrying a tough workload. Why the job?"

I circled the town square, looking for an empty spot. "Someone has to buy the pasta."

"You must have other income."

"I get survivor benefits from the military. Mom and Henry get money from Social Security. Our checks cover the mortgage and not much else."

His fingers drummed on the armrest. "Why did you pick a job in a bookstore?"

He sure was *Mr. Curiosity* today. "A lot of reasons."

"Such as...?"

"Mostly 'cause I like being around books, but I also like that Mrs. Lubis lets me do my homework when it's not busy. And the store's close to home for those days when the car won't start." I felt his sudden, tense gaze rake my profile. "What?"

"You walk alone at night?"

"Sometimes."

He grunted.

"Magnolia Grove is perfectly safe. Nothing bad is going to happen. I'm within shouting distance of neighbors the whole way." After pulling into in a parking space, I cut the engine and fumbled with my seatbelt, while I thought about the route to my house. There were no street lights and, on moonless nights, it did get really dark.

I'd never worried much about it until he introduced the concept. Lovely.

"Grant?" I shifted sideways in my seat. "If I needed your assistance, is there any way to contact you?" It felt odd to have someone I could count on for help.

"I don't carry a phone, if that's what you mean."

"No…" I meant something more metaphysical, but I felt stupid admitting it. "Can you hear me from a long distance if I call?"

"Not exactly." He half-smiled. "But I could give you a panic button."

The offer relieved me more than I would've expected. "Will it take a wish?"

He hesitated a second, then shook his head. "What are your thoughts on henna tattoos?"

Not sure where this was going, but I was willing to follow along. "Love them."

"Good. Hold out your left wrist and close your eyes."

I did as he said and waited. A touch like the flutter of a butterfly's wing tickled my wrist. It wove in and out, tracing curves and circles. I remained still long after the fluttering stopped.

"Done," he said. "When you want to contact me, touch your tattoo and call my name."

I opened my eyes, peered at my wrist, and gasped. "It's gorgeous, Grant."

"Thank you."

Twisting my arm first one way, then the other, I studied the design. It had tiny, overlapping leaves. Or were they hearts? The tattoo glowed against my skin, crisp and intricate in a beautiful coppery-brown. It made me feel happy and protected. "How long will it last?"

"Twenty-five days."

I smiled at him. "Why did you do this?"

He frowned and looked away. "I suppose I was feeling generous." With fast, efficient movements, he snicked off his seatbelt and slid from the car. Before I could get out of the car, he'd already crossed the street.

It was odd, letting him leave this way. The last few minutes had seemed almost friendly. I wasn't ready to have them end. "Grant?"

He stopped on the sidewalk opposite me. "Yes?"

I waited for a truck to pass. It gave me time to decide what I needed to say, because it had been nice having a normal conversation with someone who didn't mention college plans or soccer balls. I went with something simple. "Thanks for today."

He nodded and then disappeared into the shadows gracing the courthouse grounds, blue smoke blending with the trees.

Status Report #5
Tuesday's Wish: Auto Repair

Dear Boss,

I can't imagine what you expect Chief to teach me.

Her behavior is rather unpredictable. She is the most closefisted teen I have ever met, yet she frequents a full-service gas station. She wants to control how I dress around her family, yet she has not warned them of my existence.

Is her mother my real mission?

Humbly submitted,
Grant

6

An Epic Disaster

Wednesdays were always pure chaos in the cafeteria. Pizza somehow made the crowd louder. I looked around for a reasonably quiet corner and noticed an almost empty table in the back.

I started that way, hesitating when I noticed that Sara Tucker was already sitting there.

Should I find somewhere else?

No. I hadn't approached her like this in several months, but we had spoken at the art gallery on Monday. That had been civil enough. Here was another chance to not-ignore each other.

I slid onto a seat at her table. "Hey." Cool. That hadn't sounded too nervous.

"Hi," she said without taking her attention away from her book.

I waited a few seconds to see if she was finishing a paragraph or something, but she flipped the page and kept reading. Okay, awkward. If she was going to pretend she was alone, I could do the same. Reaching into my lunch pack, I pulled out a plastic bag of raw veggies and munched.

The book lowered slightly. Her eyes flicked to the bag, widened, and returned to her reading.

I could understand her surprise. The old Lacey hadn't been much of a health nut. Actually, the new Lacey wasn't either, just less choosy about how I got my calories. "Want some?"

"No, thanks."

The silence stretched. Underneath the table, my foot tapped in rhythm with the thuds of my heart. We had to move past the thing that had happened between us—a fight so rare and so awful that it would've taken a lot of groveling from both of us to get over it. We would have if Josh hadn't died a few days later.

Usually I was the one to say "I'm sorry" first, but I hadn't for this argument. Asking for forgiveness could be exhausting, and I didn't have any energy to spare.

But plenty of time had passed now. She knew it. I knew it. Why didn't she kick off the apologies? Hadn't I done my share by coming over here?

She stared at her book. I picked up another carrot. The cafeteria slowly emptied, and still we said nothing, like we barely knew each other.

Was she as sad about it as I was?

Sara flipped the page, unconcerned about me. Should I take the hint to leave or make her speak to me?

Enough already. If she could act like we'd never been friends, then I could act like it had only been days—instead of months—since we'd talked.

I would start with the reason for our fight and get him out of the way. "How's Gryphon?"

Her gaze met mine. "We broke up."

Wow. There must be something wrong with the school's grapevine. That should've been all over the place. I pinched my leg to keep from smiling. "When?"

"In April. And June." She snapped her paperback shut. "And a week ago."

Volatile as ever. Boyfriends like Gryphon were an addiction for her. She'd always loved being half of a beautiful couple, and he was definitely pretty. If only he'd deserved her in some other way. From the very beginning of their relationship, he'd acted like he was doing her a favor, which was stupid. He might have been a champion swimmer, but Sara was the cool one. Cute, smart, funny, and bubbling over with charm. Gryphon was popular mostly because of *her*, but his ego was too big to realize it. "What happened?"

"I got tired of…" She pressed her lips together and looked away.

Something wasn't right about this whole thing. I wanted to ask her for more details, but I couldn't. Whatever the secret was, she would only tell it to a best friend, which I wasn't anymore. But I wouldn't hide that I thought their breakup was a relief. "Gryphon was always—"

"Stop. Don't say another word. I don't need your opinions about Gryphon or any other guy I date." She popped to her feet, clutching her backpack to her chest. "You've been invisible for a long time, Lacey. Why did you bother to come over here?"

She'd acknowledged the weirdness between us. Good. That was a start. "Because I want to know why you disappeared."

"*I* disappeared? It was the other way around."

"You know where I live."

"I haven't moved either." Her hands shook. "You changed your phone number without telling me."

"I don't have it anymore." My heart pounded so hard I could feel the pulse in my ears.

"Why not?"

I didn't want to admit it. I'd worked hard to keep the truth about my family confined to the inside of our house. Yet Sara had been my best friend for years—the person that I'd once told *everything* to. I could trust her, couldn't I? "We can't afford mobile phones."

"Oh." A flicker of something—pity, maybe?—flashed in her eyes. "Why haven't you said something?"

There were so many reasons. She'd been wrapped up in a guy I couldn't stand. The money thing embarrassed me. And if Sara had ever discovered how bad off we were, she would've insisted on helping out, and I would've refused. "I've been trying to handle it myself."

"It's nice to know how little you thought of our friendship." There was an edge to her voice. "You haven't wanted to be around me in months. What's the point in talking to me now?"

"Excuse me?" I met her glare with one of my own. "Life's been hard."

"Life is hard for everybody." She snorted. "I'm sorry about Josh, but he's been gone almost a year. You can't hide behind his death forever."

My head whipped back like she'd slapped me. Wow. Had she really just said that? "You don't know what it's like at my house."

"Yeah, and you don't know what it's like at mine." She stalked away.

I watched her weave her way through the cafeteria, wondering what she meant. Everything about her family was perfect. Sara and her brother Sean were the perfect twins. They had perfect parents who had never been married to anyone except each other. They had a perfectly big house on a perfectly small yard in Magnolia Estates. There were four brand-new cars in their four-car garage. And they owned three perfect cats with better lives than most people. Okay, so maybe her father—the big, important businessman—had more frequent flyer miles than the average airline pilot. But still.

I'd have to corner Sean. He'd tell me what was going on.

I arrived home from school a little later than normal and found my mother standing in the center of the kitchen, her face pale, her trembling hand clutching the collar of her blouse against her throat.

"We have an intruder, Lacey."

"We do? Where?" The adrenaline was pumping. I dropped my backpack on the floor and looked around for a baseball bat. I had to settle for a broom.

"In the backyard."

"The backyard?" I inched closer to the window and peeked out.

Grant was pushing the lawnmower. Crap. I should've warned her already. Not that I would ever tell Grant he'd been right. "Mom. Intruders come *inside* your house. They don't mow lawns."

"Why would a stranger mow our lawn?"

"Grant isn't a stranger." What had I been thinking? I knew he couldn't do any landscaping without being seen. Sometimes, though, it was just easier to avoid conflict until it was forced on me.

"You *know* him?" Her voice rasped.

"Yeah. I asked him to cut the grass."

"Without telling me?"

"I forgot," I said, distracted by how amazing our backyard looked. There was fresh pine straw spread around the flower beds. Weeds gone. Bushes trimmed. Even the flowers seemed perky.

Wait a minute. *Fresh* pine straw? We didn't have that in the budget. I took off outside, yelling and waving the broom until I had Grant's attention.

He shut off the mower. "Yes?"

"Where did you get the pine straw?"

"Good afternoon to you as well. Miserably hot day, wouldn't you agree?"

I paused in the middle of my tirade. "Oh. Right." It was miserable out here in the full sun, although his chest looked dry. "You're not sweating."

"Supernatural Beings do not sweat. We do, however, experience high temperatures."

"Sorry." I lowered the broom and leaned on it for support. The heat shimmered above the ground in a dusty haze. Deep breaths were impossible, and Grant had been out in this all day. What was wrong with me? "Nice job on the yard."

He inclined his head. "As you were saying?"

Tirade back on. "Today's wish wasn't supposed to cost anything."

"I haven't spent a dime. I didn't have one to spend."

"Oh." Tirade off again, for good this time. "Where did the pine straw come from?"

A smug smile appeared. "Mrs. Williford has dozens of pine trees."

"Mrs. Williford? What did you have to sacrifice?" Our nosy across-the-street neighbor had never given away anything for free. Not even a hello. I didn't want to be in her debt.

"I bartered." He rolled his head around, then flexed his arms, his face contorting in discomfort. "Half of anything I raked up in her yard I could keep."

He didn't have on a shirt, and his upper body was, well, perfect. No wonder Mrs. Williford was nice to him. The sight of all that bronze skin stretched over sculpted muscle must have bewitched her. "You worked on her yard before doing ours?"

"Indeed."

Should I apologize? Hug him? Offer to give a foot massage? Henry's shout saved me from making a decision.

"Hey, Lacey!"

I looked over my shoulder. My family was tramping across the yard. When they got a few feet away, my mother halted. Henry kept going until Mom grabbed his arm and yanked him back to her side.

"Are you going to introduce us?" she asked.

There was no logical way to explain a Benevolent Supernatural Being, so I would skip the details and hope for the best. "Mom, Henry, this is Grant. He's going to help around the house for a few days."

Mom crossed her arms, bristling with suspicion. But not my brother. Released from his mother's stranglehold, Henry darted to Grant. "What kinds of things can you do?"

"Ask."

"Do you play soccer?"

My BSB crouched to Henry's level, his expression calmly curious. "I do."

"Would you practice with me?"

I tried to catch Grant's eye, shaking my head violently. Bad idea. Bad.

"Certainly," he said. "Early in the evening, perhaps? About seven?"

"Great." Henry started to walk away. Then he glanced back, worry reflected on his face. "Are you any good?"

"I am. Quite good."

My brother smiled. "Awesome. See you later."

We watched Henry swagger toward the front yard. My brother was happy. I was horrified. The last thing I needed was for my family to bond with a genie.

Mom waited until her little boy was out of earshot before launching her interrogation. "Who are you?"

"I'm Grant," he said, rising slowly, "and I'm here to help."

"I picked up that much from Lacey." She frowned. "Grant what?"

"Just Grant."

She glared. "Why are you here?"

"My profession requires me to serve humans in need."

Humans? He used the word *humans?* I had to take over. "He's a handyman, Mom."

Her glare shifted to me. "How much are we paying him?"

"Nothing." For some reason, her question irritated me. As if she ever thought about where the money came from. "He's doing it for free."

"Nothing is ever free."

For months, my mother hadn't questioned anything. The decisions I made were fine as long as I left her out of them. Now, all of a sudden, when I didn't want her involvement, she had pulled herself together enough to act like a normal parent. "Please, Mom. I have this under control."

She gave me an insincere smile. "Where did the two of you meet?"

"At the flea market. About a week ago."

"I cannot agree," he said. "We met in the studio."

I swung around to face him. "Are you correcting me?" *In front of her?*

"Indeed."

Mom snorted. "Who do you work for?"

"Me," I said in a rush.

"I have a boss," he said.

It was all I could do to keep from gagging him. "Could you shut up and let me handle this?"

He clamped his lips.

"Thank you." I turned to Mom. "What else do you want to know?"

"How old is he?"

Of course she would ask something I didn't know the answer to. Vagueness would have to work. "He's legal."

"Eighteen," he said.

Grant was only a few months older than me? I frowned at him. "That's all?"

"How old did you think he was?" my mother asked.

"Older than eighteen."

She chewed on a thumbnail. "Why aren't you in high school, Grant?"

"I've already graduated."

"Are you planning to go to college?"

"There would be no point."

Wow, we were straying off course. I had to stop the questions before *Mr. Honesty* ruined everything. "Mom, could you quit the inquisition? Grant's here to help, and he's free. Can't we leave it at that?"

"Are we some kind of charity project to him?"

"Hardly, especially since our family doesn't accept charity." This conversation was making me itchy. It had to end. "He works for a group like the Peace Corps. We're doing him a favor. He doesn't stand to gain anything."

Grant suppressed a sigh. "You're mistaken, Chief. I hope to receive a promotion after your case."

I rounded on him. "A promotion?"

"You didn't know about that, did you?" Mom sniffed in vindication.

"I did *not*."

He took a step closer to her and smiled. "Are you displeased with the quality of my work, Mrs. Jones?"

She blinked several times. Then slowly, deliberately, my mother surveyed the yard, giving each flower bed and bush her full attention. Her gaze rested longest on the wrought-iron bench under a cluster of trees, a favorite spot of hers and Josh's. There was nothing fuzzy about her scrutiny. She was really here. Really thinking about this issue. "No, you've done a wonderful job."

"Thank you." He held out his hand. "Trust me, there is no charge."

She clasped his hand. "Okay, then, but you must let me do something in return..."

As her tension melted away, mine rose. I looked from her to him and back again. She was acting normal. It was oddly upsetting. Why couldn't she act normal when it was just me?

"…would you like to eat with us tonight?"

I gasped a loud "*No.*"

"Indeed, I would," he said over me.

My mother frowned at me. "Lacey, where are your manners?" She nodded toward Grant. "We'll see you around six," she said and then hurried toward the house. The screen door slammed behind her with a *thwack*.

I was frozen with shock. How had things gone so out of control?

Grant bent over the mower. It roared to life.

"I'm not done with you," I yelled.

He straightened. "Yes, Chief?"

"Did I hear you right? Are you getting a promotion because of me?"

"Not at all. There are skills I'm expected to learn on this assignment. I shall receive a promotion based on *my* performance. *You* are incidental."

I let this new piece of data sink into my brain, feeling more stupid the deeper it settled. I'd been naïve enough to think that *I* mattered. But no.

Why did this knowledge hurt me so much? Why should I care that I was nothing more than a stepping stone? Either way, my family benefited. "Nice. Glad we could be of service."

His mouth tightened. "May I finish the lawn?"

"Not yet." Even though Grant had executed this wish perfectly, this day had turned into an epic disaster. I didn't want him hanging out with them. Henry craved the kind of guy-attention he couldn't get from us. And Mom? She was fragile in every way possible. They might make the mistake of caring for Grant, and in a month he'd move on to his next project. "I need you to avoid Mom and Henry. Understand?"

"Certainly, I understand." His eyes glittered. "I am, however, under no obligation to follow your instructions."

"I thought I was the mistress."

"For one wish per day. Otherwise, your whims have no effect."

He gave the mower a push and left me in a cloud of dust.

Status Report #6
Wednesday's Wish: Landscaping

Dear Boss,

I acquired and distributed pine straw around the flower beds. It was more than Chief asked for, but I didn't mind the effort. If that is how generosity feels, it is quite an intriguing sensation.

I had to barter for the pine straw. Mrs. Williford is a kind but lonely woman.

The vegetable garden received a special application of compost. It should be exceptionally productive this fall.

Henry Jones has a real talent for soccer.

Chief has claimed that her mother is hollow. Now that I have met Mrs. Jones, it is my opinion that the opposite is true. She is saturated with pain. May I reveal myself to her?

My mistress has serious control issues. I allowed her to goad me into accepting a dinner invitation. The meal turned out to be pleasant. Chief had to work tonight and could not attend.

I detected an odd note in her voice when she uttered the word "charity," as if it were an expletive. Is her attitude part of the family's problem?

Humbly submitted,
Grant

7

Natural Personality

For the second night in a row, Grant ate dinner with my family. And, like yesterday, I had to work. Under normal circumstances, I could've rushed right home to make sure he didn't hang out too long with Mom and Henry. But not tonight. It was Thursday and I'd promised to meet with Kimberley about the APUSH project.

I needed to chill. Grant wouldn't tell them who he really was. Right?

The French glass doors separating The Reading Corner from its sister business, The Java Corner, swung open with a creak. I looked up to find the owner, Mrs. Lubis, scanning the bookstore, her lips set in a thin, angry line. The evening barista hadn't shown up and hadn't called, which meant Mrs. Lubis would have to substitute.

Satisfied that all was well, she gave me a sharp nod and returned to the coffee shop, shutting the doors behind her.

The door chime alerted me to a customer. Then another. I put away the duster and hovered near the checkout counter at the front, prepared to offer assistance. The after-dinner flood had arrived.

Someone nudged my shoulder. "Hi, Lacey."

I looked around, surprised to find Kimberley. "You're a little early."

"When does your shift end?"

"In another ten minutes, as soon as my replacement arrives." Kimberley must not have been planning on making much progress tonight, because she hadn't brought a purse or backpack. Just the obligatory iPad.

"Good. I'll text Mom."

While she played on her tablet, I cut a sideways glance at the glass doors. If Mrs. Lubis saw me talking to a friend, I'd get a lecture and maybe a dock in pay. "Look, Kimberley—"

"My mom says fine."

Okay, totally confused. "What?"

Kimberley smiled. "It's been a long time since I've been in this place. It smells like damp cardboard."

I didn't have control of this conversation, but it didn't seem like she did either. "Do you want to wait over there?" I indicated a leather couch.

"I'll wait here."

Politeness hadn't worked. I'd have to try again. "I'm on the clock. If my boss sees us talking, it won't be good."

"I'll pretend I'm buying something." She picked up a bestseller from a display on the counter. "I want to do our project on cooking. Do you mind?"

This was Kimberley. Just roll with it. "No, I don't mind."

"Good. My granddad has access to a collection of kitchen things." She bit her lip. "I mean, kitchen utensils."

"From the colonial period?"

"Yes. The collection belongs to the history department at Piedmont College. Granddad works there. They said he could borrow the reproductions."

"Rather convenient for us." My gaze made a quick sweep of the store. We were busier than usual. To my left was a young couple with a stroller, a fussing baby, and a growing stack of picture books. In the center, an elderly woman browsed through self-help manuals. Near the front, a man in a business suit scowled at a shelf of romance novels. Sara Tucker looked through the poetry section.

No one looked interested in shoplifting. I relaxed my vigilance. "Mr. Jarrett loves politics. We're not likely to get an A if we do anything else."

"I think we can agree that anyone on *my* project team should not obsess over getting a good grade." Her face scrunched as if in deep thought. "Why did he pick me to abuse?"

Her blunt honesty with me demanded blunt honesty in return. "You challenged him about your iPad in front of the entire class."

"I see." She sighed. "That's about the brain damage."

I would've laughed if she hadn't been staring at me so solemnly. Wow, oh wow. She meant it. "You're not joking."

"Wish I were." She frowned at her tablet. "My mom's out front to pick us up."

"We're not studying here at the shop?"

"My house would be better."

A customer cleared her throat. "Excuse me."

Sara waited in front of the cash register. I pasted on my sales-associate smile. "How may I help you?"

"I'll take these." She handed me two paperbacks and some cash.

Curious, I checked the titles. *Turning Your Hobby into Revenue* and *Midnight Meditations*. Hmmm. Was someone starting a small business at the Tuckers's? I handed over the bag and the receipt.

Kimberley craned her neck to watch Sara exit the store, then asked, "Do you know her?"

Maybe. "Since first grade."

"She looks familiar. What's her name again?"

"Sara Tucker."

"Her brother is my dance partner in PE. Ballroom dancing."

"Yeah, he's great." Sean was the perfect blend of sweet, careful, and determined. If he tried something, he didn't give up until he succeeded. "Everybody likes Sean."

"Has it been ten minutes yet?"

I laughed. "Yeah."

Once my replacement took over, I followed Kimberley to a silver SUV in the parking area. She introduced me to her mother and climbed into the back seat.

Did I sit with Kimberley or ride shotgun?

I made the safe choice and crawled into the back.

It only took a few minutes for Mrs. Rey to drive us to their home. It was located midway between the college and downtown, as far away from my house as we could get and still be within the town limits.

Their yard looked like someone had clipped it with a pair of scissors. A spotlight on the front porch shone on big pots of flowers in yellow and fuchsia. The garage was spotless. The floor had been swept. A single bike hung suspended upside-down from the ceiling.

Kimberley and I entered the kitchen and dropped our backpacks onto the table. Yanking open the refrigerator, she pulled out two bottles of water and handed one to me.

The obsessive cleanliness spread across the room. The counters had nothing on them. No containers, rags, or small appliances. There was not a dust mite or tiny insect to be found, quite a feat in North Carolina. Her mom must have worked on the house all day long.

Kimberley laid her tablet on the kitchen table. "I've drafted a few slides. Want to see?"

Okay, but she couldn't expect me to leave her earlier bombshell alone. "Let's talk first."

She froze for an instant and then nodded.

I took a deep breath, bracing myself. "How long have you had brain damage?"

"Ten years." She watched me, her dark eyes big and round. "My short-term memory is impaired."

I wasn't one hundred percent sure what that meant, but it sounded bad. "Permanently?"

"Yes."

"So the iPad...?" I gestured at her computer.

"If I don't key in everything I hear, I might not remember it." She picked up her bottle of water, unscrewed the top, and took a sip.

"What caused it?"

"Chemotherapy." She relaxed into a seat and wiggled for comfort. "I had leukemia when I was a little kid."

"Is that why you moved away after first grade?"

"Yes." She watched me carefully. "Don't be sad for me. If I weren't damaged, I'd be dead."

"I won't be sad for you, but let me know how I can help."

"Just try to treat me normal."

"Sure." I nodded. Since Kimberley didn't seem to mind this topic, I would keep trying—but gently. "May I ask you something else?"

"Go ahead."

"How do short-term memory problems affect you?"

"It's like being a person who is sleep-deprived. I can't trust my brain to keep track of everything that I need." Her response was crisp and immediate, as if rehearsed. "I often walk around in a fog. I have to make decisions slowly. Repetition helps my brain remember things, so I take everything down and then reread my notes until they stick." Her face flattened into calm acceptance. "It takes a lot of work to succeed, but I can."

"When did you move back to Magnolia Grove?"

"This summer. We had been living near DC. The hospitals there are very good." With a sudden hitch forward, she pulled her chair closer to the table and looked at her tablet. After tapping at it some, she added, "Mom moved here first. She's a mural artist and had a commission to work on. Dad decided to stay in Northern Virginia. I was up there with him until last week."

Kimberley was so matter-of-fact. Was that part of her natural personality? Or part of the…?

I couldn't go there. "Are your parents divorced?"

"Not yet." She looked over at me. "What happened to your stepfather? I heard he died."

A fast and unexpected transition. "Yes, in an accident." *Motorcycle hits tree; rider without helmet.*

"Did you like him?"

My eyeballs ached. "I liked him a lot."

"Cool. I don't know many kids who get along with their steps." Her fingers fluttered. "Enough personal stuff. Let's take a look at these slides."

I sat back and watched. She'd gone to extraordinary lengths to research and contrast colonial utensils with their modern-day equivalents. The whole presentation was brilliant.

Apparently, my sole contribution would be my name. Given how little I cared about "Daily Life in the Colonies"—and the high probability Mr. Jarrett had predetermined the score for the Linden/Rey Team—I went along with this. Flipping to a clean sheet in my notebook, I doodled pictures of toasting forks and tea kettles.

After an hour of tweaking colors and fonts on the slides, Kimberley was still not satisfied. "Do you think we have enough?"

I paused in the act of doodling. "We have the slides, plus we're demoing with reproduction utensils. It's twice as much as anyone else will do. We're fine." This assignment was only worth five percent of our final grade. Why was she trying so hard?

"The project doesn't feel complete yet. You need a bigger part in the presentation."

Anything would be bigger than what I was doing now. "What's left? The only thing we're lacking is a reproduction kitchen maid."

Her eyes widened. "Great idea."

"Wait. I was joking."

Her fingers flew across the computer. "My mom has a costume. It's more like a pirate's damsel, but we could modify it. It looks something like this." She angled the screen around to show an image of a serving wench in a mob cap, dark skirt, white blouse, and a red corset stopping just below the breasts. "Would you wear it?"

It was…wow. "Possibly," I said in a strangled voice.

"Good. We're done."

Kimberley changed into a cleaning machine. She folded up her tablet case, collected our water bottles, and tossed them into a recycling bin. Maybe I'd been wrong about who the perfectionist was in this house.

"I haven't given up," Kimberley said in a monotone as she wiped the condensation circles from the table before me.

"On what?"

"My mom and dad getting back together."

"Uh-huh." I kept still. Mr. Rey lived hundreds of miles away from his wife and daughter. That made reconciliation difficult.

"Dad is an architect."

Kimberley watched me, like she was expecting something.

Was she inviting me to ask more? I looked at the clock. Already past nine. It was getting late. I had laundry to do and Henry's homework to check over. But it felt like I needed to keep the conversation going. "How often do you talk to your dad?"

"Most nights." She pulled out her phone and checked through her messages. "I have two texts from him today."

"Are you going to call him back?"

She nodded. "He's in Norfolk this week. He's been asked to design an amphitheater for an art museum." Her lips curved a tiny bit, like she wanted to smile but couldn't quite go all the way. "He likes to work on projects involving nature."

"Norfolk's not very far. You should visit him."

Kimberley shrugged. "Are you ready to go home?"

"Sure. Are you taking me?"

"I decided long ago that I shouldn't get a license. Mom will have to drive."

Status Report #7
Thursday's Wish: Plumbing

Dear Boss,

The plumbing is like new.

I repaired all leaks and added insulation to the pipes. The utility bills should yield an improvement.

There was an infestation of insects under the house. Since I didn't care to share the crawl space with them, I persuaded them to find other accommodations.

Henry helped me. He confessed to a phobia about confined spaces. I am proud to report he triumphed over his fears and joined me for part of the time, primarily in a supervisory capacity.

I walked with him to his soccer practice. On the way, he discussed his father. As I was unsure if he expected me to respond, I chose to remain silent. It was a relief when he didn't press me for comments.

Mrs. Jones didn't sleep well last night. I could detect the scent of exhaustion on her skin. I offered to cook supper, and she accepted. The lack of variety in their pantry limited me to pasta with tomato sauce.

Afterwards, she and I sat on the deck, watching Henry kick a ball around. He was delighted to show off for an audience. She shared stories from his childhood, but none from Chief's. It was a pleasant yet puzzling hour.

The needs of this family are great. I struggle to remain detached from them.

Humbly submitted,
Grant

8

Shiny Eyes

*C*hirping birds awakened me on Saturday morning. Strange. Shouldn't the alarm have gone off already?

I opened an eye, checked the clock, and rocketed into a sitting position. Quarter past nine.

The game had started at nine. Henry's *first* game.

I jammed my legs into a pair of shorts, yanked my hair into a limp brown ponytail, and ran down the stairs. The house was quiet. I ran into the kitchen and skidded to a stop. Mom huddled in her sour bathrobe, sipping coffee and staring glassy-eyed out the kitchen window.

"Where's Henry?"

"Soccer."

"How'd he get there?"

"On his bike."

Yesterday had been Repairing Bikes Day, which meant Henry's was in good shape, but the soccer field was a mile away across major roads. "Mom. You can't let Henry go that far by himself. It's insane."

Her head turned slightly, her gaze brushing mine. "He didn't go by himself."

"Who went with him?"

"Grant." She stood, tightened the belt on her robe, and pushed past me. "I'm not *that* far gone, Lacey," she bit out.

Grant took my brother?

Henry was our responsibility. I didn't want Mom to pass him off on others. It was wrong, especially when the other person was *Mr. I'll Be Gone In A Month*.

Why hadn't anyone gotten me up?

I threw on a pair of sneakers and jogged to the soccer field. My BSB leaned against a tree, partially obscured by the shadows, separated from the crowd.

I approached him in his spot in the shade. "Hey," I said.

"Hello." He didn't look my way.

"You can go now."

"No, thank you."

It took a real gift to make a polite phrase sound so incredibly insulting. "I insist."

He turned toward me and stared down his nose. "Is it worth a wish to you?"

No, it was not worth a wish. I gritted my teeth and focused on the game.

The field was bathed in hot, bright sunshine, but the players didn't seem to care. They charged back and forth, kicking the ball, running into each other, and moving on. Since I didn't know anything about soccer, I couldn't tell how much longer they had to go.

When the referee blew his whistle, the adult spectators screamed and the two teams raced to their respective sides of the field to cluster around their coaches.

Excellent. I could get some answers without missing Henry's game. "Why didn't Henry wake me up?"

Grant pushed away from the tree and stood in his subservient position, hands behind his back. "He found me instead."

"I told him I would bring him."

"He knows you don't get to sleep in often."

That disturbed me. I didn't want my brother worrying about my sleep. "It's not okay for him to bother you on your off-hours."

"I don't mind."

"This is Henry's first game. I wanted to see it."

His gaze strayed to the field. "You don't like soccer."

"I like Henry."

A whistle squealed. I looked at the field to see that the game had resumed. My brother got the ball, kicked it away, and ran like the wind in the opposite direction. "Did he do the right thing?"

"You can't tell what's happening?"

"No."

There were screams from the stands. Grant applauded. "Good play."

"How's he doing?"

"He's one of the finest players on the team."

"Cool." I wanted to believe it.

Henry kicked the ball hard, paused, and leapt in the air. His team surrounded him, laughing and punching.

"Your brother scored a goal," Grant said, his words nearly drowned out by the screaming of the crowd.

Being on the winning side turned out to be a lot of fun, and it was easy to know when to scream with *Mr. Perfect Sports Fan* standing next to me.

I was about ready to escalate from screaming to obnoxious dancing when it occurred to me how relatively isolated we were. "Grant?"

His gaze never left the field as his face tightened with impatience, but at least he spoke politely. "Yes, Chief?"

"Why are we standing over here instead of sitting on the bleachers?"

"I can't answer for you, but I am here to avoid sensory overload. The noise and odor over there are more than I wish to bear."

I stayed in the shade with him, too lazy to bother moving.

Before much more time had elapsed, there were both moans of defeat and shrieks of joy from the stands. Henry and his teammates ran to the sidelines, screaming and slapping each other and generally looking victorious.

"I guess this is the end of the game," I said.

"It is."

"And we won?" Just wanted to be sure I was interpreting correctly.

"We did."

Grant and I crossed to the side of the field where a crowd milled around the kids on our team. Henry's gaze darted among the people, his head swiveling in tiny jerks. When he spotted us, he rushed over. "Lacey, did you see me play?"

"I did. You were brilliant." I opened my arms to give him a hug, but Henry backed up before looking around to see if his teammates were watching, which some of them were.

No hug. Ouch. My arms dropped.

"What do you think?" he directed at Grant.

"You played a fine game. Exceptional technique." They fist-bumped.

Eli hobbled over, giving Grant a curious glance before nodding at me. "The team's going to McDonald's to celebrate our first game. Want to come?"

Crap. I hadn't brought a purse. "No thanks."

Henry peered at me with anxious eyes. "Can I go? Please?"

"I don't know." I hated to embarrass my brother, but I didn't have enough money to cover a fast food meal. I dug into my pockets anyway and prayed.

Not good. Only coins.

Eli touched my arm. "Coach Makanui and I are treating."

Relief. "Go ahead, then. When should I pick him up?"

"I'll drop him off." Eli crooked his finger at my brother, and they rejoined the team.

Grant and I, along with the rest of the crowd, trickled toward the parking lot, dodging a new set of spectators and players arriving for the next game. When Grant paused to retrieve Henry's bike, I stopped to watch Henry and his teammates swarming about a gorgeous black Mustang and a trio of minivans.

"The young coach is interested in you."

"No, he isn't." I could hardly concentrate on what Grant was saying, not while my brother was climbing into that beautifully restored Mustang with Eli.

"Indeed, he is. He prickles with awareness around you."

That got my attention, especially because it was completely wrong. "Why do you think that?"

"He made an overture, and you, as the expression goes, 'blew him off.'"

We fell silent. Traffic was heavy around the park. While we waited to cross at a major intersection, my brain buzzed with jumbled thoughts. What overtures? Eli had smiled and praised my brother. And he was just being nice about McDonald's. Junk food with a dozen wiggling third-grade boys was not an overture. "I can't afford to eat out."

"His treat."

"I wouldn't have let him pay."

Grant made a disgusted sound in the back of his throat. "Perhaps I am behind on the dating rituals of the twenty-first-century North American teen, but I thought that was how dates worked. If the guy asks, the guy pays."

"It wasn't a date."

"Whatever you say."

Traffic had cleared by now. I took off across the street, uncaring if Grant kept up or not.

When Eli had arrived our freshman year, I'd watched him with hopeful curiosity, like most girls in our class. He was gorgeous, new, and adorably shy. But in this town, a college professor's kid was automatically popular. And when Eli turned out to be a soccer star, he'd had too many popular girls hanging on him to look outside his circle.

"Guys like Eli don't notice girls like me," I said, "at least not in that way."

"Perhaps you misjudge him."

I halted in the middle of the sidewalk. "You're not human. You can't know how Eli feels."

"A male mind is a male mind. Natural or supernatural."

"Really? It's hard to remember that you're a guy sometimes."

He flinched, his eyes burning into mine. "How do I seem to you?"

"Like a very efficient machine." The intensity of his gaze made me uncomfortable. I walked away, from him *and* from this conversation.

Where were Mom and Henry?

I should never have given in about the two of them going to the mall on a Saturday night. The only explanation for why I caved was my own distraction.

Things had been going well for the last week. I hadn't felt as...fractured. Henry was happy about the game. Mom had lucid moments, and Grant had been solidly confident, watching from the background, making anything seem possible.

Now it was after eight, and they still hadn't come home.

I couldn't call. Mom didn't have a phone.

I couldn't go after her. She had the only car.

And *Mr. I Have Rules* couldn't fly me there on his magic carpet or whatever BSBs used these days for transportation. So I was stuck.

I stood in the bay window and monitored the street. It remained stubbornly empty. Where were they?

She'd promised they would only be gone an hour. Just a little window-shopping in the air conditioning. A free way to celebrate Henry's win.

But they'd been gone too long. I couldn't fall for her promises again. Breaking them was so predictable. It was my fault for wanting to believe her. From now on, I would have to hide the keys.

I went back to the kitchen, got a glass of water, and carefully avoided looking at the clock. Probably only a couple of minutes had passed since I last checked.

The grind of brakes alerted me to their return. I'd already sucked in several calming breaths by the time my mother walked through the back door, a shopping bag over one arm.

Wait a minute. She *bought* something? It almost made me speechless. "Mom," I said with deceptive calmness, "what did you buy?"

"Towels. They were on sale." She pouted like a naughty child, just like she used to try with Josh. It hadn't worked on him either. "The ones we have are falling apart."

My hands curled into fists. I jammed them into my pockets because, otherwise, I couldn't be sure what they might do. "How did you pay?"

Her chin jutted out. "I'm not saying."

"We don't have any cash, and I destroyed all of your credit cards." There was a flicker in her eyes. Why was she so smug? Unless… "Did you hide a credit card from me?"

She shrugged.

How had I missed those bills? How much had she run up on this secret account? The thought made me sick. "Hand it over, Mom."

Her lips formed a tiny pucker of victory. "Make me."

Really? She was daring me? "Fine. We'll do it your way." I snatched her purse and ran out the back door.

"Let me have that," she screamed.

I was in the garage studio before she even made it out of the house. With a snap of my wrist, I dumped the contents of her purse onto the worktable.

There it was. A small rectangle of red plastic. The desk held no scissors, but there was a pair of hedge trimmers hanging from a hook on the wall. I had just chopped the credit card in half when she burst through the door.

"Stop it, bitch."

My hands froze. I gaped at her, hoping that I'd heard wrong but knowing that I hadn't.

Over the past year, I'd grown used to thinking of my mom as the ghost living at my house, an adult-sized toddler standing in the way of getting stuff done. With a single word, she ripped that mirage away. I was a normal teen again—whose mom had just called her a bitch.

"Oh, baby. I'm so sorry. I didn't mean that." Her face crumpled like a contrite child's.

I could hardly gauge my emotions. How could I be numb and sad at the same time? "I hope Henry didn't overhear." It would crush him if he knew.

"Henry?" Mom's mouth rounded in a wide O. She glanced over her shoulder into the yard. "Henry?"

Her voice sounded panicked. It frightened me more than anything I could've ever imagined. "Mom, where is he?"

She looked at me, sickly pale in the light of the bare bulb. "I don't know."

My head felt so full it might explode. "Did Henry go with you to the mall?"

"Yes."

"Did you bring him home?"

"I can't remember." She took a hesitant step into the yard, the shopping bag slipping from her arm. She started toward the car. "I . . ."

"The mall closed a few minutes ago." I swayed with the effort to stay controlled. "Did you leave Henry there alone?"

"I don't know." Tears rolled down her cheeks. "Maybe."

"Grant," I yelled, rubbing my tattoo. "Grant."

"I'm here," he said, stepping from the shadows.

"Did you—?"

"I heard it all. Let's go."

I snatched the keys from the worktable and chased him to the car. Within seconds, we were peeling out of the driveway.

"Please, please, don't let there be a cop," I said, racing through an intersection with no pretense of obeying traffic laws.

"There won't be."

He was right, whether by design or prediction, I didn't know. We made it to the mall in record time.

The parking lot was deserted—a big yawning asphalt wasteland. The darkness was nearly complete, except for the streetlights casting eerie amber circles on the pavement.

I roared up to a department store, peering into the shadows surrounding the building. "Where is he?"

"Stop the car."

My heart pounded so hard that my whole body was quaking. "Why? Do you see him? I see *nothing*." I slammed on the brakes anyway. "Do you see him?"

"No. You're driving too fast. I can't tell where he is." He shifted on the seat to face me, his expression grim. "Pull over to the curb."

I parked where he indicated, in front of a drug store. The doors were closed. The lights were out. There were no little boys in sight. I leaned my head against the steering wheel and tried not to pass out.

"Calm down and listen, Chief. You have to trust me."

"Okay," I whispered. "He must be terrified."

"Not helpful." He touched me gently on the shoulder. "Remember that I have superior senses. If you'll drive slowly around the perimeter of the mall, I'll be able to divine his location. And when I say 'stop,' you stop. No questions."

I nodded and put the car into motion. Slowly.

We crept by dark, silent storefronts. All ghostly shapes and shadows. I put on my high-beams, which permitted us to see *nothing* more clearly.

As we drove past the food-court entrance, Grant tensed and leaned forward.

"Stop."

Before I'd completed braking, he slipped off his seatbelt and leapt from the car. "Henry."

I punched it into PARK and jumped out. "Henry. It's Lacey. Are you here?"

Grant was running toward the dumpsters. I focused with every fiber of my being on that area. A shadow twitched and stood.

"Lacey?" a small voice called.

"Henry." If we'd been trains, there would've been a colossal wreck. A full-steam-ahead collision. The force nearly knocked me down. I hung onto his trembling body and hugged him tighter than anything I had ever known. "I'm so glad to see you," I said and breathed in his sweaty, greasy, little-boy scent.

"Me too."

I held him as if I would never let go. He was safe and real and I loved him.

Easing out of the embrace, I knelt to inspect his whole little person. "Are you okay?"

In the glow of the headlights, he looked wrinkled and flushed, like a newborn baby. But there were no tears. Just shiny eyes. "Yeah."

I couldn't help it. I hugged him again. "Were you scared?"

"No." He hiccupped. "Not much."

"That's okay. I was scared enough for the both of us." Over Henry's shoulder, I could see Grant waiting, hands behind his back. I mouthed "thank you." He inclined his head.

Henry squirmed in my hold, pulled away, and turned to look up at our BSB. "I hid over there." He jerked his head toward the farthest dumpster.

"Wise choice," Grant said and held out a fist. They bumped.

"I thought so," Henry said.

When I struggled to my feet, Grant offered me a hand. I brushed dirt off my knees and gave in to the anger filling the void where my fear had been. "How did this happen, Henry?"

His chin wobbled. "It was my fault, Lacey. I wasn't paying attention to what I was doing. I went into this toy store, and when I came back out, she was gone." He nodded, over and over again. "You don't need to be mad at Mom. Really."

"Nice try." My mother had totally done it now. I'd put up with her skulking around. Her insomnia and coffee-mania and crying fits. I'd tolerated being in charge, paying for everything, and hiding us from prying eyes. But I could not let her hurt Henry, no matter how much he wanted to protect her from my wrath. "When I get home—"

A hand cupped my shoulder and squeezed hard.

Surprised, I looked up.

Grant shook his head. "Stop," he said.

I did.

For now.

Status Report #9
Saturday's Wish: Heating, Ventilation, and Air Conditioning

Dear Boss,
   I completed a reconditioning of the HVAC system this afternoon. It was installed only two years ago and was already in good repair. I did not point out to Chief that she had essentially wasted a wish.
   The other parts of the day were unusually eventful.
   I enjoyed Henry's game. He's a natural on the field and a leader for his team.
   Afterwards, Chief called me a machine. I did not like that description. It is hardly accurate.
   Chief stayed at home to watch a movie while her mother and brother paid a visit to a shopping mall. I thought that was a promising sign. My optimism was misplaced, however. Crystal Jones forgot her son. I can only imagine the terror Henry must have felt as he awaited his rescue.
   As we hunted for him, Chief's desperation thickened the air like smoke, filling me with every breath. If that is how empathy feels, I do not care for it.
   Do you truly believe that emotional engagement will help on this case? The idea makes me uncomfortable. I do best when my thinking remains logical and objective.

   Humbly submitted,
   Grant

9

Chained Hearts

*I*t was past midnight, and I still couldn't sleep. My brother was safe in his bed. I knew this because I'd checked a dozen times in the last two hours. But I wouldn't be able to relax until I figured out how I was going to keep him safe from *her.*

Why did things have to get so backwards in our house? Since she couldn't be the adult, I knew that it had to be me. But that didn't stop me from hating it—from wishing it was just over. I'd give anything to be a kid again and not to be the responsible one in the house. It was like I was trapped in a horrible virtual-reality game, except there was no way for me to quit.

I listened to the noises of the night. The whir of the fan blades. The hum of bugs hitting my window screen. The occasional bark of a dog. I lay on top of my quilt in my nightshirt and couldn't rest.

At one o'clock, I gave up. Good thing it wasn't a school day tomorrow. Or rather, today. I slid off the bed and tiptoed down the stairs. The sixth stair creaked as usual, but no one stirred. I paused at the bottom. Mom's door was closed, as it had been all evening.

She did poke her head out when we brought Henry home and followed him into his room. Grant and I hovered outside the door, watching as she tousled Henry's hair, kissed his brow, and whispered apologies over and over. My brother kept reassuring her that it was okay, although I thought his voice sounded a little quivery. After a few minutes, she came back out again, smiled vaguely at Grant, and then disappeared into her cave. She'd avoided eye contact with me.

Now, I nudged Henry's door yet again, wanting to check one more time. The door swung inward with a soft suck of air. I crept to the side of his bed and concentrated on his breaths. They seemed regular enough. He had recovered.

I had not.

Where could I go to calm down?

Outside. I wanted to be outside. Carefully, I twisted the lock on the front door, pulled it open a few inches, and slipped through.

The temperature had dropped dramatically. At this hour, the air was cool and dry. A light breeze ruffled my hair, wrapping me in the scent of cedar from the trees edging our yard.

I perched on the top step of the front porch and savored the night. I wasn't sure what it said about me, but I liked the solitude. It felt bold, sitting out here all alone.

My eyes strayed to the wrist tattoo. Overlapping leaves. Or chained hearts. Which was it? Or maybe I was thinking too hard.

"Hello," said Grant.

I hadn't consciously summoned him. Yet here he was and I was glad. Because I liked being bold and not alone. "Thank you."

He plopped onto the step beside me. "She needs professional help."

Maybe being alone wasn't so bad. "Not an option at the moment."

"Her depression is serious. She may require medication."

As if I hadn't thought of that already and nagged my mom until we were both worn out about it. "She has pills. She doesn't take them."

"Someone must persuade her to start again." Concern radiated from his body. "This night's lapse of judgment endangered her child. You have to get her help."

Shut. Up. "No."

"It could be worse next time."

I sprang to my feet, too agitated to sit still. "We can't afford her psychiatrist."

"There are free mental health clinics."

"No." Free clinics were too nosy. I couldn't have them getting curious about my family.

He rose too. "What is wrong with finding another therapist? A new one might convince her to resume her medication."

"Why are you pushing this?"

"Why are you being so stubborn? I don't understand how you can give up on her."

"I haven't, but I can't *make* her act like a grownup." I whipped around to face him, disturbed by how judgmental he was being. Did he honestly believe I would give up on my own mother? Didn't he see that this was much bigger than her? "What if helping my mom backfires for Henry?"

"Henry?" Surprise colored his voice. "How could helping her possibly *hurt* him?"

I didn't want to explain, as if speaking the words made them more likely to come true. But there Grant stood, waiting. I couldn't have survived this evening without him. We were his business now. He deserved to know the real reason.

"They could take him away." The statement floated on the air, a faint whisper. It was my greatest fear, and it sounded far worse spoken out loud than it ever had inside my head.

"Who would take him away?"

"Child Protective Services…"

A tall, lovely lady appears in the doorway of the guest room. Her name is Mrs. Miller. She says I can call her Mary, but I don't want to.

"Lacey?" she asks in her soft, kind voice. She looks into the shadows and spots me, huddled on the carpet, pressed into the corner. "Do you want to eat something, dear?"

I shake my head. "Where is my dad?"

"He can't… He won't…" She smiles, but it's a sad smile. "Your mom will be here soon."

I scramble to my feet. This is good news. Nobody will tell me why the policeman brought me here or where Dad is or why I'm staying in this strange house, but Mom will. "Is she coming tonight?"

"No, dear."

"Why would you think that, Chief?"

"I spent some time in foster care after my dad died. I know what it feels like." I had to wait three days for the judge to release me from temporary custody and turn me over to my mom. It had been terrifying, even though the people who took me in had been nice. My sides ached with the effort to breathe. "I'm not eighteen. I'm not old enough to be named Henry's guardian. If they decide my mom can't care for us, CPS could put him in foster care too." There were other possibilities that were even worse. I'd heard horrible things about group homes where they housed boys of all ages. Most of the time, the boys were returned to their families—but in the meantime, scary things could happen.

"Then don't go to the government. There are local churches that will have private therapy groups."

"I don't trust them to keep quiet." Unable to remain still, I paced a few steps out into the front yard and then back again. "I don't mean for this to hurt my mom, but I can't risk losing Henry. I couldn't handle that."

Grant waited in silence, still as a statue, shielded by the night. I hadn't convinced him.

I ought to go in and try to sleep. "Goodnight," I murmured, stepping past him.

"When is your birthday?"

I hesitated. "Six more weeks."

"What will you do about Henry until then?"

"I don't know." October twenty-eighth couldn't get here soon enough for my peace of mind. After that, I could be the legal adult in the home, and Henry would be safe. We had to hold out a little longer, and the incident tonight made it harder. My mom had barely been helping with Henry, and now I couldn't let her help at all. "I can't leave him alone with her, and I can't afford to quit my job."

"Can you ask one of your neighbors for help?"

"No. Mom took care of that. Not long after Josh's funeral, when she was having a really bad day, Mom told a lady down the street not to bother us with questions or casseroles. Word got around fast. We haven't been 'bothered' since."

"What about family members?"

I snorted. Josh's parents were dead. Mom's parents had disappeared, whereabouts unknown. And while my Linden grandparents might help *me*, they had made it clear that Henry was not their problem. "Family isn't an option."

"I can stay with Henry when he's at home."

An automatic refusal sprang to my lips, but I bit it back. His suggestion had potential, at least temporarily. It would give me three weeks to figure out something better. "Will it cost me any wishes?"

He released a noisy sigh. "It's on the house."

They would bond big time, and Henry would be crushed when Grant left, but the time had come to trust my BSB. He'd proven himself worthy of it tonight, and I could use his help with Henry.

I shivered. What I was about to do terrified me. Once I got used to leaning on Grant, his departure might crush me too. And then where would my family be? "I accept," I said. "Thank you."

His lips twisted. "You're welcome."

"What's wrong?"

"Nothing." He raised his head to look at the stars. "I was reflecting on how consistently grateful you are."

Ouch. "I didn't know consistency was a problem."

"It isn't. That was a compliment." His gaze returned to my face, although his expression was impossible to read in the dark. "*Thank you* is not something I've heard very often. In my experience, human masters limit our conversations either to their demands or to criticism of my results."

Had I ever criticized the quality of his work? My brain was too tired to think it through. "I guess I should head to bed now."

He walked me to the porch and stayed at the bottom of the steps. As I entered the house, though, his voice halted me.

"Lacey, why haven't you used a wish for your mother?"

"It would violate your guidelines," I said, unable to hide the resignation in my voice. "It's not humanly possible to help her get better."

Update to Status Report #9

Dear Boss,

What is happening with this case? It is unprecedented in the challenges it brings.

My previous assignments were focused on specific, personal goals. I learned discipline beside a mistress training for a cross-country race. I observed passion in a master pursuing an acting career.

I cannot recall working for a teen who wished so desperately to tend to the other people in her life, and not herself.

Why have I been assigned here? I am only an apprentice. Surely the severity of their problems deserves a Being with more experience in helping families.

Although I acknowledge Chief's concerns about her brother, I don't believe her fears are well-founded. Surely the local government would not separate Henry from his family when he is so clearly cared for.

Chief underestimates the depth of her mother's illness. Crystal Jones requires professional mental health care. Her need is urgent.

For the first time since the League instituted the revised rules, I find myself fretting under their restrictions. This family could use so much more than the guidelines permit.

I have never asked for an exception before, but I wonder if it might not be warranted for them. May I use my powers on their behalf?

Humbly submitted,
Grant

10

Disconnected Images

Mom didn't come out of her room in the morning, not even for coffee. Henry, who had recovered from his ordeal, was begging me for an extra slice of toast before racing out the back door to kick around a soccer ball.

Time for chores. I cleaned up our breakfast things, made a quick harvesting foray into the vegetable garden, and started a pot of soup.

I was too fogged over to remember what today's wish was supposed to be, so requesting it would have to wait. Besides, I wasn't in the mood to talk to Grant. I'd had enough discussion about my mom to last me a while.

With my brother out of the way, I would take on his bedroom. It desperately needed its monthly airing-out. Almost mindlessly, I opened the windows, swept the hardwoods, and changed the sheets on the bed. It was already smelling fresher when I noticed the bottom drawer of his dresser was ajar. I plopped down, prepared to refold the dresser's contents.

Sleep deprivation must've dulled my thinking because I sat on the floor for a full minute, staring at his things, before I could absorb the condition of Henry's clothes. His old shorts lay next to his soccer uniform shorts, which were not only newer—but also wider and longer. I gave my head a hard shake and refocused.

Henry's regular clothes were a mess. They were either faded, torn, or—and this made my heart hurt—too small. Had we taken him shopping since Josh died? "He needs to stop growing," I mumbled.

"How do I do that?"

I glanced up to find anxious eyes on me. Crap, I didn't mean for him to hear that. When did my brother sneak into the room? "I'm joking, little man."

"These are fine." He grabbed a pair of shorts and held them against his body. They would barely cover his butt.

"Nice try, but you know they're not." He was just a little kid. He shouldn't have to deal with stuff like this. I'd forgotten to include this problem on the master plan, but it would be added now. "I'll ask Grant to take care of them," I said, my fingers brushing the tattoo.

"Great. He can do anything."

"Did I hear my name?" Grant stood in the doorway.

"Yeah. Lacey says you're going to fix my clothes."

My BSB made eye contact with me. "Indeed, I shall."

"Good. Maybe the guys at school will shut up about it." Henry darted from the room.

I slumped against the bed and stared at the empty doorway, stricken. "My brother is being teased?"

"Of course he is," Grant said.

How could this weekend get any worse? "I didn't know. He's never mentioned it." Why hadn't he? Henry could've talked to me anytime he wanted. I would've tried to figure something out.

"He didn't care to bother you."

"Did you know?"

Grant nodded.

"He should've told me, or you should have."

"Henry told me in confidence. It wasn't my right to tell you."

My brother discussed a serious problem with Grant but not with me. Why? Henry was my responsibility. Had I somehow lost his trust?

I would have to do something to make this right. I didn't know what. But something.

My brain slogged through the possibilities. It was too late for the Labor Day sales, but maybe I could find some pants at a thrift store. "Can I wish for you to make them brand new?"

"No." He towered over me as he studied the stack. "However, I can turn those jeans into shorts."

"What if I gave you more of Josh's old clothes? Could you make little-boy pants from them?"

"Do you have a sewing machine?"

I nodded. "Mom has a great sewing machine." I'd never seriously considered cashing it in at the flea market. Sewing had been too important to her in the past. Maybe it would be again one day.

"Then certainly, I can fashion new clothing for Henry." He reached down to help me to my feet.

I rose too quickly and fell into his body. When his arms closed automatically around me, my hands were trapped between us, splayed against his chest. It was, I had to admit, a very nice chest.

Wait. No.

I pushed away and staggered backwards. "Sorry." I scrubbed my palms against my shorts to stop them from tingling. "That's my wish today. What you said. About Henry's clothes."

His gaze went from my palms to my face. With a suppressed sigh, he snapped his fingers. The pile of jeans jumped into his arms.

I ran from the room, needing to escape. Once in the hallway, though, I stopped and leaned against the wall. What had happened in there?

Grant was gorgeous, and he had a great body. But I'd known that from the first moment I saw him. What was different about today?

It wasn't as if I *liked* him. What would be the point? I was his mistress. He was my genie. *Like* wasn't part of the agreement. Grant surrounded himself with an attitude as approachable as a barbed-wire fence. No way did I want a piece of that.

Maybe what I was feeling was respect. He'd shown such strength and kindness last night.

Wrong. That wasn't it either. Respect didn't make me want to scrub the tingling from my palms.

What then? Gratitude?

Yes, that had to be it.

Of course. I had someone to share problems with. He was helping me with Henry. I was flooded with gratitude. Even Grant had commented on it last night. Unlike his previous masters, I was consistently grateful.

I needed to show him, and I knew how. He hadn't spent all of the money we'd budgeted for the air conditioning unit. We could spare a few dollars. "Grant?"

He appeared in the doorway. "What is it?"

"Do you like ice cream?"

"The invention of ice cream was one of humanity's finest hours."

I smiled. "I'll take that as a *yes*. Why don't you come with me and Henry to get a treat?"

The Super Scoops Ice Cream Parlor was located on a side street behind The Reading Corner. My brother beat us there by half a block and had stopped on the sidewalk to talk with his soccer teammate, Reynolds.

Some girls from my senior class were exiting Super Scoops as we arrived. Grant held the door for them, shocking them into silence, whether from the jaw-dropping sight of him or from the fact he was with me, it was hard to tell.

It would've been easier if my genie had been ugly. Or twelve inches tall. Or green. But no. I had to end up with the BSB who was every girl's dream. There might be questions tomorrow at school. I would have to spend some time tonight making up answers.

I entered the shop ahead of him and Henry. "What should we get, guys?"

"Peach," Henry said as he ran to the glass case holding huge tubs of ice cream.

Grant said, "Vanilla."

"Vanilla?" I gave Grant a pained smile. "Please tell me you're not serious. You ought to try something radical. Like caramel-fudge-brownie. It's a symphony of flavors."

"Vanilla is about all I can stand. My sense of taste cannot take anything stronger."

I preferred anything with chocolate. Henry wanted peach, and Grant could only tolerate vanilla. Three flavors. Since I had a Buy-One-Get-One-Free coupon with me, we'd only be able to get two flavors.

I stood in line to order while Grant claimed a table in the front corner. It had a good view of the entire shop, with its black, white, and pink 1950s decor. He positioned himself with his back to the wall and waited until I placed both dishes in the center of the table.

"Hey, Lacey, can I sit outside with Reynolds?" Henry asked loud enough for the whole store to hear.

"Sure, if his mom doesn't mind."

"She doesn't. I already asked her."

I handed over his dish and watched as he ran to an outdoor table occupied by Reynolds and his parents.

Elizabeth Langston

"All right," I said as I pushed the other dish nearer to my guest. "It's our turn to eat."

Grant shoveled in his first spoonful like he was afraid someone would take it away. It was cute and unexpectedly endearing. "How often do BSBs get ice cream?"

He swallowed and smiled lazily. "Not often. We only eat human food when invited."

I licked my spoon and paid extra attention to the taste. Creamy, rich, and delicious. I would hate only having ice cream when someone else asked. It was bad enough to wait until I saved up the money.

My BSB didn't get invitations or gratitude very often. Instead, he received criticism for the free services he provided. Was this why he needed a league?

Behind us, a group of people burst into laughter. Grant's gaze shifted in their direction. He stiffened and set down the spoon, his expression fierce.

I turned to see what had upset him. Some of my classmates were sitting nearby. Four half-eaten banana splits crowded the table top. The guys were flinging bits of pineapple and strawberry at each other. The floor under their table was disgusting.

I swung back around. "Don't watch. They're being stupid."

"I have experience with behavior like theirs. It's the reason the League developed guidelines for our assignments."

"To protect you from humans?"

"To protect us from the shallow ones. We're no longer obligated to indulge pure greed." He scooped up more ice cream and savored it as he watched Henry through the window.

"Do you like being a genie?"

He nodded. "There were several job options available to me. I made a conscious choice to spend my apprenticeship by granting wishes."

"Why?"

"It gave me the greatest opportunity to study humans in depth. I wanted to learn as many emotions as possible."

He seemed grumpy so much of the time, I'd assumed it was because he didn't like what he was doing. It was surprising that he'd asked for this job. "What kinds of things have you done?"

"Most of my masters have been teens applying to college or athletes training for competitions." His lips twisted, then relaxed. "I also had a mistress who entered beauty pageants for the scholarships."

"I wonder why none of those people were grateful."

"*Consistently* grateful." He gave a small shake of his head. "I suppose I'm treated no differently than most people in service jobs, like teachers or waiters. If we don't meet your expectations, you complain. Otherwise, our performance goes unnoticed."

I'd worked for the past year at The Reading Corner. I totally got that. "Does it bother you?"

He nodded slowly. "I think perhaps it does, and I can't say why. I am required to execute my tasks well regardless."

Yep. Got that too. "How long have you been an apprentice?"

"Two years."

"That much?"

His mouth strained to hold back a smile. "Time is relative."

"Uh-huh." Two years seemed long to have to wait for a promotion. Relatively speaking. "What does an apprentice get promoted to?"

"I'll be promoted to the principal level. The tasks are more difficult, and I won't require supervision." His lips curved slightly. "I've asked for a job in situational security."

"Huh?"

A full laugh. "You know it better as guardian angel."

I tried to imagine him with wings and a sword and couldn't do it. "Will you get to use magic when you're a guardian angel?"

"I use my powers at present. I just don't use them for you."

His pleasure in reminding me was annoying. "Why do you have the *humanly possible* rule?"

"Our goal is to assist people in solving real problems, not to make them rich or beautiful, but humans couldn't grasp that. They wanted income without working or plastic surgery without the consequences. When Beings suggested establishing guidelines, our leaders agreed. However, to ensure that we truly make a difference with our assignments, they changed several policies. For instance, when they narrowed the types of wishes that can be granted, they increased the allotment to thirty."

"Yay for me." Sounded like a good plan—unless the problem was how poor we were. "Why don't you just use the title of genie? Why not call yourselves what humans expect?"

"Very few apprentices fulfill wishes. It is not typical for a Being at the apprentice level to choose such extended exposure to the same human." He frowned. "Overall, Benevolent Supernatural Being feels more descriptive of our mission. It implies our unity."

Right. I wonder if BSBs included the tooth fairy? I'd take her leftover change. "Did you know 'genie' comes from the same Latin word as 'genius?'"

"Fits, don't you think?"

I refused to be sidetracked. "I looked up 'genie' on Wikipedia."

"Ah. The collective wisdom of humankind." He relaxed against his chair, cupped his hands behind his head, and gave me a satisfied grin.

"It says 'genie' means a 'spirit or magical being.'"

"True."

"It can also be the English translation of the Arabic word 'jinni,' which are hidden spirits who can be good or bad."

He grunted.

"So which are you?"

He popped up straight in his chair, the relaxed posture gone. "Truly, Chief, this is a pointless exercise. I've arrived to grant you a month's worth of wishes. Any further labels are unnecessary."

It was an impatient response for him, but one phrase in particular stood out. "What do you mean you *arrived*? I *found* you."

"It has been my experience that I arrive at the precise moment when someone needs me."

Grant's appearance was planned? Not likely. Too many things had come together. The money. The candlesticks. Madame Noir. The music box. If any one of those things had been left out, Grant and I would've never met. "Are you sure that I didn't just stumble across you?"

"There are no coincidences." He looked away, as if bored.

Wow. Didn't want to pursue that. "What do you do between your gigs?"

"Between *assignments*, I attend training, visit with other Beings, and read nonfiction, primarily human psychology."

I tried not to smile. "You don't understand us automatically?"

"Not at all. I find humans to be illogical." His gaze snapped to mine. "Fortunately, I expect you to be my last such assignment."

"The promotion?"

"Yes."

"What do you still need to learn?"

He half-smiled. "In order to be an effective servant, a Being must understand the spectrum of human emotions. The League has designated fourteen basic emotions in which we must be proficient before qualifying for the principal level. I lack three for promotion."

"Which emotions are you missing?"

The smile disappeared as his gaze left mine. "Generosity, empathy, and judgment. Or—" His lips pressed together.

"Is there a fourth?"

Faint color rose in his cheeks. "There is a wildcard emotion."

"What is it?"

"Love." He averted his face. "If we experience human love, we may trade it for three of the basics."

"So love is like a shortcut to promotion?" At his nod, I said, "That sounds like a good option."

He grunted. "Not at all. Most Beings are intimidated by the thought of human love. It is too…"

"Complicated?"

"Painful."

I couldn't argue with that. "Is the principal level the highest you can go?"

He shook his head. "There is another. It is quite elite. You must be chosen."

"What's it called?"

"I don't know. Only members know its name."

"Do you aspire to the level with no name?"

Something determined flashed briefly in his eyes, but his response was carefully mild. "Perhaps."

The conversation ebbed while I finished my share of the ice cream. Grant kept watch over the shop, presumably getting in some early practice on guardian techniques.

He pounced the very second the last drop passed my lips. "What do you aspire to?"

"In a career?"

He nodded.

"I'd like to own a small business one day."

"What type of business?"

"Graphic design, maybe." I shrugged to make the answer sound more casual than it was. "I'd like to make things that are pretty and useful."

"So you don't plan to follow your father's lead?"

"Into the military? No." I frowned, not sure whether to be uneasy with where these questions were headed.

"Were you close to your father?"

"Yeah. Real close." I put down my spoon and inspected the chrome top of our little round table. "He had custody of me."

"If he was in the Marine Corps, how could that work?"

"Probably like any single parent. I was in daycare when he was working at the base. And if he was busy somewhere out of town, either my mom or grandparents had me." I looked out the window, not really seeing anything. Grant's question had dredged up memories of my father, like a digital photo album of disconnected images.

Sitting next to Dad on a picnic table.

Washing his truck.

Lying on a towel at the beach.

My father had been a lot of fun. "I don't think he was gone often, because my memories of him from back then are so strong. I wasn't anxious or concerned. I knew when to expect him, and he always showed up." Until he didn't. But I wouldn't go there.

"When did your parents divorce?"

"They never married." I'd been a surprise to my parents from the beginning. "Dad was stationed in Jacksonville. When Mom found out she was pregnant, she moved in with him. After I was born, they continued to live together, but it didn't work out. They both agreed that Dad was better prepared to be a single parent than Mom. So when she moved back to Magnolia Grove, I stayed with him at Camp Lejeune." My gaze took in my brother, talking intensely with his friend while Reynolds's parents watched, smiling proudly.

Even though my parents and I hadn't been the typical kind of family, we'd found a way to be happy. It always felt right. I could still remember the handoffs on Friday and Sunday nights. It had been exciting, like I got to live in two exclusive overnight camps. Dad had a tent in his living room. Fort Lacey. And Mom, not to be outdone, had pulled out her sewing machine and decorated the most incredible bedroom for me, with a matching lavender satin quilt, pillowcases, and curtains.

It had been perfect. Two parental moons orbiting planet Lacey.

"I'm surprised your grandparents haven't offered to help you."

"They don't know what's going on."

"Of course not. You are determined to reject all charity, even if your family suffers."

Wow. Where had that come from? It had been a nice conversation until that attack. His comment had been perfectly designed to transform my overly sensitive feelings to something stinging and raw. "Maybe you could give me some pointers. You're the expert at using people."

"Pardon me?"

How dare he ruin my one calm afternoon? After a bad night, Henry's clothes, and the tingling gratitude, I needed a break from emotion. Was it too much to expect that Grant would hold off on judging me for thirty whole minutes? "You're a fake. We both know my problems aren't the real reason you've shown up."

His face tightened. "Not true."

"Don't bother acting like you care. Humans are just tools for you—the next rung in your supernatural career ladder."

"You are quite wrong." His gaze flicked over my shoulder and returned to me. "We'll have to continue this conversation another time. Someone is headed our way."

I clamped my lips together and frowned at the table. A chair scraped beside me.

"Hi," Kimberley said.

I tried to smile. "Hi. Are you here with your mom?"

"Yeah, she's standing in line."

I glanced over my shoulder to find Mrs. Rey watching us. When I waved, she waved back. I turned around to find Kimberley staring fixedly at my BSB.

"I don't remember you mentioning that you're dating someone," she said.

"We're not dating."

"You argue like people who date."

"Kimberley, this is my *friend*, Grant."

"I am her employee," Grant said in his stiff, British accent.

My head whipped around so quickly that a pain shot down my neck. "Employee?" I hated that word. It sounded so impersonal. "That isn't the right word."

His eyes narrowed on me. "Neither is friend."

Wow. That stung.

"Then what is the right word?" Kimberley asked, her face eager.

He turned his attention on her. "Perhaps helper."

"What do you do to help Lacey?"

"Whatever she wishes."

I had to grit my teeth to keep from saying something I would regret.

"Do you have a specialty, Grant?"

I snorted. "He's good at everything. Just ask him."

Her gaze didn't waver from his face. "If you're good at everything, you must be expensive."

"Indeed not. I don't charge her family."

Kimberley smiled. "I need free help. Can you come to my house next?"

He shook his head. "I'm not sure of my schedule."

She looked at me. "When will he be done?"

"Soon." Why had this afternoon gone wrong? It had been so nice. So fun. So *friendly*.

Kimberley stood and patted me on the shoulder. "I have to leave now, and I left my tablet in the car. Can you remind me later of all the stuff we said?"

"Sure." I shot a steely-eyed glance at Grant. "I won't forget."

Status Report #10
Sunday's Wish: Repair Henry's Clothing

Dear Boss,

It was an unusually long day.

When I asked to borrow the sewing machine, Chief's mother volunteered to do the stitching. We spent the evening turning old clothes into shorts and jeans for Henry.

I can barely contain my desire to help Crystal. She has confided her despair over losing her husband. Perhaps I have gained some influence with her. Since Chief won't permit me to seek assistance for Crystal, may I intervene on my own? I would keep my efforts to humanly possible actions, if you think that best.

I hoped there would be a positive change in our relationship when Chief treated me to vanilla ice cream. Her face as she remembered her father was lovely to behold. Yet what began as a pleasant conversation was ruined by her theories about my motivation.

It is maddening. A fake, indeed. My interest in humans is genuine. She is utterly mistaken.

Humbly submitted,
Grant

11

Huge Confession

*M*s. Dewan stopped me as I was leaving second period and asked me to drop by her room after school. She did not look happy.

So here I was. She still looked grim. "You can do better work than this, Lacey," she said, slapping my last assignment on the desk.

Her razor-sharp disapproval sliced through me. I stared at the paper, not touching it, not meeting her eyes. "I don't know what you mean. It's a C."

"You are capable of A-quality work." She nudged the sheet closer to me. "Lacey," she said, her voice softening, "you're a phenomenal writer. What's going on?"

I'd never gotten a C before on a major assignment. I hated that it had happened now, but I couldn't help it. I'd worked most nights last week. It was hard to get to the county library since they closed at nine. I'd done the best I could, considering I lacked the necessary research, time, and sources. However, I wouldn't explain any of this, because one explanation would lead to another. Something private might slip out, and Ms. Dewan might try to intervene. I couldn't trust her to treat my secrets the way I wanted them handled. So I answered her with a shrug.

Her lips pinched. "You're doing well enough to pass this class, but more marks like this will affect your final grade."

"Okay." I picked up the paper and slid it into my backpack.

"That's all you have to say?"

"Yes, ma'am."

"That's not good enough for me." She leaned forward, searching my face. "It's not like you to do so poorly on a writing assignment. Is there something going on that I need to know about? Something I can do to help you?"

I could think of several things. She could cut me some slack. She could find me some family assistance that wasn't official. She could wave a magical wand and make Piedmont College more affordable. "No, ma'am."

"Lacey, it's too soon to lose your intensity. You won't impress competitive universities unless you keep your grades up."

This was my second year of English with Ms. Dewan. I'd watched her enough to know that she was one of those teachers who really cared, but today, it was getting in the way. I would tell her as little of the story as I could, just enough to keep her from bugging me about it for the rest of the semester. "My grades are fine for community college."

"What?" Her eyes widened. "I thought you had your sights set on William & Mary."

Not a chance after this weekend. I couldn't be a four-hour drive away from here. "I've changed my mind."

"Why? You could easily qualify for the best four-year schools." She gave me a pained look. "Is it the money? Because if it is, there are millions of scholarships out there. I could help you find some."

"It's not the money." When Dad died, his life insurance policy turned into my college fund. He'd known Mom well enough to tie up the funds so they could only be spent on education. The amount would cover the out-of-state tuition of a school like William & Mary but not somewhere as expensive as Piedmont.

No, my problem wasn't the money. It was the distance. I had to stay close to home until I trusted my mom to take care of Henry. "Really, Ms. Dewan, Magnolia Community College is great."

"You're making a big mistake, Lacey. At least apply to other places. You might reconsider next spring and—"

I interrupted. "I appreciate the concern, but don't worry. I'm all right." I stood up and spun around to leave.

Eli waited in the doorway. He stepped aside to let me pass.

How much had he heard? As I retreated, he slid onto the chair I'd vacated. I took off at a run, my footsteps pounding along the deserted hallways. I didn't pay attention to where I was going, only that I got far from Ms. Dewan and her dismay over that big red C.

Somehow I made it to my locker just as my shaking legs gave way. I slid to the cold tile floor, leaned my head back against the metal door, and closed my eyes.

Why couldn't I have a week where nothing bad happened? Where school went well and Mom was functional? Where I could look forward to community college without someone reminding me of the universities I was giving up? Where no one was upset with me over something I couldn't fix?

If I couldn't have a week to forget, I would take a few moments.

I had to be at The Reading Corner in twenty minutes, but until then, I would stay right here and be completely alone.

There were no rude customers, no noisy classmates, no helpless family, no disappointed teachers.

Just me and the silent hallway.

Dimming into a void.

Quiet. Dark. Still.

Perfect.

"Lacey?"

It was Eli's voice, intruding into my haven of emptiness. "Yes?" I spoke around a lump in my throat, not ready to emerge from sweet solitude.

"Are you okay?"

"Yes." My eyelids fluttered open.

He was standing above me, his face reflecting concern. "Do you need help getting up?"

Having Eli see me at my worst was becoming a habit, yet it hadn't stopped him from being friendly. I hesitated only briefly before accepting his hand and letting him haul me to my feet. "Thanks."

"Are you sure you're okay?"

"Yeah." I lifted my backpack and headed for the front door.

"Hey, wait." Eli fell into step beside me. "Has Henry mentioned snack day?"

"No."

"Do you know if your mom received the email from Coach Makanui? She hasn't responded yet."

"My mother doesn't have an email account."

"Okay, then. Did you receive the message?"

"I haven't checked email in a while." Email required a computer, and I hadn't had a chance to spend much free time at the library recently. None of which I would explain to Eli.

I pushed through the exit door and halted on the sidewalk in front of the school. An ice-cream truck was parked on the street, with a line of students waiting for frozen treats. Some popular kids were hanging out in the bus lane. Everybody was laughing. Having fun. I wished I could—

"Coach Makanui put Henry down for this Saturday."

His words penetrated my daze. I stopped to frown at him. "What exactly is snack day?"

"Your family provides the after-game snack."

Anxiety prickled my skin. "What are we supposed to bring for an after-game snack?"

"Actually, snack is the wrong word." Rolling his eyes, he said, "If your mom came to any of the games last year, she'd know. It's evolved into a small meal. Chips. Juice boxes or Gatorade. Fresh fruit. Homemade cookies."

My stomach twisted into knots. "For how many people?"

"If everyone shows up, sixteen."

A feast for sixteen hungry eight-year-old boys? I made fast calculations and got dizzy. Even if I bought bargain brands from the dollar store, it would devastate our emergency fund. "I could swing lemonade and crackers."

"Have you seen what the other moms do? They go all out. It's like a competition. You didn't notice last year?"

"I did not. Soccer was something Henry did with my stepdad." This was like some kind of bad dream, and I just wanted to wake up. "I'm sorry, but no."

"No what?"

A faint buzz rumbled at the base of my skull, like someone was holding a mixer against it on low power. We barely had enough to eat now. I couldn't rob our food budget to compete against some moms I didn't know or care about. "No snack day for us."

He frowned. "It's not a choice."

The buzz got louder as panic swamped me. "It has to be, because we're not doing it."

"You agreed to it when he joined the team."

"*I* agreed to nothing."

"Your mother knew. Maybe I should talk to her."

"The answer'll be the same."

He jammed his hands into his pockets and stared me down. "It's a rule, Lacey. Everyone on the team will notice."

"Will he have to quit?"

Eli's mouth dropped open, as if in disbelief. "What's the problem here? Snack day isn't hard."

I couldn't take any more. Eli was about to walk away thinking that I was randomly mean to my brother and that I believed my family was too good to follow the rules. As much as the thought of him knowing our secrets made me sick, the only way to make Eli understand would be to tell him the truth. It felt like my eyeballs were swimming in tears. I would not let them fall. "We don't have it," I whispered.

A tense silence followed.

"I don't understand. What don't you have?"

If I were a normal girl, I'd have been crying already. I'd shed pretty tears and make tiny, pitiful gasps. But I was too tired, too overwhelmed, too in-charge to be normal. My face might ache, but the tears wouldn't flow. "We don't have the money."

"You can't afford snacks?"

"We really can't afford lemonade and crackers." I lifted a shaking hand to tuck a stray lock of hair behind one ear. I'd told someone. And not just any someone. My brother's coach. A classmate I had to face every weekday morning. A guy I thought was hot.

"Hey. I didn't know." His voice was kind. "What can I do?"

"Nothing." My voice cracked on the word. I covered my face with my hands.

He muttered something, dropped a light arm across my shoulders, and pulled me to him.

It had been so long since someone had hugged me that I didn't know how to react. I hunched stiffly, dizzy and sad and resistant.

"It'll be okay," he said. "I'll think of something."

Closing my eyes, I rested my forehead against his shirt, as if I could hide from him and the world. *I can't believe I told him.*

He murmured, "It's okay," a few times.

People passed by, spoke to Eli, and moved on. And still I stood there, tuning out everything except the gentle cocoon of his arms.

The voices stopped coming by. I wiggled slightly and inched back. His hands steadied me until I regained my balance.

"Hey, Lacey. Are you going to be all right?"

"Yeah, thanks." I studied my feet. "Do you know what time it is?"

"Almost three o'clock. Why?"

"My job. I'm late." Unable to meet his gaze, I smiled in his general direction and then turned away, embarrassed that I'd lost control.

"Lacey?"

I looked over my shoulder.

"Are you walking?"

I nodded.

"Can I give you a ride?"

A real smile tickled at the corners of my mouth. "That would be great. I work at The Reading Corner."

"Let's go."

His Mustang waited in the senior parking lot. He held the door for me as I slid in. I drank in the sight, smell, and feel of his car with a reverence that rendered me speechless.

Eli got in, slipped on his seatbelt and shades, and then cranked the engine. Even that sounded amazing.

He didn't say anything until he'd pulled into traffic. "Henry's a big asset to the team."

My little brother was about the only subject that could drag my attention away from the Mustang. "Thanks."

Eli shifted gears smoothly. "Your friend has brought him to practice a couple of times."

"My friend? You mean Grant?"

"Yes."

"He's not a friend. He's just helping us out." Enough about Henry. I wanted to talk about this car. I would've already touched the dashboard if I hadn't been afraid to. "What year is this?"

"It's a '64." There was pride in his voice. "You like Mustangs?"

"From the cradle."

Eli laughed as he pulled into a parking space on the town square. "How long is your shift?"

"Today, it's six hours." I slid from the seat and stood in the open door, admiring the car just a little longer.

"When do you study?"

"What?" He was still talking. *Focus.* "I'll study after I walk home from work."

"You walk?" His voice held a surprised edge.

I nodded. That made two guys who didn't like the idea of me walking in the dark. It was a little weird. I wasn't sure how to process all of this concern about me. "Well, thanks for dropping me off."

As I entered the shop, I watched his taillights disappear around the corner. That ride—and Eli—had been sweet.

Tonight was my turn to close the shop, which I didn't mind doing except that it took forever. I locked the front door behind the last few customers, ran the day's register, and deposited the receipts in the office. After taking one final look around, I shut off the lights and exited the bookstore through The Java Corner.

Mrs. Lubis gave me her version of a smile and tapped the lid of a to-go cup on the counter. "On the house."

"Thanks," I said with a smile and picked it up. She had my favorite drink ready—a skinny decaf cappuccino with a dash of cinnamon. As I took my first sip, my gaze lazily surveyed the room. A single customer sat at a corner table with a coffee mug and a tablet computer. He looked a lot like Eli.

I refocused. He *was* Eli.

"Hi," I said, crossing to him. "What are you doing here?"

"Giving you a ride home."

A warm glow trickled through my veins. I perched on the empty chair opposite him, suspended somewhere between shock and pleasure. "Thanks. That's really nice."

"We can go as soon as I finish my coffee."

"Sure."

I sipped my cappuccino while he stared into his mug. Silence ruled.

We needed conversation. Something we had in common. With him, that meant school or soccer. "Were you meeting with Ms. Dewan about an assignment today?"

"No, the essay contest."

"Really? I wouldn't think you needed the money."

"Ms. Dewan does."

Wow. I hadn't thought of it that way. Maybe I should reconsider writing one. I took another sip of my drink.

He looked up from his mug and smiled.

I relaxed. This was fun. Comfortable. "Is this the first year you've coached for Henry's league?"

"Pretty much. I had knee surgery this summer on my ACL. It'll take several months to heal, so I thought I'd coach for the fall season."

"Will you go back to the varsity team next semester?"

"I hope so. Since I want to play at Duke, I need a good spring season."

"Will you get a soccer scholarship?"

"I'm not interested in that. I just want to make the club sports team."

"What do you plan to major in?"

"Biology. Eventually, I want to go to med school."

In every class we'd been in together, he asked lots of questions, not giving up until he understood. An important quality to have in a doctor. "You'll be great at that."

He gave me a half-smile. "What are your top schools?"

"I haven't narrowed the field yet." *Liar, liar, pants on fire.*

"Are you considering Piedmont?"

I nearly spat out my drink. Had he not processed my huge confession? My family could barely afford milk. A private college with insanely high tuition was completely out of our league, even with everything my father had left in my college fund. "Eli, really."

"What?"

"Piedmont is nowhere on my list. Magnolia Community College is more my speed."

"You can do better than MCC."

"It's a good school."

His eyes narrowed on me. He might not agree but didn't come right out and say so. After gulping down the last of his coffee, he set the mug on the table with a *clunk*, rose, and helped me to my feet.

The drive to my house was completed in silence. I didn't even have to give directions. He'd given Henry rides home and knew the way.

When he pulled up to the curb, he cut the engine and turned toward me. "Lacey?"

There was an odd note in his voice. It made me nervous. "Yeah?"

"I want you to know that…" he hesitated, his gaze going past me. A smile curved his lips. "We have an audience."

I looked toward the house. My brother waited in the bay window. A shadow shifted in the background. Was that Grant or my mom? "Yeah. He's probably wanting some help with his homework."

"He talks about you all the time."

I whipped around to face Eli. "Really? Good or bad?"

"Great." His smile widened. "He thinks you're the best big sister ever."

I settled into the smooth leather of the passenger seat and allowed myself to take that in. Today had been hard. I'd disappointed Ms. Dewan and revealed secrets I'd hated sharing, but the evening had ended so much better. A cappuccino. A ride in a vintage Mustang with a good guy. And a brother who said nice things about me behind my back. I could get used to this.

"Thanks for letting me know that," I said as I slipped out the door.

His car door squawked open. "Lacey, wait."

I stopped on the driveway and turned to face him.

"Don't walk home in the dark again," he said. "Call me if you need a ride."

Wow. He just kept getting nicer. I wasn't likely to take him up on the offer, but I absolutely loved that he'd made it. "I'll let you know if I do," I said and then hurried for the house.

As I closed the front door behind me, Henry charged me from the living room, talking about soccer practice and Eli and homework. I nodded and smiled, only half-hearing what he said, my ears focused on the rumble of a Mustang fading down the street.

After three years of being friendly classmates, maybe Eli and I were on our way to being just plain friends.

Status Report #11
Monday's Wish: Painting

Dear Boss,

I painted the doors and shutters today. There were five partially filled cans of paint in the garage. Once I'd mixed them, the color was an unappealing gray. And, yes, I did use my powers to change the gray to blue. It was truly my wish.

Crystal cleaned the deck furniture. You were correct, of course. She enjoyed being outside and feeling productive. How else might I help her without violating the conditions of my assignment?

Eli accompanied Chief home from work, for which I am grateful. I had planned to do the same, but I had also promised to stay with Henry, who was quite happy to see his coach and sister together. Frankly, I find the improvement in their relationship both predictable and oddly unsettling.

Humbly submitted,
Grant

12

An Empty Quiet

I walked home from school Tuesday afternoon, mentally recalculating our budget as I tried to come up with some way to squeeze out a few more dollars. Maybe I could work another shift at the bookstore. Maybe Grant could create some junk that I could sell at the flea market. There had to be something we could do to cover a snack day without humiliating Henry and destroying our tiny emergency fund.

Lost in thought, it took me a moment to realize that a huge silver pickup truck hugged the curb in front of my house. I stopped and frowned as recognition dawned. It belonged to Mr. Taylor. This was strange. Even though he'd been my dad's best friend, he'd always seemed uncomfortable around my mom. He hadn't been by our house since last spring.

I hurried, taking the porch stairs in two bounds. As I skidded through the front door, I found him standing in the foyer, arms folded over his chest. Mom stood a few feet away in shorts and a stained T-shirt, her hands fluttering nervously.

"Hey, Mr. Taylor," I said.

He scrutinized me from head to toe before saying in his deep, slow drawl, "Good to see you, Lacey. How've you been?"

"I'm fine." I smiled at him tentatively. "It's nice to see you too."

Mom said, "Allyn is worried about you."

I frowned at him. "What are you worried about?"

"Just wanted to make sure everything's okay," he said.

Wariness tickled at my throat. What brought him over here today? "Everything's great. Why would you think there is anything wrong?"

"Lacey," Grant said.

I glanced toward the opposite side of the living room. Grant was leaning against the mantle. He'd used my first name. Of course. We had an audience. "What?"

"It has been implied that my motivations for being here are inappropriate."

"Mr. Taylor is here about you?"

"Indeed."

Okay, that was unexpected. "He's our handyman," I said, facing my almost-godfather. I'd already explained this. "Grant is helping us around the house."

"Which is generally what a handyman does," Mr. Taylor said. "It just seems a little odd to me, so I thought I would check in. What are you paying him?"

I stared at Grant. How could we compare notes without making things worse?

My mother jumped into the conversation. "He's working free of charge." Her forehead scrunched in concentration. "Well, we do give him room and board."

Shut up, Mom. Too much information would lead to more questions.

"Oh?" Mr. Taylor grunted. "Where does he sleep?"

"In the garage."

"There's no bedroom out there." He focused a hard stare on Grant.

"No, there isn't." Mom looked at Grant. "What do you sleep on?"

He gave her a light smile. "A hammock. I brought it with me."

"Oh. Good idea." She smiled back and then turned to our visitor. "Really, Allyn, you can chill about this. I have it under control."

"Yes, I can see that." Mr. Taylor straightened to his full height, his face tightening with skepticism. "Are you missing any valuables?"

"No, we're not," I said, ready to take control of this conversation so that I could end it as quickly as possible. "We don't own anything worth stealing."

His eyebrows shot up in surprise. "You don't? Since when?"

Wow. Big mistake. "What I mean is…" I paused and looked up at him with my most nonchalant grin. "Our family heirlooms have more sentimental value than anything else."

"But Lacey—" my mom started.

I silenced her with a fierce frown. "We're *fine*, Mr. Taylor. Really."

His face softened. "Darlin', please. What's going on here?"

My thoughts raced. What could I say to get him to leave? I had to come up with something fast—before my mother got Grant in more trouble.

Maybe I should just tell him a modified version of the truth.

I hurried to Grant's side and linked my fingers with his. He hesitated briefly and then closed his hand around mine.

Wow, did that feel nice. We were only touching with our hands, but his felt so warm and secure. My palm was tingling like it had on Sunday, and this time, I allowed myself to enjoy the feeling.

"Grant is sweet to be here for me. Aren't you?" My smile of admiration wasn't fake.

"Indeed, I am," he said, his voice sexy and deliciously British. "Whatever you wish."

My shiver was real.

Mr. Taylor's voice intruded. "Are you dating?"

Okay, I'd avoided lying up until now but couldn't anymore. "Yes, we are," I said, keeping my gaze locked on Grant. Not that I minded, because the way Grant was looking at me was seriously hot. Too bad it was an act.

"Where did you meet him, darlin'?"

"We met..." My brain went blank.

Grant glanced away from me with apparent reluctance. "We met at the flea market. Lacey and I were charmed by the same music box. She's the one who brought it home."

"Uh-huh. Crystal, did you know they were a couple?"

She stared at us in confusion. "No."

"We hadn't clarified the exact nature of our relationship with Mrs. Jones yet." Grant kissed the back of my hand before releasing it. "Perhaps you would like to see some ID, sir."

"I sure would."

Grant crossed the room to pause beside the visitor. "If you would follow me." The two men disappeared down the hallway. Seconds later, the screen door thwacked.

Even after he left, the imprint of Grant's lips lingered on my hand. It unsettled me and made me want something more.

"Lacey?"

I looked up. "Yeah?"

My mom had slumped into the corner of the couch. "What was that all about?"

I flopped down next to her. "Mr. Taylor feels responsible for me."

"I meant about Grant." Her eyelids were drifting slowly down, as if she were trying to fight off sleep. "Is he really your boyfriend?"

"No, I was hoping it would make Mr. Taylor feel better so he would go away."

"It made things worse."

"I get that now."

She laughed and wiggled deeper into the cushions. "That was exhausting. I need a nap."

I got up and headed straight for the windows in the kitchen, straining to see what was happening out there. Grant and Mr. Taylor stood beside the garage talking. Well, Mr. Taylor was talking, and Grant was nodding calmly at intervals.

A few moments later, Mr. Taylor spun around and headed down the driveway without looking back. Grant crossed the lawn toward the house. The back door creaked briefly.

"What did he say?" I asked, meeting Grant's gaze anxiously as he entered the kitchen.

"His attitude lightened somewhat. He jotted down my name. I suspect he'll research me on the web."

"Is your ID real?"

Grant gave me a patient look. "Naturally, it's real. It must be able to satisfy law enforcement agencies. There is also a minor amount of information about me on the internet."

"Nice." Of course. I should've thought of that. I slipped onto a chair, my legs giving way now that the danger was past. "I wish Mr. Taylor hadn't done this." I shuddered at how close we'd come to having a mess.

"I don't agree. Mr. Taylor's concern was overdue, in my opinion. I hope you see more of him."

I went upstairs to begin a homework marathon. It could've been minutes or hours later when I heard Henry bang into the house, stomp around, and bang out the back door. Probably looking for Grant.

Once Mr. Jarrett's latest stupid APUSH assignment was done, I picked up my English textbook. Ballads tonight. Ugh.

"Lacey," Henry shouted up the stairs. "Grant and I are going to the park."

"Fine." I registered what he said. Barely.

After I finished the ballads, I took a break, thumping down the stairs to the kitchen. As I sipped a glass of water, I relaxed and allowed myself to absorb the peace.

Actually, the house went beyond peaceful. There were no human sounds, only an empty quiet. It didn't even have the dullness that often seemed to radiate from my mother.

I walked to her room and pushed the door ajar. Stale air flowed past me. It was hazy and dark, the curtains drawn tightly. Soiled sheets were bunched up on the bed. Clothes were piled on every surface.

My mom wasn't here.

Disappointment made my skin prickle. She'd been a little better lately. She ate her meals, went to bed before midnight, showered every third day. And she'd even been busy today helping Grant clean the attic. What had gone wrong?

I wandered from room to room. Where could she be? Her favorite mug sat on the kitchen table, a white skin from old milk floating on top of the coffee.

A flash of movement in the backyard caught my eye. I looked out the window. My mom perched in the middle of the wrought-iron bench. *Their* wrought-iron bench. She stared blankly into space. Josh's hairbrush lay cradled on her lap.

It hurt me to see her like that. What could I do—what could anyone do—to blow away the gloom that shrouded her?

I had to try.

When I approached her, she didn't acknowledge my presence. "Mom," I whispered, trying not to startle her. "How are you?"

She didn't say anything, just shifted to the far end of the bench. Taking the movement as an invitation, I lowered myself beside her, close but not quite touching.

"Why are you out here, Mom?"

She held the brush up to her nose. "I can't smell him anymore." Black strands clung to the bristles.

Josh's hair. I looked at my knees, at the grass, anywhere but at those bristles. "There's a full bottle of his cologne in the medicine cabinet."

"Not that smell. *Him.*" She fumbled with the brush, then let it fall back to her lap. "I don't like living this way."

The words were flat. Unemotional.

Frightening.

The guidance counselors at the high school taught us to treat sentences like that as something dangerous. *Get help*, they would say. But it didn't seem real somehow, coming from my mom. Getting help would be an overreaction. She didn't mean what it sounded like. She was just missing him.

My mom wouldn't hurt herself. I was positive about that. Completely positive. "I miss Josh too."

"We all do." She took a shuddering breath, her gaze surveying the backyard. The trimmed hedges. The bursts of wildflowers. The garden overflowing with vegetables. But she seemed blind to the beauty and the order. "It wasn't supposed to be like this. He was the one. I can't imagine a future without him."

Another suspicious statement, nearly back to back. What should I do?

If I said something and I was wrong, she'd be all defensive and mad. But if I didn't say something and I was wrong...

I couldn't let the second statement slide.

Deep breath. Be calm. "You're scaring me, Mom. You don't plan to do anything serious, do you?"

"What do you mean?"

"Like harm yourself?"

"What?" She focused hard on my face. "*No,* baby. Of course not. Henry still needs me."

Relief. She said it like I was the one who was crazy. Good. She was missing him. That was all.

But once the relief faded, hurt took its place. She mentioned my brother and not me. "I need you too, Mom."

"I don't think you need anyone." She rose on a heavy sigh and drifted toward the house.

Wow. My whole body felt suspended somewhere between frustration and despair. Did she really think I didn't need anyone?

"You're wrong," I said, but she was too far away to hear.

Status Report #12
Tuesday's Wish: Attic Storage Area

Dear Boss,

Crystal asked if she could help me today. Per your suggestion, I accepted her offer and coached her through the chore. I detect a small improvement in her mood.

She participated in the cleaning of the half of the attic used for storage. Her goal was to organize one trunk. We uncovered many useful items, some of which belonged to Josh. After a good deal of persuasion, she has agreed to sell his things in a yard sale. I was initially concerned that she might react badly to parting with his personal items, but she handled the decision surprisingly well.

An old friend of Eric Linden's dropped by for a visit. Mr. Taylor was understandably suspicious of my appearance. He left after reassurances from Crystal and a review of my ID, although he had clearly not shed his concerns.

Chief is a good actress. When she pretended to be my girlfriend, I found it remarkably easy to follow her lead.

Henry and I kicked a ball around at the park. I enjoy my time with him.

Humbly submitted,
Grant

13

The Serious Shot

*I*t had been a grueling shift at the bookstore.

First there was the couple making out in a dark corner, not realizing (or not caring) that we had a security camera back there.

Then we had a toddler whose mom abandoned him for half an hour, figuring she could have a little free babysitting while he sat there tearing through picture books.

Finally, the old-lady shoplifter. I tried to be sympathetic until she took a swing at me.

When I staggered home at eight, it was quiet in the house. I ate cold pasta and sorted through the stuff in my backpack. I had five pre-calc problems and the definitions of thirty words in Middle English to complete tonight. Two hours or more of homework. I flipped open my English Lit book and grabbed a pen.

Grant walked into the kitchen, glowing like someone had turned on a switch. "It's haircut day," he said.

"Yes, I know. Feel free to get to it. I'm busy here."

"And how are you?"

If he was trying to make me feel bad, he was not going to succeed. "Never been worse. How about you?"

"My day was quite relaxing, thank you. I had a nap and caught up with my friends."

That caught my attention. "What kind of friends?"

"In the League."

"Ah." It was time for the pleasantries to be over. I was tired and the clock was ticking. "I'm busy here."

"So you've said."

I tapped my pen on the table and sighed. "Why don't you start with my mother? Or Henry?"

"Your mother has not made a decision regarding her hair. Henry, however, is positive that he doesn't want to cooperate."

Henry looked like a ragged little street kid next to his soccer mates. He and Mom just had to accept these haircuts. Otherwise, this would be a major loss of a wish, and Grant wouldn't force them. "I suppose I get to be the dictator who brings the reluctant humans to you."

"Indeed."

I dropped my pen onto my lit book and sighed. Loudly. "What tools do you need?"

"Brush. Scissors. Broom."

I popped out of my chair. "Fine. Follow me."

We collected a broom from the pantry and a brush from the bathroom. Next I led the way to my attic bedroom, where I fumbled around inside my desk drawer until I located the monster scissors Nana Linden had given me. They were versatile, cutting everything from denim to sheet metal to the shrubs in our yard. Grant could make them work with hair.

I held them out at the same instant he reached. The tip of the blade gouged his forearm.

A groan escaped his lips—a raw, spooky sound, like a wild animal in pain. Clutching his arm, he fell against the bed and collapsed onto the floor.

Crouching at his side, I said, "I'm so sorry, Grant. What can I do?"

He shook his head, his lips pinched and eyes squeezed shut.

"I could get the first aid kit."

The muscles in his jaw quivered with the effort to hold back groans. His silent suffering launched me into action. I ran downstairs to the bathroom, grabbed a box of bandages, and raced back up. "Here," I said.

"Please don't touch me." The words were barely above a whisper.

"Okay, I won't." I knelt on the floor in front of him, feeling helpless. "Does it hurt?"

"Yes." He lifted his hand to reveal a nasty gash seeping blue fluorescent goo.

"A lot?"

He gave me a glazed look. "Yes."

My insides ached with the desire to make it better. But there didn't seem to be anything I could do. I shifted onto my butt and dropped my head into my hands, angry at myself for being so clumsy. Stupid, stupid, stupid. Each labored breath tore into my heart. I tried not to think about the clock and tried not to think about my homework because no way would I leave him alone while he was in so much pain.

It was all my fault.

My fault—

"Chief?"

"Huh?" I blinked and yawned. I must've dozed. "What time is it?"

"Almost nine."

I rolled my neck around, hunting for kinks, but there weren't any. "I can't believe I fell asleep."

"I can."

"Did you have anything to do with it?"

His lips curved. "That would require magic, would it not?"

"Oh. Of course." How could I forget? Grant only used magic for *his* wishes.

He rose in one smooth movement and held out his hand. In the light from my bedside lamp, I studied the spot where the wound was. Or should have been. There was a scar-like pucker where I'd stabbed him. I wanted to touch it but didn't dare. "Has it healed already?"

"Yes. Thank you for your concern." He waved his hand in a move-it-along gesture, his smile widening. It transformed his face into a look that was nearly breathtaking. "Let's cut your hair, and then we'll find your mother and brother."

"You don't have to do this." I let him pull me up.

"Indeed I do. You made a wish."

"But you're hurt."

"Not anymore. I'm fine, and it's close to Henry's bedtime." He waited at the door. "Shall we?"

Once downstairs, he carried a barstool into the bathroom, then lifted me easily and set me on top. The action surprised me and I clung to his arms, the muscles rock-hard beneath my hands.

Wow. I flexed my fingers to check again. Just to make sure the first impression was correct.

"Chief?" The word growled deep in his throat.

Right. I dropped my hands and looked away, anywhere but at him. My face glowed red-hot. What was wrong with me? Had I, the person in charge, really just felt up the BSB?

Learning how to disappear would come in handy about now.

"Did you have a style in mind?" His voice was mild.

"You choose."

"May I wash your hair first?"

"Yes." I twisted around to glance behind me. There was a significant gap between me and the sink. "How is this going to work? We don't have a salon chair."

"We won't need one."

I took a peek at his face. He looked almost happy. "What will you do?"

"Trust me."

At my nod, Grant closed the door and then gently cupped the back of my neck with one hand as he gathered my hair with the other. The stool tilted backwards, but I didn't fall. As promised. Instead, I was cradled on a cushion of air.

I closed my eyes and yielded as his fingers massaged my scalp with silky shampoo. The scent reminded me of the lotion Nana Linden used to wear. Chamomile and lavender. *Soothing and rejuvenating*, the bottle had said. Too true.

And the touch of his hands? Strong and gentle and perfect. I shivered with delight, never wanting it to end. When I peered through my lashes at him, his expression was absorbed, as if this task was the most important thing in his world. It had been a long time since someone had taken care of me, and I loved it.

The shampoo was over far too soon. I sat up slowly and waited, my back to the mirror, as Grant trimmed my hair. Snip by snip, it fell, creating dark splotches against the white tile floor.

"Chief, you can look now."

I didn't want to, scared at what I might see. Grant was an expert at everything humanly possible. What if his talents hadn't worked this time? What if I still didn't look good? It would be my fault then. Couldn't blame the hairdresser if the raw materials sucked.

Okay, time to look.

I glanced in the mirror, avoiding the face, focusing on the hair. It lay in shiny, sculptured waves about my shoulders. When I tossed my head, there was a bounce to it I'd never noticed before. And the color had changed too. Ten minutes ago, I would've called my hair medium brown, but that didn't fit anymore. Now it was more of a sienna.

I couldn't put it off any longer. Reluctantly, I dragged my gaze to the center of the mirror.

Awe rippled through me. I looked…good. The hairstyle curved around my face in a soft oval. My cheekbones seemed higher, my eyes bigger, my lips more lush. How could a haircut do all that?

Was it vain to keep staring at myself? This had to be why people agreed to go on those makeover shows. They hoped, like me, that underneath their boring exterior was a gorgeous person waiting to be discovered. And that the only missing ingredient was the right makeover artist.

"You used magic, didn't you?"

"Indeed not. You were already lovely. I merely added the frame."

Blinking to fight off the sting of tears, I shook my head. I had never been lovely, but I felt like it right now.

Grant's face joined mine in the mirror. Our reflections held such contrasts. My sienna hair shone next to his rich chocolate brown. Then there were our eyes—mine gleamed like dark pools while his glittered like green glass.

We could've been a still photo, the kind from a booth at the mall where two dollars went in and a strip of three shots came out. Our image wasn't the first shot, the one that was always frantic and unfocused. It wasn't the second shot either—laughing and silly. No, this was the final image— the serious shot—where the couple realized they wanted a good picture to remember the moment by and couldn't afford to screw the last one up.

"You are beautiful, Chief."

Please don't let him be mocking me. I searched his expression but found only sincerity. The sweet thrill of it eased a wistful place inside me.

He looked away and collected the tools. "I'll find your brother."

I stayed behind in the bathroom, sweeping up the dark splotches, savoring what he'd said. Three simple, genuine words. Did he realize how much they meant to me? I liked thinking that I might be beautiful, and he gave that to me.

I located Grant and his next client in the kitchen. Henry was not a happy little man, but he bore the punishment bravely and then took off for his bath.

Grant waved the monster scissors suggestively at my mother. Chop, chop, chop. "Crystal?"

Crystal? When had he started calling her that?

She perched on the edge of a stool, hands on knees, shaking her head. "I don't know what I want."

"Short and professional," he said, "for reentering the business world."

I gaped. *Professional? Reentering the business world?* The last time I'd hinted to my mom about getting a job, I'd received the silent treatment for two days. But with Grant she didn't cower or whimper. She didn't tear up or storm out of the room. Instead, she scowled at him boldly and said in a stubborn tone, "I've already told you. I'm not ready."

"You underestimate yourself." He met her gaze calmly. "We think you're ready."

We?

She sniffed. "Have you discussed me with your boss again?"

"Yes. Earlier today."

Grant discussed my mother with his boss? Why?

"He's sure I'm ready?"

"Positive."

She looked at me. "What do you think?"

Would she really cut her hair off? And did she really want my opinion? This was so awesome and unexpected. If I could be sure it was welcome, I would've hugged her. "I think short hair would be great on you, Mom."

She gave a nod. "Short, please."

He laid a towel around her neck and caught her hair in his hands.

I couldn't believe she was going through with it. Her long, beautiful hair. *Brown kissed by moonlight,* Josh used to say. I touched her shoulder. "Are you sure?"

She nodded determinedly. "It'll be easier to take care of."

Grant clipped so quickly, she didn't have time to change her mind. Not that there was any need to. The cut was adorable. As Mom gazed in the handheld mirror, she laughed and primped her hair with her fingers. "It's wonderful, Grant. Thank you." She was still admiring herself as she walked from the room.

I watched her walk away, frozen with shock. My mother had laughed. It had been so long since I'd heard that, I'd forgotten how giggly and bubbly it sounded.

An overwhelming sense of inadequacy shot through me. For a brief moment, my mom had been happy, and Grant had brought it out in her.

Not me. Not Henry.

Grant.

I had to put it out of my mind. There were hours of homework stretching before me, which I would give anything to skip. But it wasn't an option, at least not for English. No way would I disappoint Ms. Dewan again.

After pulling out a chair, I flopped down, opened my notebook, and willed myself to concentrate.

Grant sat on the edge of the kitchen table near me, his leg nearly brushing my arm. "Do you not like your mother's haircut?"

Was my reaction that obvious? I'd have to be more careful. "It's perfect for her."

"A very precise and noncommittal response. Is anything else wrong?"

"I'd rather not talk about it."

"Certainly." He leaned over and stared at my paper. "What are you doing?"

I looked up at him. "Why?"

"Humor me. Is it Middle English?"

"Unfortunately."

"Would you care for some assistance?"

"Do you know Middle English?"

"Fluently."

Of course he did. How incredibly lucky for me. "Is it on the house?"

"Indeed," he said with a sigh. "I should like to help you, Chief. May I?"

"Cool. I accept." Tutoring by an expert and it didn't cost me anything. Maybe I'd get to bed before midnight for once. I patted the empty chair next to me. "Have a seat."

He slid onto the chair and dropped his arm along the seatback behind me.

This evening was ending so much better than I could've imagined. I smiled at him. "How many languages do you know?"

He smiled back. "All of them."

Status Report #13
Wednesday's Wish: Haircuts

Dear Boss,

I received an injury today. Suffering is a human experience that I do not care to repeat. At least physical pain heals with hardly a trace.

Chief was kind throughout the ordeal. I can never recall anyone offering to delay a wish on my behalf. It was extraordinary.

Though anxious to start her homework, she remained at my side until the pain eased. I reciprocated by allowing her a quick nap and a brief bit of tutoring.

She was shocked by her appearance after the haircut. How can she be so utterly unaware of her own beauty?

This day has been the most productive of my assignment.

Humbly submitted,
Grant

14

An Obvious Follow-up

*A*fter school on Thursday, Kimberley and I planned to meet and practice with the kitchen utensils for our demo. But we'd have to get them first, and they were at the college. She asked me to wait for her in the media center.

I arrived first, so I pulled out my pre-calc book and did my best with the homework assignment. It only took about two minutes to tear a hole through the paper because I'd erased the first problem so many times.

A chair scraped beside me. "Hey, Lacey," Sean Tucker said.

I glanced around the room. There were plenty of empty seats. He'd come to this table to talk to me. Interesting. "Hey. How are things?"

"Fine." He drummed his fingers on the tabletop. "No, that's a lie. I'm not fine, because Sara's not fine. She'll be here in a minute."

"Why?"

"So the two of you can talk."

"Sara wants to talk to me?"

"She doesn't know yet."

I felt a twinge of disappointment. "How is she going to feel about this chance encounter?"

"It's not chance."

"How'd you know I'd be here?"

"Kimberley."

My newest friend might struggle with poor memory, but she had a good mind for everything else. Sometimes I wondered if her body had overdeveloped her perception as compensation, because I'd never said anything to her about my feud with Sara. "I'm not in the mood for hostility."

"Look, Lacey." He did a quick survey of the area around us. Nobody was within hearing range. "I don't know what's going on with you and my sister. But could you be nice when she shows up?"

It was the first time he'd really talked with me in months, or mentioned the thing between his twin and me. I could understand him taking her side, but did he have to assume *I* would be unreasonable? "I'm always nice to Sara."

"Right. Whatever." He frowned. "It's just that…things are tough at our house right now."

"Like what?"

"Sara will tell you one day. Just…be patient." He bobbed his head sharply and then tapped my textbook. "Having problems?"

I looked down at the book. Should I go along with the change in topic? Yeah, I should. No use taking this out on Sean and, besides, I could use his help. "It's pre-calc. I don't understand my homework."

He looked over my shoulder at the page. "Who do you have?"

"Mrs. Leech."

"It's not you. It's her."

"Glad to hear it." I was willing to accept his explanation.

"Let me show you."

"Sure."

He hijacked my pencil and proceeded to finish my homework. Not much learning on my part, but he did talk out loud as he went. In theory, when I stared at his calculations later on, I would absorb them.

I leaned back and studied his profile. He seemed thinner and paler than I remembered. The Tuckers had a beach house up near Nags Head. Maybe they hadn't spent much time there this summer.

From the corner of my eye, I saw someone approach. Sara hurried toward our table, focused on her brother. When her gaze flicked to me, she stopped, her nose wrinkling as if she smelled something gross.

"Sean?" She glared at her brother. "Ready to go?"

The pencil kept scratching. "In a minute." His bony elbow jabbed me in the side.

I didn't like this situation any better than Sean, but did he have to be so obvious? Still, I was going to play along, if I could think of something to say that wouldn't lead to an argument. "Hey, Sara."

"Hey."

She hadn't exactly ignored me, but close. "When did you start working for Mrs. Bork?"

"A couple of months ago."

That was a longer answer—and it had been polite. A little progress. "She seems like she'd be a nice boss."

"She is." Sara hugged her backpack and looked around the media center, as if searching for someone. "But I won't be there much longer. I'll work for my mom when her store opens."

"Your mom has a store?"

"Yeah." She swung back around to scowl at me. "Is that a problem?"

"No, I'm just surprised." Mrs. Tucker was the world's most perfect mother. She had a gorgeous home that she cleaned herself. She cooked multi-course meals from scratch. She threw the best parties ever, and she didn't do it for show. She loved being surrounded by people. But in the whole time I'd known them, the only paid work Mrs. Tucker had tried was a couple of terms on the town council.

Sean put the pencil down. "Our parents have separated."

Sara smacked his shoulder with the back of her hand. "Shut up. It's temporary."

"Is not."

"Is too."

He looked at me with a *no it isn't* expression.

Was this what Sean had meant earlier? Because if it was, the news surprised me. It was true that Mr. Tucker wasn't at home very much, but that had never seemed to bother any of them. Maybe Mrs. Tucker had finally gotten tired of being alone. "What kind of store does your mom own?"

Sara met my gaze coolly. "Did Sean put you up to this?"

"Not exactly. I was ambushed like you."

"So why do you keep asking questions?"

My smile dimmed.

Her brother shot out of his chair. "Grow up, Sara. It's not Lacey's fault that Dad's a jerk and Gryphon's an—"

"Stop, Sean. Don't say it."

His eyes narrowed. "If you have to be pissed at someone, go after me, but leave her alone."

They stared at each other, seething and silent. A long moment passed.

Sara caved first. "Okay, okay, I'll be nice. For now." She turned to me. "Mom is opening an upscale consignment shop."

I wasn't sure how much to trust her rapid change of attitude, but I was genuinely curious about the store. "For clothing?"

"Yeah." Her voice lightened a little. "We'll also carry home décor."

It was a great idea. Anyone who knew Mrs. Tucker would love to get her advice on decorating or fashion. "When will it open?"

"In October. We're still painting and setting up the showroom. The store is one block off the town square, on Peach Street."

"The old Harley House?" A beautiful, historic landmark in this town.

"Yeah."

That hadn't come cheap. "Good luck."

The suspicious gleam in her eyes faded slightly. "Thanks."

Sean nudged me and pointed at my notebook. "I'm done with your homework. Do you understand?"

Not at all. "Sure. Thanks."

Kimberley passed the Tuckers in the entrance to the media center. When she joined me, she was smiling. "Everything okay?"

"It is." I gathered my stuff. "So you plotted that with Sean?"

"We did." She leaned closer and lowered her voice. "I think he's hot. What do you think?"

He wasn't hot in the gorgeous sense. But I knew what she meant, because Sean's kind of smart could be sexy. "I agree."

"We're learning the waltz in PE, and Sean's the best partner in the class. He's just...wow."

We exited through the exterior door. Mrs. Rey was leaning against her silver SUV, waving us over. We were hardly inside before she screeched out of the parking place and drove like the wind, talking nonstop about a new mural she wanted to paint. Once we reached campus, she puttered along, bounced violently over two evil speed bumps, and parked without hesitation in a space marked RESERVED in front of the Administration Building.

I waited until Mrs. Rey was ahead of us and out of hearing range before asking, "Why did your mother park in a reserved spot?"

"Don't worry. It belongs to Granddad."

Very interesting. "Is he here today?"

"Yeah. He likes to walk to work."

We entered the main building and crossed to a glass door with "Office of the President" painted in black. Inside the lobby, it was quiet, cushioned by thick carpet and decorated with paintings of landscapes looking like smeared storms. A beautiful woman sat behind a chrome desk, which was too neat for her to get any work done. The woman kept her gaze on her computer screen for a few seconds before glancing our way. She dismissed me without hesitation. But when her eyes fell on Kimberley and her mother, they widened in recognition. "Hello, Mrs. Rey. Miss Rey. Is Dr. Carpenter expecting you?"

"He should be," Kimberley replied in an equally formal tone.

"I'll let him know you're here."

It was a jaw-dropping exchange. Dr. Carpenter was Kimberley's grandfather? Baird Carpenter, President of Piedmont College?

"Ladies, you may go in."

I stumbled after them, taking in this unexpected information. We stepped into his office, an elegant room with floor-to-ceiling bookcases holding leather-bound books, an entire wall of glass overlooking the main quad, and uncomfortable chairs sprinkled about. The desk was huge, made of dark wood, and covered by messy stacks of folders and journals, plus a series of mismatched coffee mugs.

A man bent over this desk, a pair of half-glasses resting at the end of his nose. He was reading a magazine, his brow furrowed in concentration, his face pinched into a forbidding glare. When the door swooshed open, he looked up.

"Kimberley. Teresa," he said. Pushing the magazine aside, he rose and flung his arms open for my friend. She launched into him.

The transformation in Dr. Carpenter was astonishing. He'd gone from intimidating professor to adoring grandfather in a second. Mrs. Rey crossed to his side and they kissed the air near each other's cheeks.

"Hey, Granddad. This is my friend Lacey."

"Nice to meet you, Lacey." He extended his hand.

"Hello, Dr. Carpenter." As I shook his hand, I soaked in details. The expensive gold watch obscured by a starched white cuff. Manicured nails. Dark tailored suit and boring tie. He looked exactly the way I would've expected the president of an ultra-expensive private college to look.

"You're helping Kimberley with the history project."

"Yes, sir," I said, shooting a miffed glance at Kimberley. Why didn't she warn me that we were coming *here?* I looked like a refugee from a homeless shelter today, except for my hair, which was still gorgeous.

She scrunched her forehead, puzzled, and then turned to her grandfather with a shrug. "We're here for the kitchen tools."

"Excellent." He reached behind his chair and hauled out a small duffel bag. It clanked as he set it on the desk. I watched in fascination to see if any of the piles of paper would fall over, but they held their position.

While Kimberley was handing her tablet to me, Mrs. Rey was pulling a sophisticated digital recorder from her purse. It didn't take much logic to figure out who the film crew was.

The next fifteen minutes were spent in demonstrations of how the tools operated. Kimberley seemed as engaged by those metal rods as her grandfather. The only thing that was missing was a hearth and fire.

When they were done, she hauled the bag of utensils to her mom's car and loaded it into the back. Mrs. Rey twisted around to look at us. "Kim, didn't you want to ask Lacey something?"

"About what?"

Her mother nodded her head meaningfully. "The handyman?"

I bristled. Nope. Not a topic I wanted to discuss with them. I looked away from Kimberley and watched the houses blur past on the way to my neighborhood.

"How did you find the handyman?"

I debated whether to ask them to butt out, but maybe a few simple answers would be enough. "We met at the flea market."

"Do you often pick up strangers at the flea market and bring them home to live?"

That was an obvious follow-up question that I'd never thought of before. I had to stall for time while my brain caught up. "Why are you asking?"

"He seems suspicious."

I didn't like this conversation a bit. Whipping around, I met her gaze with a look that ought to intimidate her into shutting up. "He's a good guy."

"How can you be sure?"

"He's been nothing but nice. Everything we ask for, he does perfectly."

"That's great, but the whole thing still doesn't make sense." She shrugged. "He's the world's hottest handyman. Even though he doesn't look old enough to have graduated from high school, he's an expert at everything. And he doesn't get paid, yet he won't work for anyone but you."

"He's part of a group that helps families in need. It's like a local Peace Corps."

"Is your family in need?"

I hadn't meant for that to slip out, but I couldn't leave it alone now. "Why else would he be helping us?"

"My point exactly. Are there things your family needs that he can't help with?"

I'd handled our mess for months without anyone asking anything. Why were they all asking now? "No, Kimberley. We're fine."

"You're fine except for the things a complete stranger is fixing?"

I took a deep breath. No matter how mad I looked, she wouldn't let this go until I reassured her. "Grant is not a stranger. He's shown me his identification. There is no problem here."

Mrs. Rey parked the SUV next to the curb in front of my house. I grabbed the handle and swung the door open. "Thanks for the ride," I mumbled as I slid from the car.

"How do you know Grant's ID isn't fake?"

Why wouldn't she drop this? "It isn't fake!" First Mr. Taylor. Now the Reys. All of these questions were a bit insulting. I wouldn't dream of letting anyone around Henry or Mom unless I thought he was safe. I turned to scowl at Kimberley. "I have this under control. Can you please stay out of my family's business?"

Mrs. Rey gasped.

"Sure. My mistake." Kimberley tilted her head, eyeing me thoughtfully. "I thought we were friends, and it was my job to have your back. I didn't know that you're allowed to care about my brain damage but that I'm not allowed to care about your safety. I'll butt out." She reached over, grabbed the handle, and slammed the door shut before I could say anything. The SUV pulled away from the curb, and they sped off.

Status Report #14
Thursday's Wish: Restoration of a Stained Glass
Window

Dear Boss,

I found the day's assignment to be entirely satisfying. Stained glass is a new skill, with both dexterity and creativity involved. It is a lovely addition to the house and will certainly broaden its appeal.

Chief argued with a friend. I couldn't help overhearing the end of it. Kimberley Rey is a true friend to show such concern for Chief's welfare; it's a shame that Chief will not allow herself to accept such concern.

It has surprised me how little interest the neighborhood has shown over my presence. Did the Linden-Joneses keep to themselves so much?

I hope Chief makes things right with Kimberley soon. May I introduce the topic?

Humbly submitted,
Grant

15

Frills and Camouflage

I had plenty of time last night to brood over my conversation with Kimberley. I knew she was just trying to be nice, and I had blown her off pretty badly. If I'd learned anything with Sara, it was to make sure that I didn't let fights like this fester. I had to fix this today.

Kimberley avoided me all day. That had to be intentional. She arrived in the classroom at the last possible moment for APUSH and raced out again before I had a chance to speak with her. She always had Sean walking with her in the hallways between classes, and she didn't show up for lunch.

I even tried to ambush her in the parking lot after school, but I waited ten minutes and neither she nor her mother ever appeared. I would just have to drive to their house.

When I got home, my mom, my BSB, and the car were gone. They hadn't left a note, and my brother would be home around three-thirty.

I was too anxious to see Kimberley to wait for Grant and Mom to return. Glancing at the clock, I figured I could bike over to Kimberley's house, apologize for my rudeness, and bike back in thirty minutes, plenty of time to get back for Henry.

I tossed my backpack into the studio, grabbed a bike and a helmet, and took off.

Mrs. Rey was pushing a manual lawnmower across the front yard. When I slid off the bike, she stopped, dabbed delicately at her face with a pink bandana, and glanced my way. Her lips thinned as recognition dawned.

I waited at the curb. "Is Kimberley here?"

"She is." Her voice and expression were belligerent. "Why do you want to know?"

"I want to talk with her."

Mrs. Rey crossed her arms and watched me silently. She did attitude really well.

The stare-down continued, without her saying anything. Guess that left the next move up to me. I walked up the driveway, in through the garage, knocked once on the door, and stepped into the kitchen.

Inside was hushed, dim, and immaculate. Where had their obsession with cleanliness come from? The chemotherapy?

"Kimberley?"

A recliner creaked in the adjacent den. She stood, an iPad in one hand. "Yes?"

"I'm sorry."

"For...?"

"Being rude to you yesterday."

Her eyes widened. "Am I still supposed to mind my own business?"

"If it's about Grant, yes." Maybe this would sound harsh, but it had to be said. "I want you to stop worrying. My family needs him, and I am one hundred percent sure that he's a good guy. Please trust me about this."

She shrugged. "Okay."

"Okay...what?"

"I accept your apology." She smiled. "And I'll drop the thing about Grant."

Relief flooded in. This was easier than I expected. "Will your mom let it go too?"

"Yeah." She set her iPad on the table and then gave me a hug.

After a moment's hesitation, I hugged her back. It felt good.

When she released me, we were both still smiling. That was the quickest fight I'd ever had with a friend. It had always taken Sara a long time to get over anything. Hopefully, my next question wouldn't ruin things again. "I don't mean to be rude, Kimberley, but how did you remember to avoid me all day?"

She held her hand out, palm up. Something was written on it with black marker.

"Really? You wrote a note on your hand?"

"It worked, didn't it?" She laughed.

I laughed too.

When Mrs. Rey came in five minutes later, we were in the kitchen, raiding the snack drawer and still laughing.

The car was parked in the driveway when I arrived home. As I was putting the bike away, Grant appeared in the door to the studio, his arms full of boxes.

"What are you doing?"

"Preparing for today's wish. May I set up in the living room?"

Clean The Hall Closet Day. A rush of adrenaline hit me. No telling what was in the hall closet. I'd been putting it off for months, scared and excited and worried about its contents. "The living room is fine. But why are you starting so late?" I would've expected him to finish this morning.

He continued across the back yard. "I was busy earlier."

"Doing what?"

"Shelving canned goods."

I followed him in the back door. "Where did you shelve cans?"

"At the Food Pantry. We heard that—"

"*We*? We who?"

"Crystal went with me."

"You took my mother to a food pantry?"

He nodded. "It was a good exchange. We supplied labor. They let us fill a bag with groceries."

My good mood fractured at this news. Grant and I had been getting along so well. It had been lovely for the past couple of days. But he *knew* that I wanted to keep our problems private. I felt betrayed. "Why did you do that? Did Mom see anyone she knew? You can't let people know we need free food—"

"Stop, Chief. It's done." He set the boxes down in the living room, his face tight. "Crystal provided for her family today. Leave it at that. Now, if you'll excuse me, I'll get started on this wish."

"I'm not finished."

"Perhaps not, but I am, so unless you enjoy talking to yourself, I'd suggest you move along."

Our stand-off lasted a good fifteen seconds before I decided to change tactics. I might not be able to make him talk to me, but I did have something else I could control. "You can bring the stuff to me and I'll sort."

"From the closet?"

I nodded.

He tensed. "Does this imply that you will assist me?"

"Not exactly." I dropped onto the couch and propped my feet on the coffee table. "This implies *I* am in charge, and *you* are going to assist *me*."

"I prefer to complete wishes on my own."

"I *wish* you would help me clean the hall closet."

Grant had this way of locking his face into marble sculpture mode. All hard angles and stony expression. It was kind of hot. Not that I'd admit it to him.

Items appeared on the coffee table, organized with precision. He made no comments. He made no eye contact. It was far more effective at expressing frustration than anything he might have said.

For the first half hour, nothing emerged from the closet but junk—things like *National Geographic* magazines older than my mother, empty soda bottles, and chocolate wrappers (somebody named Josh had had a serious Godiva addiction). The junk went straight to the trash can and recycling bin.

Then the items became more interesting.

Grant pulled out a half-dozen unmatched women's shoes. I tossed them under the bay window.

He handed me a bag with thirty or more movie DVDs from the previous century. There were some decent ones—animated films, war movies, and a few black-and-white classics. We could sell them all at the flea market.

I paused when he held out the tuxedo jacket. It was still in good condition, but where were the pants? I patted the pockets and squealed with joy. Josh had left behind several crumpled twenty-dollar bills and a handkerchief.

"Chief?"

I looked up. Grant had a shoebox full of sewing supplies tucked under one arm. "Those are my mom's."

He nodded and set the box on a nearby table. "What about this?" He dropped a large, thin book on the coffee table.

A scrapbook. I opened it.

The first page held a photo of my dad in his Marine Corps dress uniform. He looked stern. Tough. Inscribed below the picture was his name in Nana's handwriting.

Jonathan Eric Linden

I curled my legs up on the couch and turned the pages. There were pages with my father as a baby and a toddler. His kindergarten report card—Good Conduct had not been easy for him. A staged photo in his baseball uniform. Several shots from his high-school graduation. One had him in the center, my mom wrapped with one arm, and Mr. Taylor with the other.

Grant continued to come in, dropping objects in a pile at my feet and leaving again, but I didn't look up, too absorbed by a picture of my dad wrapped in a hospital gown, holding little swaddled me. He was laughing. I was screaming.

Eerie. I flipped through the remaining pages. My dad with me at my first Christmas. My third birthday party. Reading a story to my preschool class. The final picture in the scrapbook had been taken at the military base with me all dressed up and my dad in uniform. Frills and camouflage. I looked a lot like him. I'd never noticed.

My mother came in and hung over my shoulder. "I'm glad you found that. I've wondered where it was."

"Whose is it?"

"Yours. Nana Linden made it for you."

"It's amazing." The memory of that final picture tickled at my brain, hazy and silent, like a movie on mute. It had been a windy day. Just before Grampa snapped the photo, Dad kissed my cheek. His breath had smelled like cinnamon.

"Eric thought you were the cutest thing that had ever been born. I loved to see the two of you together. He was a great dad." She flipped back a page and pointed. I was riding on my father's shoulders, laughing from pure delight, my fingers holding tightly to his ears—since he hadn't really had any hair to hold on to. My father was grinning, even though he had to be hurting. "You spent most of your toddler years being carried by him. It's a wonder you ever learned to walk."

"Chief," Grant said, interrupting. "I believe you will find this rather compelling." He held out an accordion-pleated folder.

With a great deal of reluctance, I closed the scrapbook, set it on a side table, and took the folder. I brushed away a light coating of dust and slipped off the elastic tie. Inside were official-looking papers. Bills marked paid. Auto insurance contracts. Department of Defense documents written in jargon I didn't try to comprehend. "They don't look all that important." I held them up to my mother. "Do you know what these are?"

"No." She ducked her head and shuffled toward the bay window.

What was she afraid of? "I guess we should go through them anyway."

"We who?" Grant asked.

Good question. Probably I should. But what if the papers were about Eric? Or Josh? What if it told me things I didn't want to know? What if there were more bills...? "*You* need to go through them."

He glanced from my mother to me and then lowered his voice. "A new wish?"

Crap. My wants kept accumulating. "I'll put it on the list."

Mom was bending over the pile of orphaned shoes. She extracted a bronze, jewel-studded sandal. "I've been looking for this one."

"There are more closets to clean in this house, Mom."

Her gaze roamed from the collection of books to the pile of old clothes. Josh's old clothes. Her face sagged. "I think this is enough for now." She drifted from the room.

My attention returned to the folder. Maybe it held good news. I liked the idea that there might be hidden treasures lurking within.

"She could use your sympathy."

The censure in Grant's voice put me on the defensive. "I'm juggling school, debts, a job, and a little boy. I don't have time for sympathy."

"She lost her husband."

I slapped the folder on the coffee table. "I lost Josh too."

"Surely you realize your loss is not comparable to hers."

"I do realize that. I also realize that Henry lost his dad and both of us lost our mom on the day Josh died."

"You exaggerate."

"I guess you're the expert after two weeks." Why did he think he had the right to judge me? I had three parents gone. One I could barely remember. One loved me and left me with a mess. One had checked out. Maybe *I* could use a little sympathy.

I picked up my scrapbook again.

"Chief?"

"Uh-huh?" I didn't look up.

"You are right. I spoke out of turn."

I met his gaze. Was that his version of an apology? "Okay."

He returned to the foyer. I became immersed in the scrapbook.

"Today's task is complete."

Grant's voice startled me. I'd almost forgotten he was here. I peered into the closet. It looked way better. But— wow. Three big black garbage bags. "You haven't taken out the trash."

"Nor will I."

I blinked. "What do you mean?"

He dropped to the floor, cross-legged, in a pose of complete relaxation as if he were about to enjoy yoga. "You wished for a clean closet. You did not wish for hauling away trash." He closed his eyes, a smile hovering on his lips.

I should've seen that coming. Should've known he'd find a way to get revenge. "Jerk."

His expression stayed neutral, except for his lips. They gave him away, struggling not to laugh.

Okay. I had it coming. Laughing with him, I grabbed the garbage bags and carried them outside.

Next time we did a joint project, I would choose my words more carefully.

Status Report #15
Friday's Wish: Closet Cleaning

Dear Boss,

Crystal performed volunteer work today. She received food as compensation. It pleased her to contribute. She talked of her husband as we worked. She chuckled as she shared stories of their courtship.

The folder from the closet is more valuable than Chief realizes. If she neglects to add it to the wish list, I shall remind her.

I do not care to partner on a project with Chief. May I refuse next time?

Humbly submitted,
Grant

16

Liquid Mess

I stopped in the kitchen before leaving for the soccer field Saturday. My mom was there ahead of me, dressed in clean clothes that matched. With the cute new haircut, she looked almost normal.

Was my BSB granting her wishes too?

No, that wasn't possible. No way had the League agreed to give double wishes per family. Maybe my mother really was feeling better. "Why are you dressed so early, Mom?" I asked as I filled a travel mug with coffee.

She set down her mug very carefully, like drunks do when they don't want anyone to know that they've been drinking. "I'm going to Henry's game."

"Are you sure you're ready?"

"Yes, I am." She traced the rim of her mug with her index finger. "Why don't you stay home? I can handle Henry."

Crap. I'd been hoping she wouldn't notice how we never left her alone with Henry, but apparently she had. She was forcing me to say that I didn't trust her. As much as she might want a second chance, she hadn't earned it yet. "You know that Grant or I have to attend."

"I'll be careful."

"It's too soon."

"Please. I won't make that mistake again."

"Mom, no."

She crossed her arms and glared at me. I glared back, unblinking.

The fight drained out of her slowly. "You're right," she said at last, her voice rough. "He shouldn't be alone with me." She ran shaking fingers through her hair. "Maybe Henry wouldn't want me to come."

"No," I hurried to reassure her, "Henry would be happy to have you there."

"What would make me happy?" he asked as he burst into the kitchen, all dressed to play.

"Mom wants to come with us."

"All right," he shouted and wrapped his arms around her waist in a tight hug. After a moment's hesitation, she stroked his hair.

My brother vibrated with joy all the way to the park, dancing along beside my mom. I hung back, letting them talk, although it was more like letting him talk and her listen.

Mom sat in the bleachers with the other parents. I lowered myself to the ground, reclined against the tree trunk, watched as if I knew what was going on, and enjoyed a morning where I didn't have any responsibilities.

Henry's team won again, which made them undefeated so far this season.

After the game, I went looking for Coach Makanui. Eli had said that he would work something out for today, but my family still needed to do our part sometime. I would sign Henry up for a snack day later in the season.

Once I'd calmed down about the whole concept, I'd come up with a plan for how to handle our turn. I could work extra hours at The Reading Corner, watch the grocery store for sales, and use one of my wishes to have Grant bake. Knowing him, we'd have the best cookies ever. If I was careful and took my time, I might be able to throw together a pretty good snack day.

As I waited in the crowd surrounding Coach, I spotted my mother and brother near the picnic table with the rest of the soccer team and some of their families. I also got my first good look at a snack-day feast.

There were piles of food—enough for the team and any brothers and sisters who had tagged along. Juice boxes. Potato chips. Bananas and grapes. Mini-cupcakes. Chicken nuggets. No one would need lunch after this.

One of the boys started to leave with his family, then turned around and ran to my mother. "Thanks, Mrs. Jones," he shouted.

She nodded, a bewildered smile on her face.

Soon the whole team swarmed her, yelling thanks. Henry watched, eyes big, a little apart from the others. When he noticed me, he ran to my side.

"How did you do it, Lacey? I mean…" He glanced at the picnic table and then back at me. "I thought we would bring something embarrassing for our snack day. I didn't think we could afford something this good."

Before I could respond, he raced away.

Our snack day? I went still. Everyone thought that my family supplied the food today?

My eyes sought Eli and found him on the fringe of the crowd. A couple of fathers talked to him while he nodded politely. After the two men left, he looked around until his gaze locked with mine.

We stared across a gap of twenty feet or so, my face tight with outrage, his eyebrow raised in question.

I stalked over. "You bought the snacks."

His smile disappeared. "I did."

"Without warning me?"

"I told you I would figure it out."

"Why does everyone think we bought them?" I had to jam my fists into my pockets to hide their shaking.

"I didn't bother to change the signup sheet."

"Why not?"

He gave me an arrogant frown. "It's no big deal."

"It is to me." My family could have done this if he'd just given us a little more time. We weren't above the rules. We were willing to do our fair share. Eli had taken that away from me.

I leaned close enough to inhale the woodsy scent of his cologne. "We have to tell everyone that you brought the snacks."

"I have a better idea. Tell Henry, and let him straighten it out."

I whipped around, ready to march over and fix the lie, until I saw my brother. He stood beside the picnic table, chomping on chicken, the happy host. Mom waited nearby, talking with another mother and smiling. It had been a year since she looked that normal around other people.

I couldn't ruin it for him—for either of them.

What Eli had done today was incredibly generous. So why did it leave me feeling inadequate?

Eli stepped into my path, blocking me from their view. "Let it go, Lacey. This isn't about you. It's about Henry—a kid I happen to like."

"I like him too, which is why I don't want him wondering how I made the world's best snack day appear out of nowhere."

"He's not wondering where it came from. He's just glad it did." And with that, Eli took off.

I watched him as he joined the crowd, laughing with the kids, shaking hands respectfully with the parents. Even my mom approached him with a hesitant smile. Eli was a fantastic guy who had done a wonderful thing that nobody would ever know about except me. And it left me feeling more wrong than I could stand.

Until Josh died, I'd been good at all of the things that mattered to me. Good student. Good daughter. Good friend. Now it felt as if I never got the important things right. I was tired of being wrong, but had no idea how it could be fixed.

I drew back into the shadows of a nearby tree, aching and alone.

When the celebration broke up, my family went in three different directions. Henry rode with Eli to a teammate's house for a victory swimming party. Mom went home, while I walked to work for a four-hour shift. Saturday mornings at the bookstore were generally quiet, and I was ready for some easy money.

Wrong. Mrs. Lubis asked me to staff The Java Corner instead.

"Lacey, dear, I need some peace and quiet to settle my nerves."

Great. Saturday mornings were the busiest time in the coffee shop. I had to run the cash register, back up the barista, bus the tables, and break up the toddler fights being ignored by their parents.

I fumed all the way home. My first sight of the foyer put the fuming on hold.

The hardwoods were awesome. They looked practically refinished. It was Floor Polishing Day, and Grant had succeeded beyond my wildest dreams.

It was time to re-broach the topic of selling the house with my mother.

I leaned against the front door and tried to imagine the impression a prospective buyer would have. Gleaming floors. Sparkling chandelier and windows. Light, airy rooms with high ceilings and no cobwebs. Polished, antique mantle around a brick fireplace. It looked like a lovingly cared-for home in wonderful, move-in condition.

Wait.

I expected gleaming hardwoods. But sparkling windows and polished mantle?

Something was off about this picture. As far as the eye could see, there was house-cleaning perfection.

I wandered into the kitchen. It too was squeaky clean. A lace cloth covered the table and, in its center, sunflowers clustered in a ceramic vase.

Weird.

Voices murmured in the back of the house. I followed the sound to my mother's bedroom and halted in shock.

My mother stood on a stepladder, hanging freshly laundered curtains over the window. Grant waited below her, his hands outstretched to catch her if she fell.

Surprise prickled along my skin. "What's going on?"

"Oh," my mom said, clutching at the ladder. "Hi, baby. You scared me."

She'd dressed this morning, gone to a game, and washed curtains when she got home. Where had all of that energy come from?

Mom hadn't stopped talking. "Isn't my bedroom looking great? Grant's been a big help."

Why was she responding to him? For months, Henry and I had needed her. For months, I'd tried to break through. But no. She'd worn her pain like a shield, deflecting everyone. Yet Grant had arrived, and a few days later, she acted almost giddy.

Why does it hurt me to see her so happy? I didn't know, and that scared me.

"Wasn't it sweet of him to pitch in?" She gave his shoulder a squeeze. "He is so good at this stuff."

He smiled.

How had they become such easy friends, when I had to fight for his smiles outside the wishes? "It's not like he's doing us a favor, Mom. He's supposed to do his job well."

He looked over his shoulder at me, his smile fading. "Such a lovely way you have with words."

My mother's brow puckered in confusion. "What just happened?"

"Everything is fine, Crystal." He took her hand and helped her from the ladder.

There was another thing that upset me. He called her Crystal, yet he refused to call me by my name. Why was that true?

His chin lifted, as if he could read my thoughts. "I believe my work is done for the day." He skirted the bed and approached the door, which I blocked. "Excuse me."

I pressed myself against the doorframe. As he stepped past, he rasped, for my ears only, "Don't ever speak about me that way again."

Staring straight ahead, wondering how this day had gone so wrong, I listened to his tread fading away on the newly polished hardwoods. A moment later, the front door creaked.

"Lacey, I don't understand. What's going on?" My mom drew near me. She smelled like bleach.

"Why him?" The question came out as a whisper.

"Grant? What about him?"

I wanted to be part of her solution. I wanted her children to be the reason for the miracle. My throat ached under the strain. "Why does it have to be a stranger who helps you get better?"

"Grant isn't a stranger." Her voice sounded weary. "He doesn't remind me of Josh."

It was the first time I'd heard her use my stepfather's name in months. "What does Grant do that I haven't done?"

"Nothing. It's just different with him." Her fingers reached out to smooth my hair. "I'm sorry, baby. You don't get to be a kid anymore, and I can't even promise when I'll be able to be the adult again. I'm just…sorry." Turning, she shuffled to the bathroom. The lock clicked.

I stayed huddled against the doorframe for far too long, hoping she would come out. I wanted to talk more. I wanted to solve things. But there was only silence from the bathroom and a clock ticking down the hall.

My brother would be home soon. I didn't want him to find me waiting in her doorway looking sad. Pushing away, I trudged to the front porch and peered down the street. No sign of Henry.

Good. I could hide before he came home from the pool party. Time to go back inside and find something useful to do.

So why weren't my feet moving?

I looked around. There was a light breeze blowing. It was a gorgeous day, but I couldn't take it in. Grant had a right to be angry. I'd been stupid and wrong and jealous. Of his effect on her. Of her effect on him.

I rubbed my tattoo.

The porch swing squawked. I turned toward it and found Grant there, watching me through narrowed eyes. The air hummed between us.

"I'm sorry, Grant."

"Apology accepted." He hadn't snapped back at me. Instead, he chose words of forgiveness. Two simple, disappointed words. I had no defenses against them.

Like one of those summer storms that seem to pop up out of nowhere, my insides churned into a liquid mess. I squeezed my eyes shut and swallowed hard, trying to force back the tsunami of emotion roiling inside me. The effort robbed me of strength. I reached forward blindly, bumped a pillar, and hung on as if it were a lifeline.

The swing clanked and rattled abruptly. "Was there anything else, Chief?"

"No." I bowed my head, draping my face in a curtain of hair, and hoped that he would *just go*.

The tread of his feet approached and then paused on the top step. "What are you competing for? Crystal's sanity is not a prize to be won."

His words broke the dam around my feelings. Once the first moan slipped past my lips, the rest spilled over. All of the day's bad feelings pushed down, forcing me to my butt and squeezing my chest so tightly that I could hardly catch my breath.

Where was all the misery coming from? My family was surviving. We had a house to live in. We paid our bills most of the time. I had things under control. So why cry now?

"Tell me what's wrong," he said.

"I hate this." I pounded my palms against my thighs and sucked in breaths.

"What do you hate?"

"Everything." I hated breaking down in front of him. No, it was more than that. I hated breaking down, period. Yet here I sat, huddled on the top step, shaking uncontrollably and dripping tears. "I hate that Mom's depressed. I'm sick of wearing the same old clothes and eating the same old food. I've said *no* so many times that Henry's stopped asking. And I've forgotten how to let people be nice to me." I pressed cold fists to my hot face. "I'm so tired of being alone."

"You're not alone. I'm here."

"Not for much longer, and then I'll be even more lonely than before."

The boards creaked as Grant settled beside me on the top step. He didn't speak. He didn't touch me, but I could feel his presence as intensely as if he'd cradled me in his arms.

Anguish bled out through my tears. I leaned against the railing, too weary to even prop myself up. I wished I could be a boring high-school senior, the kind who worried about

GPAs and boyfriends and applying to out-of-state colleges. I wished my life could return to normal. And I had a genie, dammit. Yet the things I wanted most, he couldn't give me.

"It's okay to ask for help."

I shuddered at his statement. What if people refused? Nothing would change except I'd be embarrassed.

"They might say *yes*."

I angled my head to see him better. "You aren't supposed to read minds."

"I don't have to." His lips twitched. "Your thoughts scroll across your face like captions."

Lovely. I had no secrets from him anymore. "What a charming set of faults I have."

"You're human."

"Compared to what?"

"Lacey."

He'd called me by my first name again, yet this time he hadn't even realized it. Not that I would point it out, because I liked the sound of my name on his lips.

Before I could say anything else, a car rumbled to a stop before our house. A car door slammed. Flip-flops snapped up the driveway.

"What's going on?" Henry asked, charging up the first three steps. He put himself between me and Grant.

I scrubbed at my cheeks with the back of my hand. "Nothing. I'm okay."

My brother leaned over to peer in my face. "You look awful."

"Thanks for the honest assessment," I said, biting back an unexpected urge to giggle, "but really, I'm okay."

Henry turned to Grant, scowling. "Did you do something to her?"

Grant shook his head. "I did not. If your sister says she's fine, I suggest you believe her."

The two guys stared at each other, my brother with eight-year-old aggression, my BSB with mild patience.

It was adorable.

Henry smiled first. "Cool. What's for dinner?" He ran past us and into the house.

"Are you sure you're okay, Lacey?"

I looked up. Eli stood on the sidewalk, fists in pockets, taking in the sight of messy me and calm Grant. I rose unsteadily and wobbled down the steps, holding onto the railing for support. "I'm fine. Just having a hard day. Hard week. Hard…everything."

"All right." With deliberate care, he looked at Grant. A silent message passed between them, the air vibrating with tension.

What was that all about? It felt weird and out of place. I took a step closer to Eli and tried to smile gratefully. "Eli, I'm sorry about what I said earlier."

He nodded.

"Thanks for bringing Henry home."

"Sure. Any time." He swung around and headed for his Mustang.

Once Eli's car had hummed around the corner, I turned back toward the house. Grant had vanished. I flopped onto the bottom step and stared dazedly into the yard.

I'd left something off the list of problems I'd recited to Grant. I was tired of pushing away my friends.

Status Report #16
Saturday's Wish: Floors

Dear Boss,

You need not worry about my exposure to the spectrum of human emotion. I experienced more variety today than I care for.

There have been numerous times in my career that my masters have treated me like a common servant. It is something I ought to be accustomed to. Coming from Chief, the slight cut deeper. Crystal and Henry have treated me as an equal from the moment they met me. It made Chief's attempt to demote me all the more raw.

The scene changed so rapidly that I could hardly adjust. She flowed from angry to distraught in a matter of moments. Her loss of control—her abject misery—nearly undid me.

Why is she unhappy with Crystal's attempts to improve? Surely it doesn't matter who brings about the change.

I cannot figure my mistress out. She is unlike any human I have ever met.

Humbly submitted,
Grant

17

Polished Brass

Homework was light on Monday, and I didn't have to work. That gave me a couple of hours where I had nothing planned. I knew exactly what I would do with the time.

Slipping open my desk drawer, I rummaged around until I found the last of my favorite Pomegranate Red nail polish. After spreading an old towel over my quilt, I sprawled on the bed and tackled my toes first. I had barely started on my left hand when a car pulled into the driveway. I only half-listened, confident that the vehicle would back up immediately and drive off. It didn't.

Had someone given Henry a ride home from school? A quick glance at the clock told me it was too early.

Pushing up on my knees, I looked out one of the dormer windows. An unfamiliar car idled behind our Focus.

That was odd.

Skipping down the stairs, I flung myself out the front door and waited on the top step, tense and not sure why. A woman slid from the car, a blue shoulder bag clasped in one hand and a notebook in the other. She clopped up the sidewalk on stilettos.

Nothing about her—not the silky white designer dress, the perfect makeup, or the funky jewelry—indicated a government official, but somehow, I knew she was. My mouth went dry. "May I help you?"

She held out her identification. "I've come for a home visit. May I speak with Crystal Jones?"

I looked from her face to the image on the card. Now that I'd seen her up close, I would've guessed her closer to college age than old enough to be a government drone. I peered at the tiny print on the glossy card. Camarin Paxton, Department of Social Investigations. A shudder rippled through me. Did I look as horrified as I felt? "My mother's inside. Let me ask her."

"Thank you." The woman smiled politely, walked around me, and moved with serious speed to the door.

"Excuse me?" I hurried to catch up. "It's pretty quiet in the house. She might be napping."

"Perhaps you could wake her." From the porch, Ms. Paxton studied our car, still gleaming from Car Repair Day, and then the front flower beds. Her nose twitched.

This could not be happening. It was like someone had dropped me into the middle of a horror movie. The lines sounded familiar, just like I'd imagined them. The setting was expected, but there was no real sound, only a hollow popping in my ears.

I pushed past her. "I'll go inside and see if my mom's up."

"If you don't mind, I'll come with you."

"My mother sleeps in the nude." Lying made my neck turn red.

"All right, Miss Linden. I'll wait in the living room."

"Fine." I gestured toward the couch before disappearing down the hallway.

When I opened the door to Mom's bedroom, I discovered a disaster of epic proportions.

Mom was curled in a fetal position in the middle of her bed, wearing Josh's favorite outfit—drawstring shorts,

Carolina Tarheels T-shirt, once-white socks. More brightly colored T-shirts lay scattered about her, like a memorial-to-Josh quilt that had yet to be stitched. I closed the door softly and crossed to the bed. "Mom, what happened?"

Her fingers absently smoothed a shirt. "They still smell like him."

I resisted the urge to touch one, to bury my face in it. "Why did you take them out of the closet?"

With an effort, she shifted her gaze to mine. "I have to sort his clothes for the yard sale."

Selling Josh's things? This was the first I was hearing about it. If Mom was ready for such a big move, I would be happy for her, but it seemed like too much too soon. I sucked in a deep breath and exhaled slowly. "You don't have to do that, Mom. We'll put his clothes back in the closet." I held out my hands. "Can you sit up?"

She struggled to sit and swung her legs over the edge of the bed. Hunched over, hands pressed between her knees, she stared mutely at her toes. The new haircut clung to her head in sweaty hanks.

If Ms. Paxton got a glimpse of this Crystal Jones, Henry and I would be in foster care by nightfall.

"We have a visitor. She needs to talk to you," I said, my brain racing. What were the alternatives? *Think.*

"Tell her to go away."

At least Mom's voice was clear. "I don't think we can tell her to go away." The Carolina T-shirt had a large tear at the neck. "We need to change your top."

She didn't budge, flinch, or show any indication of having heard me. I grasped the hem and yanked it off, then found a clean one and pulled it over her head. Thankfully, she roused herself enough to slide her own arms through.

Time was shrieking past. What if Ms. Paxton came searching before I was through? How much time would she allow me to "wake up" my mother?

"Listen to me. This lady is going to ask you about our family. You have to keep the answers simple."

"Why does she want to know about us?"

"I don't know, but don't give out too much information." I tugged Mom to her feet. She didn't wobble. Good. "Let me answer the hard questions. Do you understand?"

She nodded. I looked into her eyes. They were glazed, almost lifeless.

All Sunday, she had been fine, but not today. She was too far gone to fake her way through this interview.

I rubbed the tattoo.

Granted emerged from the master bathroom. "What do you need?"

"It's my mom."

His gaze snapped to her. Masking a shudder, he strode quickly across the room and stood by her side. "Crystal?"

A sigh whistled between her lips. "I'm not good."

"It's okay." He took one of her hands and then looked at me. "What can I do?"

"Have you completed today's wish?"

"Yes."

Crap. What was I going to do?

"Miss Linden?" a voice called from the living room.

Grant's lips thinned. "Who is that?"

"A social worker."

"Indeed?" Anger blazed in his eyes.

"We have to get Mom out of here, Grant. You have to take her away."

"What do you mean?"

"I *wish* my mother would disappear for a while. Please."

"Chief, what are you asking of me?"

"Can I take tomorrow's...request today? On credit?"

"I've never had someone ask that before."

Heels clicked on the hardwoods, stopping outside the kitchen. "Miss Linden?"

I stepped closer to him. "Please. Tomorrow's wish. Right now."

He glanced at the door and then back at me, his face tightening. "The guidelines don't allow for it."

"They don't forbid it either. Please. Mom trusts you."

He gave a decisive nod. "Fine. Open the window."

I ran to the window, twisted the lock and raised the sash. When I spun around, Grant stood by the bed, my mother cradled easily in his arms. Her head rested against his shoulder.

"Where are we going?" she asked, her eyes closed.

"For a walk." He met my gaze. "Any further instructions?"

"Use your best judgment." I searched his face. Why was he angry?

The heels clopped to the bedroom door. The visitor rapped hard. "Did you find your mother?"

"No," I called back, staring at Grant in horror. If Ms. Paxton walked in, there was no way they could get out of here in time.

The doorknob turned.

Grant and my mother evaporated in a puff of blue smoke.

The woman frowned and looked around the bedroom until she spotted me. In my absence, she had donned a pair of glasses. New, cute, and expensive. Not what I would've expected from a social worker.

"Where is she?"

This woman was pretty bold. Weren't there laws about privacy or something? "I don't know."

"Can you guess?"

"I really couldn't."

Ms. Paxton's eyes narrowed behind her shiny red frames. "Are you concerned about her absence?"

I shook my head. "She's probably at a neighbor's house."

"What about your brother?"

That question made me hot and shaky. "What about him?"

"Where is he right now—with your mother?"

The idiocy of her assumption took me aback. How could someone in her position not know when the schools let out? "He won't be home from school for another half-hour."

The woman checked her watch. "Unfortunately, I have somewhere else to be. I'll return on a different day." She retraced her path to the living room and bent to gather her things.

I held the front door.

She smiled gently. "I'm not the enemy. I only want to make sure you are receiving the appropriate level of services. We're here to help."

She seemed so genuine that I was almost fooled. "I understand."

Shrugging, she turned to go. Stiletto heels clicked on the hardwoods, then the porch, then the concrete sidewalk. A car door thudded. An engine roared to life and faded away.

Relief made me dizzy. I leaned against the wall, not trusting myself to stand unassisted. That had been a close call.

There would be a next time, unannounced and probably during school hours. My mom couldn't stay hidden forever.

Status Report #18
Monday's Wish: Refurbishing Appliances and a wish on credit

Dear Boss,

The appliances in the kitchen, as well as the washing machine and dryer, are now in impeccable condition. They should last for years.

I heard a familiar voice today. I had not seen Camarin since her promotion to Principal. Did you send her to investigate my effectiveness? I assure you—it is unnecessary. Especially from her. She lacks sufficient humility to assess me, nor is she subtle enough to handle Chief's family with the sensitivity they require. Don't do this again, please.

I am puzzled over Crystal. Although her mood remains uneven, it had been many days since it had sunk quite this low. I had spent a large portion of the morning helping her plan a yard sale. It had given her great pleasure to think that she might contribute to the family's income. This was a small victory for her; I can't imagine how it could have changed so quickly.

Humbly submitted,
Grant

18

A Decent Guess

The day for our colonial project demo had finally arrived, and getting dressed put me into a seriously bad mood. Why didn't the wench costume look as good on me as it had in the photo? I hadn't bothered to try it on when the Reys dropped it off last night, and now I wished I had. The peasant blouse and long dark skirt hung about me like a tent, and the ankle boots looked like I was on my way to a construction site. I would wait to put the corset on at school—no use walking through the neighborhood looking any more stupid than I had to.

I went straight to the girls' bathroom when I arrived at school. Nobody walked in on me as I struggled into the corset, which was just as well because it took a frustrating and curse-filled five minutes to get the crazy thing on.

When I was done, I paused for a moment of painful communion with my colonial sisters. Breathing, it turned out, was optional in one of these things. Spinning around, I looked in the mirror.

Okay. Wow.

I hardly recognized me. Lacey-the-wench looked curvy and hot. The corset pulled in my waist and pushed up my boobs. If girls didn't have the whole suffering issue to deal with, corsets would be hugely popular.

Oh yeah. I was definitely feeling the magic now.

Time to find the rest of my project team. Kimberley was waiting for me in the media center with her bag of twisted iron. She wore a costume too, which no one would notice with me around—the first time that had ever happened.

She hopped out of her chair, hoisted the clanking bag, and blinked at the sight of me. "You look amazing."

"Thanks." Maybe wench-hood wouldn't be so bad after all.

We caused a sensation when we walked into APUSH, just before the bell rang. Mr. Jarrett, who lounged behind his desk absorbed by his computer, looked up at the stirring of noise that greeted our entrance. He sneered at the sight of Kimberley, flicked a glance at me, and then did a double take. He scrutinized me with a great deal more intensity than was appropriate for a teacher. Creep.

"Poodle," he said without looking at her, "would your team like to go first in the show-and-tell?"

"Yes, Mr. Jarrett. We would."

Kimberley ran the demo. I stood next to the projector attached to her iPad, smiling like a spokesmodel on a game show and paging down through the slides while Kimberley talked. She was good at public speaking. Of course, it helped that the slides had intense notes.

The presentation ended too quickly, a thought I'd never had before on a social studies project.

"Thank you, ladies. The demo was helpful. And Lacey, my compliments on your...um, assets." His gaze never moved above my chin.

Until that comment, I'd been having a good day. Why did this creep have to screw it up? I glared at him, almost choking on my outrage. He'd been mean to Kimberley since she arrived, and now he was staring at my breasts. Why did any of us put up with his crap?

Before I could think through what I was about to say, my saucy-wench mouth opened and out came, "Talk to my face, pervert."

There was a brief, shocked pause before the whole class erupted into applause.

Mr. Jarrett shouted for silence. When that didn't do any good, he flapped his arms, but no one paid attention. I tried not to gloat, but it was impossible.

When his gavel crashed on the edge of the desk, the applause died away.

His fierce gaze swept the classroom before landing on me. "Maybe you should tell the vice principal what you called me."

"Maybe you should tell him why." The boldness in the clothes must have been infecting me.

Everybody roared with laughter—except Mr. Jarrett. His face got tight enough for the veins to pop out on his forehead. "Lacey, go change your clothes. Poodle, take a seat."

The adrenaline rush faded. I spun on my heel and ran to the bathroom, a little shaky as I tried to recover from what had just happened. We probably lost an entire letter grade because of me. I'd better leave wench-hood behind before I got into worse trouble.

My hands wouldn't cooperate. I stared into the mirror, obsessed with my reflection, putting off my return to being ordinary.

Minutes passed before I prodded myself into movement. I loosened the laces on the corset and regained the fine art of breathing. Normal Lacey started to emerge.

Wait.

I wasn't going back to APUSH. If Mr. Jarrett noticed that I hadn't returned, I'd mumble "lady problems" and hope he didn't ask more. The costume stayed. I tied a bow in the loosened laces, walked out to the hallway, turned in the opposite direction of the classroom, and hid for the rest of first period in the media center.

My corset-induced confidence lasted through lunchtime. I sauntered into the cafeteria, looking for people to dazzle.

There was a line of students waiting to buy something from a booth. The attached poster announced the Dance Club's September fundraiser. They held a dance every year on the Friday night of our football team's bye week.

I positioned myself so that I would be seen.

Eli stepped out of the front of the line. As he turned to leave, he spotted me and detoured in my direction, his attention occupied with stuffing tickets into his wallet.

"Hey, Eli," I said, swishing my saucy skirt.

His gaze swept me from head to toe and then back again. He smiled. "Feeling better?"

"I am. Thanks for checking on me Saturday." Eli must've forgiven my rudeness enough to speak to me again. This costume was magical. "If Henry's team remains undefeated for the rest of the season, do they get a prize or something?"

His smile deepened. "Or something."

"Will they get trophies and stuff?"

"They will. They're good, Lacey."

"Cool." This conversation was going well. My hot look made me bold. I pointed at the wallet he was sliding back into his pocket. "Are you going to the dance?"

"Yeah."

"Do you know how to dance like that?"

"Some." He shrugged. "They'll give lessons. You can try ballroom, Latin, swing. It's fun."

"What about your knee?"

"I'll be careful."

"You got two tickets. Does that mean you have a date?"

His voice, his face, his entire body went instantly still. "No."

Heat rose up my neck. I hadn't been fishing, but it must have been what he thought. I had to fix this. "Well, have a good time. I'm not going. Dances aren't my thing."

"Really?"

"Yeah." I looked around desperately for a way to end this conversation now. Kimberley waved at me from the front of the ticket line. "Excuse me, but I'd better go. I see my friend over there."

He nodded and took off for the cafeteria exit.

A finger—with a sharp fingernail—poked me in the back. "What was that all about?"

I spun around. Kimberley was still in her costume, which was solid black except for a white scarf covering her hair. She looked like one of the nuns from *The Sound of Music*. I'd been too consumed with being a wench to think about it earlier. "Eli doesn't have a date to the dance."

"Did you ask him?"

"No."

"Why not?"

The family budget couldn't cover something like a ticket. Or the right kind of dress. Or any of the stuff that went along with asking someone out on a date. "I don't want to go."

"You're a pathetic liar. Here's your ticket." She held one out to me.

"No thanks." Spinning around, I headed out the cafeteria and down the hallway. Her footsteps plodded along behind me.

I stopped at my locker.

"Take it, Lacey."

"No."

"Look. It won't be fun if I go by myself."

I pulled my math homework out of my backpack. "The ticket isn't the only cost."

"You can borrow a dress from me. I have lots."

"No, I can't." She was smaller than me everywhere except bra size. Bad idea.

"Do I throw the ticket away?"

My locker door banged shut. She was right. It might be fun, and I would like to go. But jeans and sneakers would be out of place at the dance. "Do whatever you want with it."

"Good. I will." A wide smile lit her face. "See you." She glided away, uncaring about the other students gawking at the nun floating down the hall.

Really? It was hard to believe that Kimberley had given up so easily. I turned in the opposite direction, mulling over when she might try another assault on my decision. There were only three days left.

After school, I hurried home, dumped my backpack in the foyer, then charged up the attic stairs as quickly as the colonial skirt allowed. The costume came off. Jeans and a T-shirt took its place.

If I wasn't careful, I'd be late for work. I tore downstairs, grabbed the car keys from a hook hidden behind the bureau, and thundered into the foyer.

"Chief," Grant called.

I wanted to ignore him, but the happiness in his voice wouldn't let me. I looked over my shoulder.

He was hunched over piles of paper on the dining room table, smiling.

What was going on with him? Our Grant didn't smile very often.

"What is it?"

"Come here. You need to see this."

His excitement was contagious. "What?" I was smiling too, without even knowing why.

"I reviewed the accordion file we found this weekend."

Not what I expected. "I burned through two wishes yesterday. You didn't have to do this one today."

He gestured dismissively. "We'll catch up sometime. What I uncovered is more important. It's a key."

My scalp tingled. Maybe I hadn't heard that right. "A key to what?"

"I would guess a storage facility."

There was a loud humming inside my head. "Let me see."

Grant crossed to my side and held out his hand. On his palm lay an ornate key made of polished brass, the kind that fit into an old-fashioned padlock. A storage facility was a decent guess. But where? And why?

"Mom," I shouted.

She appeared in the doorway to the kitchen, a dish towel in her hand and a smear of flour on her cheek. "What, baby?"

"Did Josh ever mention that he put some things in storage?"

She nodded. "He took me with him once."

A wave of pleasure washed over me. What could be in there? "Where is it?"

"I don't remember."

Of course not. But never mind. There weren't that many facilities around town. I could go to all of them until I found the right one. "Do you remember what he put in it?"

Her face paled. "Projects."

"Art projects?" My stepfather had been good. Too good for this town to understand. "Are you saying that Josh stashed some of his carvings?"

"Yeah." She turned to leave.

"Mom, wait." When she hesitated, I rushed out my next question. "How many projects did he store?"

"I don't know."

"Can you give me an idea? Was it more like five or fifty?"

"I said I don't know."

Deep breath. Should I press it or not? "Why haven't you told me about this?"

She lifted a hand to her mouth. "I forgot," she mumbled around biting her cuticles.

"This could be huge—"

There was a touch on my shoulder. I cut a sideways glance at Grant. He shook his head at me.

"Okay, fine, Mom. But we have to find out what's in there. It could be valuable."

My mother gave a choked sob. A few seconds later, her bedroom door slammed.

Why did this always happen? Things seemed like they were going well and then, bam, something happened that screwed things up again.

Eager to leave, I swung around, tripped over my forgotten backpack, and fell hard on my butt.

Perfect.

Grant knelt beside me to pick up the contents of my backpack that had scattered all over the floor.

"What is this?" he asked, holding up a golden-yellow slip of paper.

A tiny ember of joy flickered inside me. "It's a ticket to a fundraiser dance." Kimberley was so incredibly stubborn. And sneaky. And nice.

"You bought a ticket?"

"No." Why hadn't she listened to me? "Kimberley did."

"I'm glad. You'll have a good time."

Reality blew out the ember. "I can't go." I took it from him and stuffed it into a side pocket of my backpack.

He sighed. "Why are you determined to live the life of a martyr?"

"It's complicated."

"I have ten days to listen."

A quick glance at my watch made me gasp. "I have ten minutes to get to work, so this conversation is officially over. I'll have to run a few stop signs as it is."

Status Report #19 & #20
Tuesday's and Wednesday's Wishes: Important Papers
and Vehicle Towing

Dear Boss,

I shared my discovery of the key with Chief at approximately four PM on Tuesday. At four-fifteen, I received a signal from her.

Chief had driven her car into a pothole and ruined a tire.

If you were watching, you might have thought I stretched the rules, but I believe my solution fell within guidelines. Duct tape is an extraordinarily useful product. It patched the tire sufficiently well to push the car home.

We did, of course, wait until after midnight so the vehicle towing task could be fulfilled on Wednesday. Chief is, understandably, upset.

Perhaps Thursday is the day to collect on the "credit wish."

Humbly submitted,
Grant

19

Unnatural Angle

What a hideous night this had been. I lay on my bed, stared at the ceiling, and called myself all sorts of creative names. Wallowing in my own stupidity was far more urgent than sleep.

At four, I gave up, rolled out of bed, staggered to the kitchen, and pulled out the wish list. When Grant and I made it originally, we'd put the most boring items at the end, the wishes that cost the least amount of money. The wishes that weren't likely to be done now.

We had to have transportation, but how could I afford to replace the tire? There wasn't much cash left from selling the picture frames. To avoid temptation, I always paid off bills as quickly as the checks came in.

I didn't really have a choice. I'd have to raid the emergency fund to buy a new tire, and I wasn't willing to do that yet. We'd have to park the car.

Folding the checklist, I pressed my cheek against the coolness of the tabletop and closed my bleary eyes.

What about the storage unit? It might be filled with carvings. Maybe it held other valuables I couldn't even imagine. That would be nice. Lots of things to sell. More frames. Or power tools. Guys liked to buy power tools.

It would be great to have unexpected income. New tires, new clothes, better food, and less fear that something would go wrong.

I could make it a wish. Grant would locate the storage unit, organize the treasures he found, and take them to the flea market.

It was a good plan.

All we had to do was hang on a little longer, and the money would show up.

Eventually...

"Lacey." A hand grasped my shoulder and gave it a hard shake.

I didn't want to let go of my dream yet. It involved a ticket, all shimmery and golden. For the dance. Or maybe the lottery. Either way, I won.

"Are you okay?" Mom's voice seemed muffled.

"I think so."

Cool fingers touched my forehead. "No fever. Did you sleep in the kitchen?"

"Possibly." My eyelids slid open halfway. Strange. The world had rotated ninety degrees. "What time is it?"

"Six."

I sat up. Ouch. My neck muscles bunched painfully, preferring the unnatural angle they'd been in for the past hour. I stretched and focused on my mother's face. Time to tell her about the car, but I didn't want to. "I have bad news."

She nodded.

"I messed up the car."

Her eyes widened. "How?"

"Blew out a tire."

"Oh."

That was all? Just *oh*? No crying fits or disappointed sighs? "Do you understand, Mom? It might be a few weeks before we can drive the car."

"I wasn't driving it anyway." She ran her fingers through her bangs, fluttering them back from her face. "I screw up often enough that I think you're entitled to a mistake every now and then."

Was my mom teasing me?

Wow, that was great. "We're good then?"

"Yes." Her smile was slight, but there. "Do you want coffee or breakfast?"

"Sure, Mom. Both would be nice." I shook my head as I tried to mentally replace the argument I'd expected with this rarely seen maternal energy.

"Go on, baby. I'll have everything ready by the time you're dressed."

As the day went on, I couldn't remember for sure whether I'd washed my hair, put on deodorant, or arrived at school on time. My classes made no impression on me either. I was too fogged over to pay attention, but I did remember my mom's too-strong coffee and peanut-butter toast.

When I got home, I flopped onto the porch swing, closed my eyes, and rested my head against the swing back. The mistakes of the previous day drifted from my mind. I gave in to drowsy relaxation.

Grant's presence swirled around me like a sweet breeze. "How was your day off?" I asked around a yawn.

"Fine." A pause. "Go to the dance, Chief."

Not what I expected. "Why?"

"You want to go."

I looked at him through my eyelashes. It would be noisy and crazy. Everybody would be dressed up and trying to learn the dances so we could all be bad together. It sounded great.

No use denying it—I did want to go. "That's not a good enough reason."

"It could be your last chance in high school."

He was right. Time was running out. I would graduate in January. Then work, work, work. There weren't going to be other chances like this in my senior year.

What was I thinking? We couldn't afford it.

But I wanted to go.

What I needed to do was consider things logically. I didn't have to worry about my ticket, thanks to Kimberley. And I didn't have to worry about a second ticket, because I didn't have a date. "I don't have anything to wear."

The swing dipped and creaked under his weight. "Make a wish."

I allowed my head to loll sideways so that I could frown at him. "I can't. I still haven't paid you back for the wish from Monday."

"I'll finish my visit a day early." He smiled. "You haven't used a single wish for yourself. Ask me to create you a gown."

Hope tickled the back of my throat. Could I? "Let's say, theoretically speaking, I agree to attend the dance. Where would the materials for the dress come from?"

"Your mom discovered two bridesmaid dresses when we were cleaning the attic."

"We should sell them at the yard sale."

"Crystal thinks they're too ugly to sell."

Really? If the dresses were too ugly to sell, did he actually expect me to wear one to my last high-school social event *ever*? "Why didn't you throw them away?"

"She says the fabric is good quality." He slid from the porch swing. "I'll be right back." The screen door slammed behind him as he disappeared into the house.

My mom knew about fabric. She'd filled my closet with frilly dresses when I was little. Once I'd moved in with her, I'd been the best-dressed kid in kindergarten.

I straightened and turned sideways in the swing, one foot on the porch. With a slight push, I sent the swing rocking and drew up my leg. The breeze whispered around me. Should I go?

Kimberley would be there. We could smirk over what everyone was wearing and shout over the band.

Eli would be there. Maybe, if I worked up the courage, I could dance with him. I was pretty sure he was too nice to reject me right there in front of everyone.

My last dance.

The screen door slammed again.

Grant held the two ugliest dresses I had ever seen. The first was a floor-length ball gown (we were talking *Gone with the Wind* here) in black lace over emerald silk. The other was a calf-length halter dress in gray satin with a big stain at the hem. I deflated in abject disappointment. "I'm not wasting a wish on that stuff."

"You doubt me?"

He sounded so insulted I couldn't help laughing. "You have my complete trust."

"Good. Then it's settled." He tossed the gowns over the railing. "Stand up."

"I haven't said 'I wish' yet."

"It'll have to wait until tomorrow. You had today's wish at midnight."

Oh. Right. "Thanks for reminding me."

"Chief, stand up. Arms out. I need to take your measurements."

When I hopped from the swing, it squawked in protest. Dutifully, I stood and held my arms out at shoulder level while he scrutinized me from head to toe. His gaze had a physical feel, like my shampoo/massage. It was delicious.

I had to snap out of it. My lack of experience had left me pathetically needy if a guy could simply look at me and make me shiver.

Grant stepped closer. He reached out, his fingers close but not quite touching my rib cage. Electricity arced between us. I gasped.

He jerked away. "Have I hurt you?"

I shook my head. It was supposed to be impersonal. This was Grant. My *friend*.

No. My *employee*. "You can keep going," I said, my voice husky.

The hands returned, hovering a fraction of an inch from my body. They traced from my waist to my hips. His fingers floated around my neck, then skimmed my arms from shoulder to wrist. It was sheer heaven. My brain dulled into a sensory explosion.

Was he done yet?

Where else did he need measurements?

I backed away from him until the swing smacked my legs. "My bra size is 34B."

He looked away. "I'll take your word for it."

Update to Status Report #20

Dear Boss,

I will not be collecting the credit wish on Thursday. Chief needs a party gown, and it must be completed by Friday.

We have reached Wish #21, and it will be the first wish that benefits only her.

My previous assignments were, frankly, dull. I knew that my masters were in need. The goals they pursued were important and required their complete dedication, but that did not alter how intensely conventional the tasks were.

Chief's home-repair requests are among the most basic tasks I have ever attempted. Yet, now that I know how much they impact her entire family, her assignments have also proven to be the most rewarding.

She amazes me.

Humbly submitted,
Grant

20

Overcome With Awe

School passed in a blur again on Thursday, but for a different reason. I was eager to see what Grant would create for me. Nothing else registered.

As soon as the final bell rang, I hurried out the front doors and cut through the parking lot. At the crosswalk, a silver SUV idled. "Want a ride?" Kimberley called from the back seat.

I hopped in. This would cut five minutes off the commute. I could see the results that much sooner.

"I'm glad you decided to come to the dance." She sighed happily.

"Thanks. Really. I love that you did this for me."

"Mom can drive."

"Great."

"Do you have something to wear?" Mrs. Rey asked.

"Yeah." And I couldn't wait to see it.

Kimberley grasped my arm. "Do you want to see my dresses?"

"Sure." Dresses? Plural? Of course. She would have plenty to choose from. All gorgeous. All expensive.

Mrs. Rey made a turn at the next corner, away from my house and toward theirs. Obviously, we were going to see her dresses right now.

We swung into the driveway and eased to a stop.

"Follow me." Kimberley unlocked the front door and sauntered down the hall toward the back of the house.

It was the first time I'd ever been in her room. Interesting. The daughter got the master suite while the mom got one of the tiny bedrooms.

I stepped in and was instantly reminded of my friend's health issues. The dresser top was covered with prescription bottles. A whiteboard took up one wall—with her week's schedule written in large letters. A corkboard had hospital memorabilia tacked to it—get-well cards, plastic wristbands, and photos.

I pointed at one of the candid shots. "Who are all those people?"

She peered over my shoulder. "My care team." She touched a photo where she sat in a wheelchair surrounded by people in scrubs. "That tall lady behind me is my oncologist, and the other two people are my nurses."

"Did you have a stem cell transplant?"

"Only chemo. I had the good kind of leukemia."

"The *good* kind?"

She gave a light laugh. "There's bad leukemia, and then there's not so bad. That's what I had—the kind with a great survival rate." Her finger moved to the next photo. "And here are my homebound teacher and lead social worker. I stay in contact with them."

The phrase *social worker* caught my attention. "Kimberley, are you still concerned about Grant?"

"No. You said he's a good guy, and I believe you."

"Did you remember to mention it to your mother?"

Her lips pressed together primly. "I did."

"Did she promise to drop it?"

She nodded. "Why do you ask?"

"A lady from the Department of Social Investigations came by our house on Monday."

She wrinkled her nose. "I've never heard of that department. Are you sure that's what she said?"

"I saw her ID card."

"North Carolina has Child Protective Services," she said with the casual air of a person familiar with such groups. "I don't know who your visitor was, but Mom and I were not the reason she came." Kimberley disappeared into her walk-in closet.

Her response gave me a prickling sense of foreboding. Next time I got to the library, I'd have to do a search on that department name.

"Here they are," Kimberley said as she walked out. "I've narrowed it to two." She held a coat hanger in each hand.

I studied the dresses. Both shimmered in the afternoon sunlight. Dress one was flame red and ruffly. Dress two was metallic gold and slippery. I cleared my throat. "You don't have to worry about anyone else wearing the same thing."

"I wasn't worried about that."

Of course not. "Well," I said, stalling for time. "The red one looks like it would be perfect for salsa."

She flapped its full skirt. "It looks great when I twirl."

"You'll be noticed. In either dress."

She laughed. "That would be the point, wouldn't it?"

"Right." I drew closer and inspected the dresses. The golden fabric was thin and would cling to Kimberley like a second skin. Magnolia Grove High wasn't ready for it. "I think the red."

Kimberley scrunched her nose. "That's what I'm thinking too." She tossed them on her bed in a crumpled heap. "Are you ready to go home?"

I returned to a quiet house, which meant it was either empty or my brother was buried in homework. As I walked past the living room, I glanced in and froze, transfixed by what awaited me on a dressmaker's form.

It was the dress. *My* dress.

I gave my head a quick shake. Yep, still beautiful.

The halter dress had a short, full, silvery skirt peeking through black lace. Black beading highlighted the waist. I was overcome with awe. "Wow. Just...*wow.*"

My mom appeared beside me. "You like it?"

"It's gorgeous." I walked closer, happy to be near it. "It has to be the most incredible dress I've ever seen."

Of course, the dress had to be accessorized. What about shoes?

Bare legs or hose?

"Can I raid your jewelry box, Mom?"

"Sure." She drew even with me, bouncing on her feet. "Are you going to try it on?"

"Not now."

"You should try it on." She smoothed a fold of lace. "What if it doesn't fit?"

"It will." Grant didn't make mistakes. I'd rather wait to see everything—hair, makeup, dress—all at once. "I can't believe how good silver and black look together."

Mom's voice had lost its sparkle. "It's pewter. Not silver." She drifted out of the living room.

That was strange. My gaze fell on Grant, who watched from the foyer. "What's wrong with her?"

"Crystal made the dress."

"Really?" Surprise whispered down my spine. That dress had taken a lot of handwork, and my mom had done it? She'd spent hours doing something this hard for me? I nearly vibrated with happiness.

"Indeed, she did."

No wonder she was disappointed by my reaction. I hadn't gushed out loud, and this dress definitely deserved gushing. I hunted her down, intent on making it up to her. She was in her usual spot at the kitchen table, sipping coffee and pretending to read a newspaper. Henry wasn't around, but the music coming from his room indicated that he had finished his homework.

Leaning against the wall, I studied my mom. This made two days this week where she hadn't been a ghost. The haircut made her look younger, she wore actual clothes, and she didn't seem quite so sad. I loved seeing her this way. I just wished I could trust it. "Thanks, Mom. The dress is beyond perfect."

"You're welcome."

"I didn't know you could sew like that anymore."

Her gaze met mine, as if she were tuned in. "It's like riding a bike. You don't forget."

Anticipation tingled along my nerves. This was the most coherent conversation we'd had in a while. "Did you enjoy it?"

Her lips curved. "Yeah. It was fun."

This was my chance. When Grant had nudged her, she got better. It could work for me too. "You should do it more often then."

"I'm not turning it into a job, if that's what you really mean," she said, her voice hardening.

I gaped in surprise. That wasn't what I meant, but maybe we should go there. "Why not? You're good at sewing. You could make money at it."

"Not now, Lacey." She propped her chin on her fists and became absorbed in a chainsaw advertisement.

"You ought to give it some thought." This was a victory for her. She should capitalize on it. "You already said it was fun."

"No."

Ideas burst from me like a geyser. "People pay a lot for party dresses. We could buy old gowns cheap from a thrift shop—"

Her free hand smacked the table open-palmed. "Leave it alone."

"Why?" Frustration gripped me. This could be good in so many ways.

She shook her head and flipped another page.

"What are you afraid of, Mom?"

She crumpled the paper with clawed hands and shrieked, "Pressure."

The music stopped. Two sets of footsteps sounded in the hallway, but no one came into the kitchen. It was just me and my mom and a completely unexpected word.

"Pressure? What kind of pressure would you have making dresses?"

"Deadlines." She shot to her feet, the movement jolting the table and sloshing coffee from her mug. "Dressmaking is hard," she said in a tight voice. "What if I made something for someone and they wanted it by a specific day and I was a mess that week and couldn't get it done?"

"You wouldn't have to do it by commission. You could create dresses on consignment."

She bowed her head, her hair brushing her cheeks and concealing her eyes. "Why are you so obsessed with money?"

Obsessed with money? This from someone who had checked out and left her underage daughter to juggle the family's problems? "Why am I supposed to feel like a jerk for keeping us above the poverty line?"

"You're exaggerating."

"I'm not."

She looked up, breathing through her mouth. "It's not that bad."

"How do you know? You don't look at the bank statements or pay the bills."

"I would be able to tell."

"Apparently not."

"We're managing."

"Yeah, on *my* back."

The anger on her face faded to confusion. "What do you mean?"

"Your check barely covers the mortgage, Mom. We'd starve without my job or Dad's benefits from the military."

Her eyes widened with shock. "I didn't..." She stopped to press shaking palms against her temples. "I can't think about this right now. I'm not well. It's hard to be me." She brushed past me and hurried down the hall.

"It's hard to be me too," I whispered.

Status Report #21
Thursday's Wish: Dress Creation

Dear Boss,

Today I created a party dress for Chief. She reacted with utter delight.

Crystal helped with the dress, making suggestions as I sketched and cut. Once the garment was ready to be assembled, she offered to stitch it. Her sewing machine is capable of intricate work, and she has a large stock of lace, trim, and beading. Crystal took such pleasure in the project that I am surprised she ever gave this skill up.

Chief revealed the truth about their finances. Until today, neither her mother nor I knew how dependent the family's survival was on her. It is humbling to realize the extent to which I have misjudged Chief's intentions.

The wishes on this assignment have been simple. I believe that I have been completing them with care and competence. Yet I can't help but wonder if I understand humans less now than when I arrived.

Humbly submitted,
Grant

21

Relative Inexperience

I awakened early and lay quietly, practicing the speech I was about to give Grant.

Today's wish had to be about my mother. She wanted to get better. I was sure of it. If my dress was any indication, she wanted to be creative again. The trick was figuring out how. Holding her back for fear of other people finding out was not working.

Dread filled me as I imagined how Grant might react. I didn't want a fight, but what if he thought my wish didn't go far enough?

I changed into jeans and a shirt, yanked a brush through my hair, and tiptoed down the stairs. Henry was still asleep, a restless ball of boy and sheets. My mother curled on the couch, staring quietly out the bay window at the empty street beyond. The table beside her held four coffee mugs and a mound of used tissues.

I slipped through the kitchen and into the grayness of the dawn. The studio was dark. With a touch of my tattoo, I called his name.

"Good morning." He stood before me, buttoning his shirt, its edges a stark white against his skin. He smelled of pine-scented soap. "Why are you here?"

"I want to discuss my wish."

"Staining the deck is next. I know what to do."

I gave a tiny shake of my head. The list had to be abandoned. What had I been thinking? I'd been so proud of myself for planning the wishes. I was organized and responsible, unlike my immature stepfather or the self-centered kids at school. By planning the future, I had it under control. At least, that's what I'd thought.

Creating the list had done nothing more than give me a false sense of power. I'd fooled myself into believing that I could hand Grant a little money, point him at some home repairs, and a month later the Linden-Jones family would be able to wave goodbye as our free handyman left.

Wrong. Our problems were complicated, and they were much bigger than selling a house.

If I'd thought the month after Josh died had been confusing, it was nothing compared to having *everything humanly possible* made available to me and having to make the right choices. When Grant first appeared, thirty wishes had seemed almost decadent. Now, I was tied up in knots about not picking well. "I wish for you to help my mom get better."

"Well done, Lacey."

His good opinion meant so much to me. I'd thirsted for it. Craved it. And now that I had it, I wanted more. Stepping nearer to him, I wrapped my arms around his waist and rested my cheek against his chest.

He didn't hesitate for even a second. He cradled me to him, his arms strong and safe.

I closed my eyes and yielded to the pleasure of his embrace. What would I do without Grant?

"Chief," he said against my hair, "I can't snap my fingers and make her well. It'll take time for your mom to improve. What do you want me to do in one day?"

"Can you do research? Can you find out what we can do that doesn't involve the government?"

There was silence. Why? I looked up to study his face. His expression was thoughtful. I was glad, because I couldn't have taken his disappointment. "There have to be things that could make a difference, stuff that Mom is willing to try and that I can keep monitoring after you're gone. What do you think?"

"May I include private groups in the investigation?"

And here it was. The big hurdle. Letting people know. Well-meaning people. People whose help could hurt. Would they feel obligated to report us? Would they be as committed as I was to keeping my family intact?

"You can include private groups."

"They might recommend medication. Will you be able to pay?"

I nodded as I stepped from his arms. "I'll find the cash. Somehow."

The sky had lightened. It was time to leave for school. Had I been clear enough about what I wanted?

Did I even *know* what I wanted?

"When you get home this afternoon, I'll have answers," he said.

"Thank you." I turned toward the house.

"She has to wish it too, Chief."

I glanced over my shoulder. "She will." I hoped.

When I reached our street after a shift at work, Grant was waiting at the corner.

I approached him, jittery with nerves. "Is everything all right?"

He nodded solemnly. "I learned a lot today. There was a book at the library about holistic approaches, like herbs and exercise. I checked it out for you."

"That's great." I wanted to smile, but his grave expression held me back. "Is there a 'but' in here somewhere?"

"Home remedies don't work for everyone. She may need professional help."

"What kind?"

"I found a grief support group at a local church run by a licensed therapist."

"Will that be enough?"

"Perhaps not, but it will be a start."

I continued down the sidewalk as Grant fell into step at my side. "Did you mention any of this to her?"

"We shared a pot of herbal tea and discussed drinking it instead of coffee. I spoke of the benefits to be gained from daily walks. She was noncommittal."

"You didn't mention the group?"

"No, that is your call."

We entered the house and parted in the hallway. Grant headed to the kitchen. I went upstairs, prepared to spend the remainder of the evening getting ready.

The new dress awaited me in my room—sophisticated and unique. Even though I had a lot to do, for a brief moment I stood quietly, smiling at my gorgeous gown, relishing the anticipation.

Needing to share this feeling with someone, I crossed to the stairwell. "Mom, can you come up here a minute?" I shouted down.

"In a sec," she shouted back.

A couple of minutes later, she thumped up the stairs and burst into the room carrying a big plastic sewing box. A hesitant smile spread over her face. "It's going to look great."

I laughed. "It really will. You did an amazing job."

An apology had been offered and accepted. Both directions.

She nodded, the efficient seamstress taking over. "Come on, baby. Try on the dress and then stand up here so I can see if the hem is right."

Our conversation centered around the dance and my dress. I stood on a chair, biting my lip against saying anything impatient to make her hurry. She poked and prodded, tugged and twisted, then snipped a couple of loose threads. When she left, we were both smiling.

Grant didn't appear to be in the house anymore, which was fine. I didn't want to see him until I was totally done, and only his complete astonishment would satisfy me.

I read over the *Get Ready for the Dance* list. First item: Downstairs to shower, shampoo, and shave. Back to the attic, wrapped in towels.

Henry sat on my bed, a huge smile on his face and a brown paper sack in his hands.

"What is it, little man?"

He handed me the bag, bouncing as I peered inside. It was a bottle of nail polish. *Pewter Pearl.*

I blinked back the moisture in my eyes. "Where did you get this?"

"At the dollar store, except it was *two* dollars." He leapt off the bed and ran over to the door. "When we were cleaning up this weekend, Mom said I could keep any change I found under the couch cushions, and I found two dollars and fifty-seven cents. So I bought that for you."

"Thank you. It's perfect," I said, my voice husky.

"Cool." He bounded down the stairs.

I added a new item to my checklist.

Makeup. Dress. Jewelry. *Polish.*

I was nearly ready when the phone rang. Henry charged up the stairs and held out the cordless. I accepted the phone gingerly, not wanting to mess up my newly painted, pearly pewter nails. "Hello?"

"Guess what?" Kimberley asked.

"Your mother will be late picking me up?"

"No. Guess again." She giggled.

I blew on my nails. They looked pretty good. "You put on the red gown with the fluttery skirt, and it barely covers your butt."

"The red one?" There was a pause. "Is that the one we picked? I'm wearing the gold one."

"The gold one is great." Nobody would look at me. Guaranteed. "Thanks for calling. Now, if you don't mind, I have things to do."

"But you haven't guessed."

"So you're not calling about how good you look in your dress."

"No." She made a rude noise with her lips. "Eli is driving us."

I nearly dropped the phone. "Eli Harper?"

"Yeah."

"Why is he driving?"

"I asked him to be my date."

The words rolled around inside my brain, beeping and clanking like those little metal balls in an old-fashioned pinball machine. I imagined Kimberley in her crazy-hot liquid-gold gown trying to salsa on the dance floor with the equally crazy-hot Eli. And I would get to watch from the side. "Congratulations," I said, trying to sound happy for her.

"Thanks." She exhaled. "I asked Sean first, but he turned me down."

I cleared my throat, but it didn't seem to want to work. "Did Sean say why?"

"No. I don't understand him, and I wish I did." She sighed. "Okay, I have a big favor to ask."

"Yeah?"

"I'm leaving my iPad at home, so I need you to help me remember what happens tonight. Can you stick close to us?"

"Yeah, I can do that." Wow. The two of them—and me.

"Thanks." A doorbell rang in the background. "Can't talk anymore. Eli is here. I'll see you soon." Click.

"Sure," I said to no one and tossed the phone onto the bed. Then I tossed myself onto the bed.

Kimberley had asked Eli to the dance. I should have been happy for her, right? And I was. They would look adorable together. But it changed my evening completely. I'd expected to hang out with a friend, and now I would be alone.

Muffled voices drifted below me. The tread of shoes on hardwood floors. The occasional *snick* of a door shutting. And still I lay there. Reorienting my thinking. Eyes closed. Mouth closed. Mind closed.

They would be a couple.

I would be the pathetic extra.

Eight-year-old feet padded up the attic stairs. A progress check.

"Lacey?"

"Yes, Henry?"

His face hovered over mine, upside down. "Something wrong?"

"Yes." At least my brother could read me.

"Can I make it better?"

My lips curved a little. "No."

He sighed. "Is it a high-school thing?"

"It is." My lips curved a lot.

"Mom wants to know when you're coming down."

"Soon." I sat up. Too suddenly, as it turned out, because a wave of dizziness rolled over me. Gripping the edge of the bed, I waited for the dizziness to pass. "Hey, little man, help me up."

He grabbed both of my hands and tugged, catapulting me from the bed. Henry was stronger than I expected. "Okay, I'm good." I looked around for my mother's jewel-studded sandals that had a little bit of a heel.

"Wow, oh wow, Lacey. You look awesome."

"You think so?" I opened my eyes wide and prayed he would say nothing else that might have the potential to mess up my mascara. "Can you hand me those shoes?"

"Man! Can you dance in these things?"

"I don't know. Guess I'll find out." I followed him down the stairs.

My mom stood near the front door, applauding. "Oh, baby. You look wonderful."

"Thanks, Mom." For a second, it was like being in our family *before*. Henry was proud. Mom was present. If dressmaking was her own special brand of therapy, she could make a dozen party dresses to hang unsold in the closet. "I'll have the best dress at the dance." I looked around. "Where is Grant?"

"Behind you," he said.

I turned to find him in the entrance to the kitchen, his face expressionless, his body still. But his eyes? They shimmered with something hot and intense.

"What do you think?" I asked.

His gaze never left mine. "You are stunning."

I smiled with pure happiness, letting his perfect words flow sweetly through me.

"When will Kimberley be here?" my mom asked.

"In a few minutes," I said, glancing back at her. "She and Eli are probably on their way now."

"Eli Harper is her date?" My mother wrinkled her nose. "That'll be awkward, hanging around and watching the two of them."

"Very awkward. I wish I had a date."

Goosebumps prickled along my limbs. Had I just said *I wish*?

My gaze met Grant's again. Locked.

How about a date with a hot guy who smoldered in my direction as if I was the most gorgeous thing he'd ever seen?

A date with Grant?

The idea became all-consuming. It took over my brain and my wants and my everything. I wanted it so badly I suspected everyone could see it on my face.

But this wasn't a wish. Not a genie/mistress wish. I'd already had one today, and even if I hadn't, I wouldn't use a wish for this dance. I wanted Grant to want it too. Like a guy and girl on a normal date. "*Will* you come with me?"

He gave an immediate nod. "Do I need a ticket?"

"Eli has an extra one." And if the universe loved me, he hadn't given it away yet.

"I'll change."

My mom put a hand on his arm. "Do you want to borrow something of my husband's?"

Henry and I both gaped. Had our mother volunteered clothing of Josh's?

"Thank you, Crystal. I accept." He followed her down the hallway. A moment later, the back door creaked.

"Is this a double date?" Henry asked.

"I guess it is. Sort of." Most double dates were planned. This one had evolved.

"Is Grant your boyfriend now?"

"No." Of course not. Silly idea. Grant wasn't human. We couldn't be more than friends. It was forbidden. Probably.

"I think it would be great if he was."

Okay. Didn't expect that response. "Really? Why?"

"Because Grant wants to be your boyfriend."

I stifled my skepticism. "How can you know that?"

"He stares at you all the time. My friend Reynolds says that means he wants you."

I tried to imagine two little soccer players attempting to assign meaning to Grant's behavior. It was cute. "Grant and I are hanging out together for the evening. That's all." It was like a fairy tale. At midnight, everything would return to normal.

"If you say so," Henry said, holding up his index finger. "Can you wait a second? I want to take pictures."

"With what?"

"My camera. Grant fixed it." His feet thudded down the hall.

Henry was posing me on the wooden swing when Grant appeared on the porch. I ached with wonder at the sight of him, forgetting to breathe or speak. He was like a beautiful, mesmerizing god.

"Doesn't he look nice, Lacey?" Mom asked as she smoothed the lapel of his jacket.

I nodded, even though "nice" was a pitifully inadequate word where Grant was concerned.

We posed on the porch for an excessive number of photos. First we were side by side in the swing. Then we leaned against the railing, sometimes with me standing in front of him, sometimes with him standing in front of me. The more pictures Henry took, the more nervous I got.

Where is the pumpkin? We needed to leave for the ball.

As if on cue, Mrs. Rey's silver SUV rolled through the intersection and slowed to a halt at the curb.

I started down the front steps, too fast given my relative inexperience on the sandals I wore. But not to worry. Grant caught my hand in his and steadied me before I could make a fool of myself. When we reached the sidewalk, he didn't let go.

How would I get through the night? I didn't know how to act around this Grant, the one holding my hand. It wasn't as if we were out on a real date, although Grant had this whole brooding athlete thing going that was kind of fascinating.

And tonight, I would not be his mistress.

Status Report #22
Friday's Wish: Mental Health Research

Dear Boss,

The research went well. There are many possibilities that do not involve governmental agencies, although it may take some persuasion to ease Crystal into cutting back on caffeine.

I have located a free clinic at a local church. They promise confidentiality as long as no one is in danger. I have hopes that they can provide a high quality of care.

There is more to report but I must keep it brief, for I have an unexpected engagement this evening. Lacey has asked me to escort her to a dance at her high school.

She is beautiful.

Humbly submitted,
Grant

22

The Right Verb

*K*imberley smiled brightly when we reached the car. "I didn't know he was coming with you."

"My plans freed up for the evening," Grant said. He held the door for me and then walked around to the other side. *Mr. Perfect Manners.* Chivalry was hot.

"Hey, Lacey, Grant," Eli said over his shoulder from the driver's seat.

Kimberley chattered the whole way to the school, unconcerned that nobody else was saying anything. The parking lot was full when we arrived. She held onto Eli's arm as she led the way in, her dress giving off an eerie glow in the moonlight, her free hand gesturing while she talked. Grant caught my elbow and let some distance grow between us and them.

When we got to the gym doors, Eli and Kimberley hadn't made it much past the entrance. The sight of them together had created a minor stir. Several popular couples had circled around them, laughing and shouting over the music. Kimberley smiled as she watched Eli like a hawk, obviously trying hard to fake her way through conversations with people whose names she didn't remember.

And her dress? It looked even more amazing on her than it had promised on the hanger. It clung to her body in ways that had Eli's soccer mates gaping and their dates jealous.

"Shall we?" Grant placed a gentle hand in the small of my back.

"Just a sec," I said and stepped forward to touch Kimberley's shoulder. "Are you okay?" I spoke in her ear.

She nodded confidently, her eyes glowing with excitement.

Linking my fingers loosely with Grant's, I walked beside him around the perimeter, taking in the nearly unrecognizable gymnasium. Someone had strung hundreds of strands of white Christmas lights in the rafters. Not very original, but I loved it.

It was too warm. Even though the air conditioner roared overhead, it wasn't making much of a difference. A DJ bounced in the corner, playing a Broadway tune while dance-club members tried to teach the waltz to a few brave classmates.

"Come on, let's stand over there," I said to Grant and headed for a location that gave me a decent view of Eli and Kimberley.

Grant watched the chaotic group on the floor and the huddled pairs dotting the bleachers. "May I ask why we are standing here?"

I gave him a mock frown. "It would be evident to a real teen. BSBs must not get out much."

His expression remained neutral. "Beings don't get out at all."

"Seriously?" At his nod, my frown turned real. "You didn't hang out with your other assignments?"

"I have never received an invitation for a human social event until now." He studied the dancing couples, his gaze sweeping the floor rapidly. "My masters wanted me to work, not play."

"Jerks," I muttered.

He focused on me, a dazzling smile lighting his face. "I shall ask again. Why are we simply standing here?"

"We're observing my classmates."

"Why?"

I laughed. "It's a sociology experiment."

"What is the goal?"

"To study the dating rituals of the twenty-first-century North American teen."

A dozen freshman girls strutted by in high heels and short, sparkly dresses. Seconds later, a half-dozen sports-jacketed guys slouched after them. The two groups met briefly, spoke loudly, and went their separate ways intact.

"Your dating rituals strike me as rather annoying and ineffectual."

"Depends on what you're hoping for."

"I'm hoping for an excuse to hold you in my arms." He gazed down at me, his expression making me shiver. "Care to dance, Lacey?"

"I'm all yours."

It didn't take long to notice the effect we had as we strolled onto the gym floor. Every pair of female eyes watched him pass. Grant all dressed up was an astonishing sight, and he was with me. For this evening, I would be stared at and talked about. I didn't mind at all.

The music changed to something more Latin and dreamy. I hesitated. "Do you know how to rumba?"

"I do."

"Are you any good?"

He smiled. "I am. Quite good." He took me into his arms, one hand warm and sure against the bare skin of my back. I closed my eyes and drank in his scent, pine-soap freshness mixing with the spicy cologne clinging to my stepfather's jacket.

This was heavenly. I relaxed against his body and lost myself to the music and the feeling of complete joy.

"Want to dance, Lacey?" the tall, handsome Marine asks.

"Yes, Daddy."

Under the twinkling lights of a crystal chandelier, I glide onto the ballroom floor, clinging to my father's hand. The other dancers part as we pass, craning for a glimpse of this most unusual couple.

"Am I the only little girl here?" I whisper.

"You are," he says, lifting me until our eyes are on the same level and my legs dangle at his waist. "When our captain told us to bring our best girl, I knew that I had to bring you."

"Are we going to dance now?" I ask, locking my arms around his neck.

"We are." He launches into a spin that swirls us around and around. I rest my head against his shoulder and laugh with delight.

"Lacey? Are you all right?" Grant asked.

I nodded, too happy to even speak. I loved dancing with him. It felt so safe and sweet.

"May I ask your thoughts?"

"I'm glad you came with me tonight."

The muscles in his shoulders bunched. "Gratitude is not what I want."

I quivered at the intensity in his voice. Tilting my head back, I met his gaze squarely. "Gratitude is not what I'm feeling."

Awareness shimmered between us. We stopped moving and stood there—absorbing each other, breathing in rhythm.

Kimberley's voice doused me like an icy shower. "Lacey, let's trade partners."

"No." I didn't want to trade partners. I wanted to stay in the circle of Grant's arms and explore what was happening between us. I looked at him to see if he agreed, but his expression had turned smoothly neutral.

She either hadn't heard me or didn't care, because there they were, standing next to us, smiling expectantly.

"Here, Grant," she said, holding out her arms.

We exchanged partners.

While they blended into the swaying mass around us, Eli and I stood still, eying each other carefully. The dim light of the gym gave his hazel eyes a golden sheen. I hoped someone got photos of him with Kimberley, because he looked as hot as she did.

If it had been any other day, I would have looked up at him in mute wonder at the thought of dancing with Eli Harper. Instead, I was on my first date with Grant, I wore a gorgeous dress, and I looked amazing. Confidence hummed through my veins. After closing the distance between us, I linked my fingers behind his neck. His hands came to rest lightly at my waist.

He moved stiffly.

"Is there something wrong, Eli?"

"No, just trying to be careful with my knee."

"Are you tired? Do you want to stop?"

"No, we're good." His arms tightened.

It was my turn to be stiff as I tried hard not to bump him.

"You're okay, Lacey. You're not going to hurt me."

I tried to match his steps, but it wasn't easy. He wasn't as graceful as Grant. Or maybe it was the brace. "So you found a date."

"She found me." He stared over my shoulder. "Apparently, dances *are* your thing."

He remembered my comment from the cafeteria. That was interesting. "I changed my mind because Kimberley didn't want to come alone."

"Oh, yeah?" His gaze met mine. "What about Grant?"

"I invited him fifteen minutes before you picked us up."

Eli smirked. "He works fast."

I looked away. Wow. I was going to let that statement pass. "So, when did she ask you out?"

"This morning. She told me that I was her second choice and Sean was her first."

I didn't know whether to groan or laugh. "Technically, *I* was the first."

"Third choice, then."

When I checked his expression, he seemed more amused than upset.

"It's okay, Lacey. I don't mind." He shifted me closer and laid his cheek against my hair.

I relaxed, glad to be back to our uncomplicated friendship, and enjoyed the song.

A girl shrieked nearby. I glanced over Eli's shoulder in time to see another couple teetering toward us, a tangle of arms and legs. Both went down at our feet. The girl's elbow jabbed into Eli's left leg.

I hardly had sufficient time to prepare, but Eli had no warning at all. He staggered forward, falling into me.

"Oops," the other girl said with a wave. Her date had already stood and was yanking her into a clinch.

I was more concerned about Eli. His eyes were closed, his lips pinched.

"Did she hurt you?" I asked.

"She got my knee," he said through gritted teeth.

Crap. I slid my arms around his waist. "Lean on me."

As he shifted his weight, he hissed pained breaths, in and out. Around us, the dance ended and some couples began to drift away.

"Do you want to sit down?"

A jerky nod.

I rubbed my wrist tattoo and then edged slowly around to Eli's side. "Drop your arm across my shoulders. We won't walk until you say."

"I'm good."

We took a lurching step toward the side of the gym. Grant materialized at his other side, gave an assessing glance, and pitched in. When we reached the bleachers, we eased Eli down. He stared straight ahead with glazed eyes.

Grant leaned close to be heard over the noise. "What do you need?"

"Ice," Eli said in a tight voice.

Grant beckoned to Kimberley. "Can you make an ice pack?"

Her eyes widened warily. "I think so. What exactly do I do?"

"Locate a plastic bag or a paper towel. Fill it with ice."

Her face scrunched with the effort to concentrate. "Where will I get ice and paper towels?"

"I saw some bottled water in the far corner. You should be able to find ice there. You can retrieve paper towels from the bathroom. Wrap the ice securely in the towels and—"

"Stop. Just stop." When she turned to me, her face had a haunted look to it. "I can't do it, Lacey. I want to help, but I can't keep up."

"Don't worry." I rested a reassuring hand on her shoulder. She was trembling. "I've got this."

"I'm sorry. It's too much—"

"You can help right here with Eli." I spun her around gently and nudged her over to the bottom bleacher. "Talk to him. It'll take his mind off the pain." Once she had settled, I threw a *don't ask* look at Grant and took off to find the ingredients for an impromptu ice pack.

It didn't take long for the ice to work. We could see the tension fade from Eli's face.

"It's better, thanks," he said.

Kimberley laid a light hand on his shoulder. "Do you want to leave?"

"That'd be great, if you don't mind."

"I don't." She rose.

Holding hands, they inched around the edge of the gym. Grant and I followed, unable to talk over the deafening blend of music, laughter, and one hundred pairs of heels hammering the floor.

I fetched the car while the other three waited by the gym doors. Grant helped Kimberley into the passenger side while Eli insisted that he could drive. "My right leg is fine."

Before I could slide out of the driver's seat, Kimberley tapped my arm. "Do you want a ride home now? You don't have to. My mom could come back and get you later."

"Not necessary. I think Grant and I will stay a little bit longer, and then we can walk home."

A minute later, Eli and Kimberley were on their way, and Grant and I were alone in the parking lot.

Finally, I could have him all to myself on the dance floor. Eagerly, I tucked my hand into his arm. "Ready?"

"As you wish."

His voice sounded weary. I studied his expression. In the faint glow of the streetlights, his face seemed strained. "Is there something wrong?"

"The noise in there…" His voice trailed away.

"Is it too much for your senses?" At his nod, I gave his elbow a squeeze. "Why didn't you say something?"

His lips curved slightly. "I am now."

"Let's go."

The walk home through the silent streets of Magnolia Grove was way lovelier than the dance would've been. I took off my shoes and tiptoed through the cool grass of the lawns, pointing out historic houses and award-winning gardens.

It was late by the time we reached my neighborhood. "I don't want the evening to end. I've had so much fun."

He laughed. "A sentiment I share."

"Oh, please, Grant," I said, smiling up at him. "Could you for once drop the British royalty act and lighten up?"

"It is my understanding that American girls admire a British accent."

"The accent, yes. The aristocratic vocabulary, no."

The house was dark as we strolled up the driveway. He paused while I unlocked the front door, then said a quiet goodnight and started down the steps.

"Wait." I wasn't sure what got into me, but I didn't want him to leave. "Stay a little longer."

At his nod, we dropped onto the porch swing. I leaned against his shoulder, linked my fingers through his, and rocked in the dark. Scenes from the dance replayed through my mind, like a slide show. Fading in. Fading out. Eli laughing with one of his soccer mates. Sara on the dance floor, wrapped around the captain of the basketball team. Kimberley hugging Sean as we were leaving, his deep brown jacket a cool contrast to her slippery gold.

It'd been too long since I'd had such a good time.

There was so much to thank Grant for, and there wasn't much time left to say it. "What happens to you once my assignment is done?"

"You have to make me available to someone else."

Instant goose bumps. I straightened to see him better. Was I supposed to discard him like a worn-out piece of junk? "How do I do that?"

"Sell the music box."

Didn't like that either. "Why the music box?"

"It's my home."

I loved the music box too. It brought us together. "Is it part of the magic, or do you just like living there?"

A long pause. "I am not tied to the music box."

I studied his profile. It came in sharp relief against the blue-gray glow of the moonlit night. Sheer perfection. "May I *give* you away?"

He turned to look at me, his face half in the shadows. "Indeed, although my boss would have to approve the next case in order for me to reveal myself."

"Would he approve my mother?" I asked in a hopeful rush.

Grant shook his head. "We're allowed only one month per household. This is the first time I've ever regretted that rule."

I caught my breath. We were so alone. So isolated. How could I be talking about our goodbyes with such calm—as if he didn't matter to me? Because he did. Too much.

Tonight had been like a real date. Laughing, talking, dancing, holding hands. When my gaze dropped to his mouth, I sighed. How would it feel...?

"I wish you would kiss me," I said, the words so soft that maybe I could pretend later I hadn't said them at all.

The look on his face was inscrutable. What was he thinking? Did he pity me? Did he feel obligated?

His arm slid along the back of the swing, drawing him nearer. He hesitated.

Why had he stopped? Our mouths were tantalizingly close. Did he think I would change my mind? Not going to happen. I closed the gap.

His lips moved over mine, firm and sweet. I pressed closer, wanting more. He deepened the kiss, his fingers cupping the base of my head gently.

Shivery sensations raced throughout my body. I didn't want the kiss to end.

He pulled away first, his breathing ragged.

It wasn't enough. With trembling hands, I reached for him and found myself pulled onto his lap, cradled in his arms. The second kiss was even more amazing.

Maybe three?

"Lacey," he said on a groan.

I rested my head against his chest, lips aching, wanting still more. We could never return to our mistress/servant relationship. Not after this. "Did you kiss me because you had to?"

"Kissing you was my choice."

That was wonderful and frightening. "Why?"

"You enchant me."

It was my turn for a ragged breath.

If this was a movie, the violins would be swelling, my eyes would be misting, and we'd be walking hand in hand into the sunset. But it wasn't a movie. This was real life. The handsome hero was Grant, and I had to give him away.

My mother's words echoed in my brain. *I can't imagine a future without him.*

Emotions swirled in my chest, overwhelming me. How did I feel about him?

It was more than gratitude. I was grateful to a lot of people. It didn't feel like this.

It was more than friendship too. He was unlike any friend I'd ever had.

Our relationship was something else—a connection with many dimensions. But what was the right verb?

Did he enchant me?

Did I love him?

Maybe it was better not to know.

He was waiting for me to respond, but I couldn't identify how I felt. "Good night," I said and slipped like a coward into the house.

Update to Status Report #22

Dear Boss,

I have fallen in love with a human. What are my options?

Humbly submitted,
Grant

23

Achy and Scared and Elated

Saturday morning brought more soccer. Henry's team played their third game and celebrated their third win.

Grant walked beside me to where the team huddled around the snacks. My brother was obviously the hero, a role he loved.

He ran up to me. "Did you see my goal, Lacey?"

"I did." Barely. I'd arrived ten minutes ago. Talk about sleeping in. I had to cut out those three AM nights with all the tossing and turning and reliving lovely memories in slow motion.

"Were you watching?" my brother asked Grant.

"The whole game."

"You weren't talking to Lacey?"

Grant gave me a half-smile. "I've hardly exchanged a word with your sister."

"Awesome." Henry punched me in the side. "Can we leave now?"

Somebody had too much energy, which an entire soccer game had been unable to drain. "I'd like to speak to your coaches first."

"Can I go to the playground?"

"Sure, I'll find you."

He gave me a thumbs-up, hijacked his friend Reynolds, and raced to the playground.

I turned to Grant a little nervously. This could be awkward—the coward facing the brave one for the first time. "Hey."

"Hello." He smiled. Not a smug one, either. A *happy to see you* smile. "I missed you."

Relief flowed, pure and sweet. I hadn't ruined everything. "You're not mad?"

"How could I be? I overwhelmed you."

We were still partners. I wasn't clear what kind, but it was all good. Still, I couldn't say his words back to him because I couldn't describe how I felt yet. "Grant? I don't know—"

"Shhh," he said. "There isn't time to say what we need to. We're fine."

I nodded, glad for the reprieve. "Come on. Let's go and check on Eli."

It was the first time I'd met the adult coach. While Grant asked Eli about his knee, I listened to Coach Makanui gush over my brother. Very cool. My mom had been right all along. Henry was an asset to the team and extraordinarily talented and lots of other glowing adjectives.

A crowd of parents had formed behind us, waiting to speak with them. Grant and I were turning away when we heard a scream.

The piercing cry twitched my nerves like an electric shock. "Henry!"

Grant was already running toward the playground at superhuman speed.

I raced after him. Henry was a short distance away, lying on his back in the mulch under a play structure. Reynolds stood, stiff and horrified, at his side.

Grant knelt. "Be still. It's going to be fine." His hands hovered an inch above Henry's head, then passed swiftly down his body. When the inspection was complete, Grant made a noncommittal grunt.

"What happened?" I asked, plunging to the ground beside my brother.

Reynolds said, "He fell off the fort. It was an accident."

Pain contorted my brother's ashen face.

"What hurts, little man?"

"My leg." Henry moaned.

I could see why. It seemed to twist at an odd angle. "Anywhere else?"

Grant shook his head. "Just the leg."

I met his gaze. "How do you know?"

"Trust me."

"I do." Completely.

Other people were running up. "What's going on?" someone asked.

"I fell." Henry groaned.

Coach Makanui squatted to take a closer look at the angle of Henry's leg. "I think it's broken, buddy."

I gasped, then looked at Grant. He nodded.

The coach rose. "Let me see if I can find something to splint it until we can get you to the Emergency Room." He took off.

By now, a limping Eli had arrived as well as both soccer teams, their families, and a few spectators who had nothing to do with us at all. One of the bystanders said, "The team insurance won't cover this. It's not sanctioned play."

I looked at the loud-mouthed parent. "Back off," I said, cold fury making the words carry. The man slid away.

My eyes sought Eli, seeking confirmation. "Is that man right?"

He gave a curt nod.

I quaked on the inside. Hospitals meant hospital bills. And while my own health care was covered pretty well because of my dad, Mom and Henry's coverage sucked.

Two fat tears rolled down Henry's cheeks. "I'm sorry, Lacey. I didn't mean to. I'm sorry."

"I know. It's all right." I brushed the sweat-soaked bangs from his forehead and tried my best to look like everything was fine and I wasn't panicking.

"No, it isn't. You don't have to take me to the hospital."

"Of course we do."

"No, Lacey. We can't afford it." He scrubbed at his eyes with dirty fists. "I shouldn't've been climbing so high."

Henry's words cut me to the quick. What had I done to my brother? Had I turned him into the same coin-counting freak I was? Had I made him afraid to be a little boy? "Don't worry, Henry," I said in the most unconcerned tone I could muster. "We can handle emergencies. I promise." My gaze met Grant's. There was real concern in the depths of his eyes. "I wish you could do something."

A sound escaped his lips—a searing, unearthly sound—as if he too suffered. One hand clamped around Henry's knee and the other around his ankle. Grant said, for my ears only, "I can fix it. It will cause him an instant of hideous pain. Then it will be over."

"Do it."

Henry's scream ripped through us all.

"Are you crazy?" One of the soccer parents grabbed Grant by the shoulder and knocked him back.

"It's okay," Eli said, gesturing the parent away. "He's a friend."

Coach Makanui had returned with a first-aid kit. Popping open a lid, he drew out a temporary splint. "This won't feel good, buddy."

"I'm fine now. Grant fixed me." Henry sat up, flexed his foot, and then stood. There were gasps of surprise from the crowd.

"Whoa. Sit back down here, please," Coach said. "We need to get that leg X-rayed."

"But it doesn't hurt." My brother waited with impatience while the older man wrapped the splint about his leg.

"Henry, you need to see a doctor, and I'm taking you," Coach said. "Is there a volunteer who can help me carry our patient to a car?"

Before anyone could respond, Henry stood, hobbled a few steps, and said, "See. I'm fine. We don't have to go to the hospital."

Eli shot me a sympathetic glance as he dropped a firm hand on my brother's shoulder. "I think it's best for us to go anyway. Just in case."

Coach Makanui and another parent carried a still-protesting Henry to the parking lot.

Eli glanced at me. "Do you have your car with you?"

"No, I walked."

"Then ride with me."

"Thanks." I started to follow Eli, but a light touch on my arm stopped me. It was Grant. I reached for his hand, needing its comfort, however briefly. "Are you coming?"

"I'll run home and get Crystal. We'll meet you at the hospital."

My brother rested in supreme enjoyment atop the hospital bed, sipping a juice box and flipping through a new graphic novel. The attention had succeeded in distracting him.

"They have to X-ray Henry's leg," Coach Makanui said.

I shook my head emphatically for the thousandth time.

"Lacey," Eli said, his eyes narrowed. "How can you be so certain?"

Too bad that nobody would believe the real reason. "Henry is walking on the leg without pain. He wouldn't do that if it were broken."

The doctor gestured impatiently. "An X-ray is a prudent precaution."

"No," I said. Henry's leg wasn't broken. I knew this to be true. X-rays would be an *unnecessary* precaution.

The doctor shrugged. "Perhaps we should wait until a parent arrives."

As if on cue, my mother rushed into the Emergency Department, surprisingly calm and take-charge. "I'm Crystal Jones, Henry's mother. Tell me what's going on."

"We think it would be wise to X-ray his leg, Mrs. Jones."

"Then go ahead."

Some of the hospital staff looked at me with smirks on their faces. I grabbed my mom's arm and pulled her to the side. "You're throwing away money. Look at him."

"The doctor recommends it."

"Grant says it isn't broken."

"Grant isn't a doctor."

"He's better than one."

She lowered her voice. "We have to be sure. Now I know your focus is on the money, but mine has to be on Henry."

Her statement stung me into silence. How could she possibly believe that Henry's health and happiness weren't the most important things in my life?

She turned her back on me and spoke normally. "Give my son the X-ray," she said to the hospital staff. To Henry, "How are you, sweetie?"

"Great." He pointed to a nearby tray, covered with many empty snack containers. "They have lots of good food here."

We had the verdict two hours later. Not broken.

"It's better knowing for sure," my mother said after the coach dropped us off at home.

Would she be saying that when she got the bill?

We barely had Henry settled in front of the TV before the doorbell rang. And then rang again. And then rang some more. By the end of the day, the entire soccer team, with their parents holding aluminum containers, came by the house. And not only wiggling third-grade boys. Most of them brought along wiggling toddler siblings.

We'd had more people tramping through here today than in the past year combined. It was weird. And nice. I liked the feel of laughter inside these walls.

The timing was good too—from the hostess end of it. The house hadn't looked this great since we moved in.

Okay, so maybe the kitchen didn't look that great at the moment. I stood in the doorway and surveyed the mess. Trash overflowed the garbage can. The table was a disaster. Puddles of juice sat drying on the floor. The kitchen needed major cleaning. I was glad of something to do. It would keep my mind off the hospital bill a little longer.

Maybe I should pull out Henry's health insurance policy. Josh had renewed it not long before he died, which meant it would expire soon. I wasn't sure what it covered in emergencies. We'd never had to use it before.

Maybe I would let it go until the bill came in.

I picked up a bottle of homemade kitchen cleaner, a few rags, and got to work.

The doorbell rang yet again. It was Eli. "I brought a few things." He had a huge fruit basket in one hand and a paper grocery bag in the other.

I led the way to the kitchen. "Thanks for giving me a ride to the hospital and for...well, just everything."

"My pleasure. How's the patient?"

"Popular."

He laughed as he considered the dishes and trays stacked on the counter. No room there. He set the fruit basket on the table and then, before I could stop him, opened the door to the pantry. He paused, taking in the still-sparse shelves. Bracing a forearm on the doorframe, he looked at me over his shoulder. "Lacey, please, can I—"

"It's the end of the month. Everything will be good in a couple of days." I pulled the bag from his fingers, slipped under his arm, and stepped into the pantry. The items went up as quickly as I could make them.

"Lacey." His voice held quiet sympathy. "What else can I do?"

I folded the bag and slid it onto a recycling rack. "Say hi to Henry."

"That's not what I meant."

"I told you. We're fine." I gave him a big, bright smile—the effect lessened by my big, flushed cheeks—and shooed him away from the pantry, pulling the door shut behind me.

His body blocked my path. I stopped, confused about what to do or say next.

He laid a gentle hand on my arm. "Kimberley explained her condition to me last night on the drive home."

I bobbed my head. Why had he brought this up?

"She hides it pretty well. I would've never guessed." He stepped back, his hand dropping away, giving me a little breathing room. "What you did last night and what you did today were amazing. You took over, and you made things better."

"Thanks," I mumbled, brushing past him.

"So where's your brother now?"

Was this horribly awkward conversation finally coming to an end? "On the deck, with Mom and Reynolds Samm and some of the others."

Eli walked to the back door and hesitated, one hand on the knob. "I want to help. Just so you know, I'm going to keep asking." The door clicked behind him.

With Eli gone, I busied myself putting away the fruit. Most of it could go on the table in a bowl, but the two ripe peaches went into the fridge, right next to four aluminum trays of macaroni and cheese and two apple pies. Both dishes were Henry's favorites, information he had apparently mentioned in front of his soccer teammates and their mothers. The Linden-Jones family would have plenty of empty calories for the next week.

It took until sunset for all of the visitors to leave. The patient and our mother retired to her room to read library books side-by-side while I scrubbed the kitchen. Once the cleaning was done, I stumbled out to the front porch, worn-out and sticky-hot.

Grant waited on the swing. He rose as I approached.

"Where have you been all afternoon?" I asked, leaning into him.

"Inside the music box." A light kiss brushed my hair. "It was best."

I nodded and yawned. "I think I'll sit."

"Allow me." A moment later, he was on the swing with me in his lap, hugged against him.

I loved being held by him. "If your sense of smell is so good, how can you stand to be near me?"

He laughed. "I hadn't noticed."

"Such a gentleman." I shut my eyes, content to drift and doze. The swing rocked gently. When his arms settled more securely around me, I snuggled deeper into them. This whole physical-contact-at-every-opportunity thing could become quite addictive.

"How are you?" His voice was quiet with concern.

"Good." I hoped he didn't want to talk. Vegging was fine.

"Are you hungry?"

I sighed. Girls were supposed to be the talkers; boys, the grunters. But, of course, our relationship would be unusual in every way. "I am a little hungry."

He stood, lifting me up with him. My hands flew from their happy position on his chest to a frantic grasping at his shoulders. "Excuse me, but maybe next time you could warn me."

"I would not have dropped you."

"My head knows that, but my body didn't."

The arm under my knees released and soon my feet touched the floor. But the arm supporting my back stayed firmly in place. "Do you have any requests?"

"For what?"

"Food."

I stood on tiptoe and kissed him. "No mac and cheese," I said against his lips.

"Deal." He stepped away. "Meet me in the backyard in twenty minutes."

I put the break to use. A shower and clean clothes were necessary. Grant didn't deserve to cuddle something as sweaty as me.

It only took fifteen minutes, but Grant was ready. He'd set up the food on a small table placed next to the wrought-iron bench. A candle glowed, perfuming the air with warm vanilla. In the center of the table waited a plate of fresh fruit, gourmet cheese, and fancy crackers. I bit into a crisp slice of apple. "Where did you get this?" I asked around a full mouth.

"Mrs. Williford brought it over."

Unexpected tears stung my eyes. "Why did she do that?"

"She wants to help. It was a pleasure for her to do this. Just enjoy it."

Was that why Eli offered to help? I nodded as I stuffed in another slice. Then another. I was hungrier than I'd realized, not just for food—but for the yummy, expensive kind that I hadn't tasted in a long time. Five minutes of silent eating (well, almost silent) passed. Finally, I'd had enough and flopped back on the bench.

"Better?" he asked.

"Much. Thank you."

His arm slid around my shoulders and drew me to him. It was odd, sitting there under the veil of darkness, watching the neighborhood settle down. Lamps burned in windows.

TVs flickered. A few houses down, the rhythmic thud of a basketball on concrete and muffled laughter alerted us to the only other people outside on this glorious fall night.

"This is a perfect date," I said.

He tensed. "You'd call it a date?"

"Sure. You wouldn't?"

He looked down at me, his eyes glittering in the faint light. "I thought American girls liked more formality in a date."

"More money is what you mean." I smiled. "It's a date. Don't argue with me."

"I never do."

"Right." A thought that had tickled in the corner of my brain all day floated into the foreground. "You didn't argue with me about fixing Henry's leg."

"Indeed."

"You used magic."

"I did."

I straightened on the bench and turned to face him. "Was it your wish to heal Henry?"

"It was."

"So you won't get punished?"

He raked his fingers through his hair. It fell back into a smooth cap around his head. "There will be a consequence."

Uh-oh. That didn't sound good. "What consequence?"

"It's not important."

Like I believed that. "Then you won't mind telling me."

He rose from the bench and took a few paces into the yard. "I will not receive my promotion at the end of this case."

Lose his promotion? Because he helped a little boy in pain? "I don't understand. You can use your powers if you want something, and you wanted to help Henry."

"True."

"So what's the problem?" I stopped, appalled, as realization hit me. "*I* wished it too. You used your powers for *my* wish."

He nodded.

Great. If only I'd kept my big mouth shut, it would've been okay. Grant could've healed the leg and kept his promotion intact. "Wow, Grant. I'm so sorry. This isn't fair, and it's my fault."

He shook his head. "I made a conscious choice. I knew I was not honoring the rule."

"Maybe I could talk to your boss—"

He interrupted. "No, I'll handle him."

Crap. It made me crazy to see him so calm when all I wanted to do was stamp my foot and swear. I bounced off the bench and crossed to his side. "Why did you grant the wish?"

"I couldn't bear to see Henry in pain."

"You should've refused."

"I don't regret my decision." His hands dropped to my hips and drew me to him. "Granting your wishes is no longer just a job. It has become *my* wish. I'm enthralled with your family. I need to see Crystal recover. I'm humbled to have Henry call me his friend. I want to be a partner in restoring laughter to your home. But most of all, I love you, Lacey, more than I could have ever imagined."

Hadn't it been just yesterday that I was his employer? No, maybe the change to our relationship had started on Thursday. Or maybe Wednesday. Or the week before that.

Whatever. This was moving fast.

I stared at his mouth, unable to drag my gaze away. *Grant loves Lacey.* The words made me achy and scared and elated, all at the same time. "Aren't relationships with humans forbidden?"

"Discouraged, yes. Forbidden, no."

"Hold me."

He wrapped his arms about me. As his strength flowed into my body, all of my nagging worries fled. I braved a peek at his face. He was smiling. A smile of delight. A smile I had put there.

Grant had served countless humans, good and bad, rich and poor, great and ordinary. And yet, from among all of them, he picked me. *Me.*

I gave in to the joy and ignored the tiny voice reminding me that time was running out.

Status Report #23
Saturday's Wish: Healing

Dear Boss,

I confess that I healed an injured boy. I did so fully understanding that the consequence for my action was to delay my promotion.

I will prepare for the next case.

You are correct. Until I experienced human love, I never understood its nature.

Humbly submitted,
Grant

24

Into the Warmth

Reynolds Samm invited Henry to spend Sunday afternoon at his house. My brother was particularly excited because we didn't have video games anymore and Reynolds had every video game system known to man. Reynolds's mother invited Mom to come too. When Mrs. Samm had visited our house yesterday, she became obsessed with our foul-smelling coffee. Apparently, Mrs. Samm was a fanatic about the health benefits of herbal tea and decided my mother was ready to be educated.

It was not much to build a friendship on, but I wasn't complaining. My mother was acting happy. Henry was ecstatic. And the invitation left me and Grant alone for the rest of the day.

"What do you want to do?" I asked.

"Whatever you want."

It was hard to know whether he was yielding to me because I enchanted him or because I was his chief. Either way, I was good with the outcome. "How about a bike ride?"

"Is there more to this request than a simple trip about the neighborhood?"

"There is." I had a glimmer of a plan to make some quick cash—a plan that required a visit to the flea market.

The ride to the outskirts of town was fun—for him. After the first ten minutes, I was huffing and puffing. He barely cranked the pedals and laughed at me a lot.

For a Sunday, there weren't many people at the flea market. We wandered along behind the shoppers while I checked out what they were buying.

Grant didn't tolerate the meandering for long. "May I ask what we're doing?"

"Hunting for business opportunities."

"You might give me more details."

"I'm a good doodler. I want to see if I can turn my doodles into money." I stopped before a table filled with Halloween costumes and trick-or-treat bags. Good profit margin, especially on the bags, but Halloween came once a year. I wanted something I could sustain for a longer period of time.

"Are you sure you want to do this?"

"Not really. The thought of getting it wrong is terrifying." The emergency fund only had sixty bucks left, which would barely make a dent in what we owed. But if I could strike it big with the right idea... "I figured if you could turn strips of wood into dollars, maybe we'll get lucky again."

Madame Noir was in her spot, reigning over the passersby, drinking sweet tea. "Lacey. Yoo hoo."

I walked over. "How are things?"

"Not good." She clucked her tongue and stared at Grant. "Do I know you?"

"No, ma'am. We've never met."

She frowned. "You seem familiar."

I did not want her going there. Time to divert attention. "Did you sell the candlesticks?"

"I did." She preened.

"Big profit?"

"You know I'm not going to tell." She pursed her lips until they resembled a plump rosebud.

She had, and it put her in a good mood, possibly enough to give me free advice. "I need to make some money, Madam. Any ideas for things I could do here?"

"You've sold about everything, haven't you, sugar?" She nodded, needing no answer. "You could work the refreshment stand. They're always looking for people."

"I was thinking about homemade items I could sell."

"Potpourri."

I shook my head. "Too expensive to buy the ingredients."

"Doll clothes."

That would take my mother's help, which I couldn't count on. "I don't know how to sew."

She fluttered her heavily mascara-ed lashes. "Accessories for little girls. Their parents spend money on the craziest things."

"Like what?"

"Hair bows. Purses."

In every photo of me as a little girl, I'd been wearing something shiny or frilly. This suggestion might be good. "Thanks. I'll give it some thought."

Grant and I cruised the aisles some more, only this time I stared at each family that passed. Madam was correct. There were lots of little girls with glittery hair bows and sparkly purses.

Unfortunately, there were also lots of booths selling such items. I halted at the end of the row, discouraged. "Look at the competition."

"Indeed."

A nearby booth had a large rack of bridesmaid dresses, all marked down to rock-bottom prices. I browsed through them, ideas exploding like fireworks. We could buy them cheap and sell them for so much more, but not while my mother feared pressure.

I spun around, eager to get away from temptation, when my gaze landed on a HUGE MARKDOWNS sign.

Beneath lay dozens of canvas sneakers, in all sizes and colors. I walked over and picked up a tiny pair in rose pink, no bigger than the palm of my hand. I'd had a pair like this when I was in kindergarten, except mine had been covered in sequins and tied together with lace shoestrings. They had been my mother's creation. My friends had been jealous.

Excitement punched me in the gut. "Here's the project." I held up the tiny pink sneakers.

"What?"

"Adorable shoes." I showed a wad of cash to the seller sitting behind the table. "How much can I get for this?"

An hour later, Grant and I stood beside the worktable in the studio, assessing two dozen pairs of toddler shoes. I only had a few bucks left and still needed to buy fabric paint, glitter glue, and sparkly jewels. But it would work, because it had to. I was investing our entire emergency fund in this project.

The decision was behind me. It was time to dream up the possibilities. I studied the shoes.

"Chief, am I to participate in the production line?"

"You are essential to the success of this operation. It's a *joint* project."

He smiled. "I don't care much for joint projects."

"If I ask, you have to obey."

"I'm aware of the rules, Mistress."

I ignored his sarcasm. Nothing could burst my bubble. "This is going to be fun. My designs. Your execution."

"Is it today's wish?"

"Tomorrow's. I have to get supplies and make some drawings." There could be themes. Ladybugs and butterflies for tiny scientists. Tiaras and kissable frogs for the little princesses. Cupcakes and ice cream cones for the dessert fans like me.

"What will I do today?"

I had to focus. Something for *Mr. Impatient.* "I'm still thinking. Maybe we could finish restoring the music box."

"Why?"

So many questions. "To give you a nice place to live."

"I already have a nice place to live." He flipped open the lid and pointed at the church. "Would you like to see inside?"

Could that possibly mean what I thought? "Inside the church?"

"Yes."

"Wouldn't that take magic?"

"I *wish* to give you a tour."

Was he actually offering to show me inside? To shrink me to the size of a grape seed? I gazed into the depths of the music box at the frozen lake and the church with its arched black doors, stained glass windows, and tiny steeple. "I would love to see inside."

"Then take my hand and close your eyes. The process is not pretty."

"What process?" I grasped his hand as ordered.

"The blue smoke. If you want to return in the same shape you leave, you must be completely still."

"I will."

There was a deafening roar. Intense pressure. Brightness searing my eyelids.

In a split second, it was over.

"We have arrived."

My eyes opened. I stood in the most color-free place I'd ever been. Everything was white or black. There were white walls with white floors, warm against my feet. Black beanbag-like furniture clustered around velvety black rugs. It was like I'd stepped into the middle of a rerun of *The Twilight Zone.*

The interior of the church was one big room. We were in the living space, our backs to the tall arched doors. There

Elizabeth Langston

appeared to be a sleeping space at the other end, with something resembling a kitchen in between.

I turned slowly. Even the stained-glass windows were dull from this perspective. "There's no color."

"I don't tolerate color over lengthy periods of time."

"But the white is so bright."

"I'm not human. I don't have the same reaction."

"How do you handle it when you're in my world?"

"I return here."

Walking further into the living room, I pressed down on one of the beanbag things. It had a springy feel. The kitchen had glossy counters and a sink but no appliances or cabinets. There were letters stacked in a white mesh basket. Black cloth napkins and black dishes.

"Where is your food?"

He pointed at a giant Pez-like dispenser on the counter. "It arrives when I need it."

I walked over and stared at its perfectly formed elephant's head, beautiful and lifelike. But when I raised my hand to touch the trunk, Grant shouted, "Don't," and wrapped an arm around my waist to yank me back. "It's not safe."

"Okay." I peered up at him. His pupils were tiny specks and his breathing was fast. "What's the deal?"

"Our food is the source of our power. Humans must not come in contact with it."

"This gives you magic?" At his nod, I peered through the translucent tube of the dispenser. It was filled with small doughy spheres about the size of golf balls. "How long does the effect last?"

"Perhaps three days. I don't know for sure since I've never gone that long without our nutrients." He stepped between me and the dispenser, blocking my view. "Please don't go any closer."

"Sure." I turned my back on the kitchen and stared next at the sleeping space. A black-and-white hammock lay partially hidden behind a silky curtain. "Do you have a bathroom?"

He inclined his head. "No comment."

There was no dust or streaky windows or spots on the floor. The walls and tables were bare. No photos or electronic equipment or books. "It's so spartan."

"Exactly."

I hugged him, trying to wrap my brain around all this new information. He could create any home he wanted, and what he ended up with was so simple. "Do you get bored in here?" I said against his chest.

"No. The human world requires a lot of energy. I need a calm place to recharge."

I tried to imagine him in here at night and failed. Much as I liked to be quiet, this seemed extreme. It would drive me nuts. "You stay here between assignments?"

He looked around the room with wistful eyes. "This is where I hibernate."

"In silence?"

"Partly. I also check in at the League."

"How?"

"There is a...place we can go. I hang out with other Beings." He drew away from me and crossed to the kitchen.

An aura of sadness trailed after him. Until this moment, I'd never been so completely aware of our differences. It was like I'd pretended he came from an alternate region instead of an alternate universe. He missed his own kind. "So you get face-to-face time with them?"

"Certainly," he said, his voice crisp and professional. He flicked an imaginary crumb on the countertop. "In addition to a boss, every apprentice has access to a team of mentors. The League hosts social events regularly."

"What do you do at them?"

"Discuss our humans. Learn new skills." His voice roughened. "Applaud promotions."

My heart sank. "Your name won't be announced next time." My fault. I owed him a lot.

"I do not regret it in the least. My turn will come soon enough." He held out a hand. "Would you care to go outside?"

I nodded. "Is it cold?"

"Indeed." He lifted two thin black blankets from pegs on the wall. "We won't stay long."

The doors swung open. He started down the steps.

Not me. I stayed behind and stood still on the stone terrace gracing the front of the church. Oh, the view. It was familiar—and yet not. A cobblestone lane curved away through drifted snow toward the village in the distance. Above, an overcast sky. No stars or moon. Just the sense that a snowstorm could roll in at any second.

And, of course, there was the frozen lake, rimmed with evergreens.

"I'm ready," I said in a hushed voice.

We crossed the lane and followed a sloping path toward the ice, sparkling in the light of an ornate gas lamp. I barely registered all of the details, my attention consumed by the Victorian couple. "They're skating."

Grant laughed. "Naturally. Did you expect them to be frozen as well?"

"Yes." They were good. Olympic good. We watched as they circled the lake, twirling and leaping. On their third trip past, they waved, bowed at our applause, and skated over.

"Grant," they said in unison.

"Magnificent as always." He indicated me. "Norah and Charles, may I present Lacey."

While Norah dropped into a curtsey, Charles kissed my hand.

"It's nice to meet you," I said. "I enjoyed your performance."

Norah gave a bubbly laugh. "What a charming accent you have. Do you live nearby?"

Before I could respond, Grant said, "She is a human."

The couple exchanged glances. "How very interesting," said Charles. They stared at my BSB with knowing smiles.

"Time to practice," he said, waving them off.

With a glide backward, they returned to their skating.

I clasped his hand and tugged him along the path. As we came around the crest of the hill, the village shops appeared. "Are they real?" I asked.

"Indeed. I must warn you, though. The goods are over a hundred years old."

"What about the prices?"

He rolled his eyes. "Do you ever stop thinking about money?"

"No." I clutched the edges of the blanket more snugly about me.

"Yes, the prices are from long ago. It is, however, Christmas Eve here. The shopkeepers have gone home for the season." With a light touch of his hand at the small of my back, he turned me toward the church. "We should go. Your lips are blue."

I stepped carefully across the ice-crusted cobblestones, climbed the wide stone steps, and followed him into the warmth.

"I think we should return to your world."

"Okay, but before we go..." I took a flying leap and landed on one of the beanbags. It was a strange sensation. Sort of floaty. Not beans or foam or air or water. It was more like going to the dentist and getting laughing gas. I wanted to giggle and drift.

"Don't get too comfortable."

He was laughing at me again, but that was okay.

"Lacey, take my hand and shut your eyes."

I took a last look around the room. Then I did as he asked. A second later I was back in the studio, a little dizzy, a little regretful, sitting high on the worktable, wondering how I would ever be able to top a visit inside a music box.

Grant stood between my legs, a hand braced against the tabletop on either side of my hips. "I have a suggestion for today's wish."

"Hmmm?" His hands were distracting me, close but not touching. I was pretty sure that was a situation that needed fixing.

"I think we should turn the studio into a production line for the shoes."

"Hmmm?" I looped my arms loosely around his neck.

"Lacey, pay attention."

I leaned back a little. "It is so hot when you give orders in your British accent."

"Lacey!"

My name on his lips was hot too. "I wish you would turn this studio into a production line for my shoe business."

"As you wish, Chief."

There it was again, that strange sensation. Sort of floaty. Completely lovely. "Why aren't we kissing yet?"

"The same question had crossed my mind." He leaned closer and pressed his lips to mine.

I could never get enough of this sweet, crazy kissing. How did anyone ever get anything done when they were falling in love?

How long would it take for the craziness to wear off? Months? Weeks?

I froze. Grant and I didn't have weeks. We had days.

He drew back. "What's wrong?"

My stupid brain. Why couldn't it live in the moment? But no. It had to ruin a perfectly good make-out session. "I wish you didn't have to leave on Saturday."

His eyes narrowed at my words.

"Wait," I said. "I know I can't have that as a real wish."

"I can stay."

Had I heard that right? "You can stay?"

"Yes."

"Really?"

"Indeed."

Joy welled up inside me. The end of the month had stretched before me like a black hole, threatening to suck him into eternity. The few times I'd tried to deal with it, my thoughts had skittered away. Final goodbyes were horrible enough. Saying it to Grant would be unimaginable. "For how long?"

"As long as you want me."

I slipped into his arms and buried my face against his chest. Below my cheek, his heart beat steady and sure. "I want you," I said. "You're sure the Boss will go along with this?"

"I am allowed to take a leave of absence."

It was almost too good to be true. "This is wonderful. I can't believe it. It's so—"

He kissed me with hungry expertise, an amazingly effective way to refocus my priorities.

Status Report #24
Sunday's Wish: Shoe Factory Construction

Dear Boss,

I confess. I invited a human into my home. If that is another offense requiring discipline, then so be it.

The leave of absence will begin Saturday, following the completion of her final wish. And yes, I am completely clear about the consequences. I don't care.

I have never been so happy.

Humbly submitted,
Grant

25

Sweet and Brief

*D*oodles poured from my pen all evening. Although I didn't expect many purchases from the male toddler population, I created a snake or two and one fabulous train. My mom nudged me away from the kitchen table around midnight.

At the crack of dawn, I rushed out to the garage and stepped inside. Since yesterday, the studio had become an artist's dream. The lumber racks had been converted to slanted shelves with plastic bins. There was a paint chest and a cabinet for undecorated shoes. The worktable had been transformed from a rough and splintery surface to a masterpiece of polish and functionality.

"What do you think?" Grant was sitting cross-legged on Josh's desk.

"I love it," I said, then gestured around the room and at the track lighting above. "How did you get the materials for all of this?"

"In your attic, I found broken-down furniture, tubs, and spools of wire. Then there was a bit of bartering with Mrs. Williford." He slid off the desk. "And perhaps a few things falling outside normal guidelines."

I sighed with anticipation. My new production space looked and smelled like success. How could the business fail when it had a "factory" like this?

He crossed to my side and dropped an arm on my shoulders.

"Thanks," I said. When he glanced down, I kissed him.

One thing I had discovered over the weekend was simply how much I liked kissing and being kissed. I hadn't had much experience with it in the past, especially not the boyfriend-to-girlfriend variety. But now that I had, I liked it a lot. And there were so many kinds. Like that gratitude kiss we'd just shared. I would have to come up with a better one before I left for school.

"Here are my designs," I said. "I wish for adorable toddler shoes."

He took the sheets of doodles over to the worktable and smoothed them flat. There was a lot of grunting and head-nodding. A couple of minutes passed before he said, "Very nice. Do you have specifics about the colors?"

"You decide." I reached into the pocket of my jeans and pulled out my last emergency fund twenty-dollar bill. "It's not much for the supplies."

He grinned. "I'll make it work. Crystal knows a craft store with great bargains."

"My mom knows about this?"

"Indeed. She's showing interest in your project." He sobered. "No pressure. We'll let it grow naturally. Okay?"

"Okay." I cast a look of longing at the room, then at the guy, gave him a better kiss (the kind that had to sustain us both for another seven hours), and left.

I practically ran home from school, eager to see Grant and the shoes. Pushing the door open, I walked in. My gaze fell on the worktable first.

Goosebumps shivered down my arms. The shoes were perfect. I admired the pair nearest me. Lavender, with silver tiaras outlined in miniature crystals. But it was the shoelaces that grabbed my attention. What had he done to them?

"I painted them too."

They were so cool. Tiny figures danced along the strings, brushed on with a device as fine as the tip of a needle. "How?" I said, looking over my shoulder at Grant, who had appeared behind me.

"I can't explain the process. It's an ancient technique that's been lost to human history."

"One-of-a-kind shoes." Twenty-four pairs. Different colors, different themes, each unique. Excitement burned deep within me. We had a gold mine here.

On the far end of the table sat a small, open box. I walked closer to peek inside. The box contained a bracelet made of copper wire links, shaped into overlapping leaves. Or were they hearts? It was gorgeous.

If Grant hadn't already said he loved me, the bracelet would've said it for him. I went from gazing in awe to flying into his arms.

"What do you think?" he murmured against my hair.

I leaned back, my tone serious. "It's the most amazing gift anyone has ever given me."

His hands slid to my waist. "Try it on."

I slipped it onto my wrist and let it rest over the nearly faded tattoo. The bracelet glowed against my skin, sophisticated and intricate in a beautiful coppery brown. Words of gratitude ached in my throat, but I didn't trust myself to speak. I loved the bracelet. I loved everything he did. I loved him.

Was my love enough?

Grant kept giving and giving. I wanted to give back. Instead, I gave him more work. When we'd been mistress and genie, ordering him around had been expected, but we were a couple now. One of us could not give more than the other. It put us out of balance.

I had to figure out some way to fix it. "Well," I said, trying to infuse a professional tone to my voice, "I'll take over now." I ducked out of his arms and walked away from him.

"Is something wrong?"

"Not at all." I knew my behavior puzzled him, but I didn't know how to explain. "You've officially completed this wish. So thank you. I'll handle the rest."

"Lacey, please—"

"Hey," Henry interrupted, poking his head in the open door of the studio. "There's a lady here to see you and Mom."

His statement bathed me in an icy stream of fear.

I didn't even need to ask him who. The social worker had returned—far sooner than I would've expected. I clutched the edge of the worktable, as my legs were as stable as Jell-O. "Where is she?"

"Right here, Miss Linden." Camarin Paxton stepped into the studio, her heels making muffled taps on the concrete floor. "Don't worry about finding your mother this time. I've already had a conversation with her."

"What?" My head swam. I hadn't seen Mom this afternoon. I didn't know if this was a good day or a bad one, and either could have its problems. On good days, she might say too much. Like...had she mentioned that Grant hid her during the last visit?

Grant was staring hard at the visitor. "What are you doing here, Camarin?"

With fingers grasping the table to keep from swaying, I looked toward him. "You know her?"

He gave a curt nod, his glare never wavering from Ms. Paxton's face.

Her expression was calm, her gaze unblinking. "I've come to ensure that this family has what it needs. Why else?"

"They are doing fine without you."

"That's not your call." She turned to me. "I'm satisfied with what I see for now. Do you have any questions for me before I go?"

"I do." I tried to calm my breathing and clear my head. I had to find out what she knew without revealing my fear. It didn't help that the tension radiating off of Grant blasted me like a hot wind. "What is the Department of Social Investigations? This county has Child Protective Services."

She smiled kindly. "Our institution is not part of your county government. It's organized at a higher level."

Grant snorted. "Indeed."

Her lips tightened, but she didn't respond.

"Will you be returning for another visit?" I asked.

"No," he said.

"It's possible," she said.

All right. I had to know what was going on. "How do you know Grant?"

Her gaze flicked from me to him. "We've worked together on projects before."

"We're not likely to do that again," he said, his voice strained.

"I hope we will." She spoke intently, as if only to him. "Your skills are exceptional, Grant. You could be one of the chosen."

He stiffened. "You can't know that."

"Yes, I can." She studied him, her glass-green eyes almost wistful behind her trendy red frames. "Be careful which path you take. Decisions have consequences."

She nodded at me, spun on her heel, and clopped to the exit. Henry had to step aside to let her pass. I'd forgotten he was there.

My brother frowned at me, his eyes widened. "What was that all about, Lacey?"

I forced my lips to curve into an unconcerned smile. "No big deal. Just a friendly person checking on us."

"Grant doesn't like her."

My BSB visibly relaxed. "Your sister's right. It's not a problem, Henry. Camarin said she was satisfied. I'm sure that's true."

"Okay." My brother darted into the backyard.

Grant turned to the worktable, busily lifting a pair of shoes and carrying them to a plastic bin. When he turned around, I was waiting. "Who is she?"

"Camarin Paxton."

"That's not what I meant, and you know it." I met his gaze unflinchingly. "Where did you meet?"

"I can't say."

"Is it a secret?"

"An oath." His chin jutted out in challenge. "I can reveal nothing else about our association."

"So she's a BSB."

He looked away from me, but not before I'd seen a flash of acknowledgement in his eyes.

"Grant, we have to talk about this."

He lifted me onto the worktable and stepped between my legs, his hands resting lightly on my hips. "What do you want to know?"

"She mentioned decisions having consequences. What does that mean?"

"Camarin had no business providing a commentary on my actions."

"But she did, so tell me."

He leaned forward for a kiss, sweet and brief, before responding. "Once I'm on a leave of absence, I'll have to find somewhere to stay besides the church."

His beautiful, comfortable, black-and-white home? "Why?"

He watched me steadily through narrowed eyes. "I can't run the risk of finding myself trapped inside it one day."

"How could you be trapped?"

"The nutrient deliveries will stop."

Not good. A whisper of unease curled inside me. "And once the food stops, you lose your powers?"

"Yes."

I locked my hands behind his neck. It was lovely, sitting here with him, entwined in each other's arms. Yet I had to think through what he'd said, even though there was part of me that was scared to learn anything else. "Will you lose your acute senses?"

"No."

"Wow, Grant. How does that work?"

"It will be fine. Trust me." His green eyes glittered with intensity. "I'll darken the windows in the studio and put my hammock up here. I'll eat bland food. I can do this."

"How long will you be able to stand it?"

He smiled. "I can stand anything as long as we're together."

I loved it when he said things like that. It took the edge off my fears. "What happens if we break up?"

"I resume my apprenticeship."

Okay. That didn't sound too bad, but there had to be more. I could hear it in his voice. "Does your apprenticeship resume where you left off?"

He hesitated. "No."

"Then where?"

"There will be a period of readjustment."

"Which means…?"

"I can anticipate new assignments."

"How many?"

"I may require several cases to reassess the stability of my emotional skills."

"Several?" Wow. My head hummed with the possibilities. "How long could that take?"

"Not long."

"Months?"

He shrugged. "Possibly."

I wiggled away from him, slid off the table, and crossed to the doorway to stare out into the yard. I didn't like these consequences. It seemed too harsh when he was only one assignment away from promotion. "You're giving up a lot."

He stepped behind me and drew me back against him. "I knew the consequences when I made the offer. I want to do this. I want to be with you. Please don't worry about it."

I didn't want to worry about it. I wanted to believe him and be happy. "Are you sure?"

He answered me with a kiss. A thoroughly hot, achingly sweet kiss.

When the kiss ended, he nuzzled my cheek and said, "Please, Lacey, let this go. It will be fine. Trust me."

"Okay." I leaned into his arms, humbled by how much he loved me. And hoping that my love for him could prove half as strong.

Status Report #25
Monday's Wish: Shoe Production

Dear Boss,

Why did you send Camarin again? Were you truly concerned about my work for this family? Or was her real goal to remind me of the gravity of what I'm about to do?

I have made my choice. After reviewing the Leave of Absence Protocol, I'm clear about its directives. I understand that I am to contact you only if I wish to return to the League—and that you will monitor me only in case of a health emergency that requires an immediate extraction.

Do not concern yourself about Lacey's family. I have met their needs well, and I will continue to serve them on my leave of absence. I resent the implication that my judgment is clouded or my skills compromised by human love.

I have unfinished business here. Crystal is at a fragile stage in her improvement. If I leave as scheduled, she will suffer. Henry and I have become good friends. I am not prepared to abandon him yet.

And Lacey? I cannot fathom the thought of saying goodbye. I love her. It makes no sense for us to part.

You encourage Beings to understand love. Why then are you throwing up obstacles when I wish to experience it for myself?

Please do not investigate again. Camarin's presence has raised unnecessary questions in Lacey's mind. I am comfortable with my decision.

Humbly submitted,
Grant

26

Five Days of Us

I finished my shift at the bookstore Tuesday around six and hurried home, eager to see Grant. I headed straight to the studio.

It was empty. I knew Grant wasn't in his music box, because I could feel his presence even when I couldn't see him.

I ran into the kitchen. It was deserted also, but there were voices coming from the formal dining room. I peeked through its doorway and gasped.

The table had been set for two, complete with a linen tablecloth, candles, and a small bouquet of flowers in an old crystal vase.

"Wow, this is gorgeous. What's the occasion?"

Mom, Henry, and Grant turned. My mother and my brother laughed and then brushed past me to disappear into the kitchen.

Grant crossed to me. "It's a date."

"Like a romantic, just-the-two-of-us date?" Could happiness make a person explode? It sure didn't feel like I could keep it all in.

"Yes." He dropped a light kiss on my mouth. "We all cooked."

"Wow." I adored him. Really adored him. How could it possibly be true that he loved me? It was crazy and wonderful. "Should I change clothes?"

"No. You're perfect the way you are. Let's sit." At my nod, he held a chair for me and then sat beside me. "Ready," he called out.

Henry walked, carefully holding two small plates filled with pickles, olives, and carrot sticks. With a big grin, he said, "I made the appetizer."

"It looks amazing." I smiled. "You know how much I like pickles."

"I do. That's why I added them." Henry smacked both plates onto the table and ran back the way he came.

I looked over at Grant and found him watching me. I caught his hand in mine and pressed a kiss to its palm. "Thank you. I love this."

He leaned closer to me and kissed me. Hard, hot, and delicious. It ended too soon. I wanted more.

"There will be time for kissing later." Grant smiled. "We'd better eat."

I nodded. "Can you tolerate pickles?"

He shook his head.

"I'll have yours."

For five days, everything had gone so well. Grant had used the word "enchanted" with me, and it was true. It was like I'd stepped into a dream, and it was too lovely to wake up.

Henry and Mom were the waiters for our romantic dinner. They served us pasta, then leftover apple pie. When the meal was over, they took away the dishes. We could hear them banging around as they washed up.

I looked cautiously at Grant, wondering what would come next because I wasn't ready for our evening to end.

He stood and held out his hand. "Shall we take a walk?"

"I'd love to."

It would be hard to describe this date to anyone. We strolled through the neighborhood, hands clasped securely, as night fell softly around us. It would probably sound boring, but it was delightful. We talked when we had something to say, kissed often, and relaxed into the silences, when the feelings were too intense to spoil with words. Each touch, smile, laugh—sweet and magical in their own way.

Eventually, we returned to the house and headed for the wrought-iron bench in the backyard, where he promptly cradled me in his lap.

The perfect ending to the perfect date.

I snuggled against him, sighing as his arms tightened about me. "I still can't believe you're staying with us."

"Believe it." His lips brushed my temple. "I've chosen you—*us*—for as long as you'll have me."

I'd want him for a long time. I lost myself to the moment, so very happy, and allowed my thoughts to drift.

Believe it.

I did.

I've chosen you.

Chosen? His BSB friend had used that same word yesterday.

I'd been too distracted at the time to ask what it meant, but I was curious to know now. "Ms. Paxton said that you could be one of the chosen. For what?"

The change in his demeanor was immediate and dramatic. He became tense. Agitated. "Special assignments." His voice was strained.

I looked up into his face, but he didn't meet my gaze. Something about my question had upset him in a powerful way. "Would you like them?"

"Yes."

"What kinds of assignments?"

"I don't know," he said with great reluctance.

"You don't know what they are, but you would like them." I laid a gentle hand on his cheek and turned him so that he had to look at me. "Are the assignments a secret?"

He gave a curt nod.

Secret assignments that he didn't know about but still wanted? The awful truth twisted inside me. "She thinks you have a shot at the level with no name."

"She cannot possibly know that." Uncertainty flickered in his eyes.

"But your boss could, and he might have sent her."

"Perhaps."

"Grant." I studied him, desperate to understand. "It's your dream to be promoted to that elite level."

"I have changed my dreams."

Wow.

Slowly I slid off his lap. He had hidden this from me because he'd expected me to react badly. He was right. I walked a few paces away and stared into the darkness of the yard. "What does it take to qualify for the elite level?" I asked, trying hard to control the quiver in my voice.

"Exceptional skills. An unblemished record." He rose and came to stand beside me. "There are others that we aren't allowed to know."

"Am I a blemish?"

"Lacey." He wrapped an arm around my waist and pulled me to him. "Stop worrying about this. I know what I'm doing."

I couldn't stop. I'd begun to believe in a future with him because the consequences had seemed manageable. But this?

"What if you knew for sure that you were trading away a shot at elite?"

A shudder passed through his body. "I would not be happy to learn such a thing. However, I think the risk is quite low. It is not logical to offer us a benefit that stunts our career."

"Grant, you're not meant to live an ordinary life." I choked on a sob. "Even a small risk is too much."

"Do not concern yourself over the unknowns. It is my decision," he said. "I make it willingly."

It wasn't his decision. It was mine.

I was screaming on the inside, and it was all I could do to keep my cries from bursting free. Camarin hadn't shown up randomly. Her visit meant something. He needed to consider this information carefully.

What if he forfeited his right to be chosen?

What if we didn't make it to forever? How long was long enough to be worth it? A month? A year? My lifetime?

How could I let him make this sacrifice? Yet the alternative was to ask him to leave.

I'd already been dreading how my mom would react if he had to go. Would his departure send her spiraling downward again? And what about Henry? How long would it take him to recover? He'd lost his father less than a year ago, and now Grant?

What about me? He'd become the center of my world. Nothing thrilled me more than seeing him smile and knowing that I was the reason.

Letting him go would be devastating, but was that enough to keep Grant from his dreams?

We were so happy together. It was hard to believe that our first date had been last Friday. After only five days of us, I could hardly bear to go to school and be separated from him. How could I send him away?

"I can't," I said, facing him fully. "I can't let you do it."

His jaw set stubbornly. "I will not leave."

"You have to." I closed my eyes, but the tears fell anyway.

"I want to stay. You're the only one who makes me truly happy. Don't take that from me."

I burrowed into his arms. I loved his strength and his determination. I loved how much pleasure he got from doing things right and how eager he was to learn. I loved that life was better simply because he was around.

I loved *him*.

And there it was—the reason I wouldn't let him gamble his future for me. "You'll have to go, Grant. I'll wish you away."

"The wish only lasts a day. I'll come back the next."

"If you do, I'll wish you away again."

"No," he said, his voice confident, "you won't."

I crept up the stairs to my room, crawled into a corner, and watched out a dormer window, waiting for midnight.

First, I watched the stars, tiny pricks of white against a blue-black sky. A sliver of moon peeked over the windowsill and slowly climbed until it disappeared from view.

The hours ticked by. I waited through each rasping breath, each hot tear, each agonizing thought.

At nine, the stairs creaked, the footsteps drawing nearer. "Lacey?" my brother called.

"Yes?"

"Are you all right?"

"No."

There was a long pause and then the stairs creaked again, the footsteps fading.

Ten. The TV flicked on in the living room below me, loud enough to vibrate the floor.

Eleven. The TV flicked off and the pacing began. I could tell where Mom was by the squeaky board next to the fireplace.

At 12:01, I stood up and stumbled outside.

The studio was dark. I turned on the light and looked around. So much had happened to this room and in this room over the last month. It was clean, organized, and ready to change our luck.

I owed it all to Grant. It was time to do the right thing. Standing in the doorway, I rubbed my tattoo.

He appeared instantly. "Why are you here so late?"

"I've come to make a wish."

"A wish now?" His expression was confused at first before changing to concern. "No, Lacey. You're tired. You don't have to decide this now. Go to bed. We'll talk in the morning."

"The facts won't change. You're sacrificing too much. I can't let that happen."

"It's not a sacrifice." He crossed to me and reached for my hands. "I want to be with you. I want to live in your world."

"For how long, Grant?" My voice trembled. This was so hard. I could barely get my thoughts out. "How long before you miss what you're giving up? How long before you resent throwing away your future for me?"

He shook his head with confidence. "That won't happen. When you and I are no longer together, I'll resume my career. It will always be there to reclaim."

"The dream career you're facing now?"

There was that flicker of unease in his eyes, quickly suppressed. "I can't know for sure, but I'm not worried." He closed the space between us and pressed his mouth to mine, his kiss searing my heart. "We're good together," he said against my lips. "We have so much left to do. Let me handle what comes after."

Yes, please.

No. Wait. I had to be strong. I pulled away from him and backed into the yard, into the shadows, his words trailing me, sweet and tempting. I wanted to believe. I wanted him to be right. If I listened much longer, I'd yield.

He followed. "I love you, Lacey. I know what I'm doing."

"You don't understand human love, Grant," I said, backing up until a tree stopped my progress. "You don't know if this is a fair trade."

"I'm willing to discover it with you." He braced his hands on either side of my head and leaned so close I could feel the heat of his body. "You want that too."

I did. I wanted more than anything to forget my worries and take what he was offering. But the memory of the other BSB shimmered in my mind. She'd been sent here to warn him. He was a rock star. He was destined for miraculous things. That's what his future should be. Since he wasn't thinking clearly, I had to, even if it tore me apart. "I love you, which is why I have to let you go."

He shook his head. "No. You don't." He cupped my face with one of his hands, the pad of his thumb lightly caressing my cheek. "You give me something I've never had before. You're all I want."

I closed my eyes and relaxed into his touch. His lips brushed my temple, my jaw, my mouth.

It would be so easy to give in...

I broke away and slipped from his arms, putting distance between us. "You're supposed to be one of the chosen. How can I be happy wondering if I'm taking that away?" This hurt so badly. I wanted it to end. "Tell me you understand."

"I don't." Even in the darkness, his eyes shone with desperation. "I accept the risk. Let me stay."

"I can't." I shook my head firmly.

"At least let me say goodbye to Crystal and Henry."

How would I ever explain this to them? "No, Grant. I know it'll hurt them, but I don't need all three of you ganging up on me."

"Please, Lacey. Don't do this. I love you."

"I love you too. That's why I can't let you ruin your life for me. I'm not enough."

"You're everything."

"I'm sorry, Grant."

"No—"

I forced the words past a throat clogged with tears. "I *wish* you would leave and not return."

There was a puff of blue smoke. A faint hiss. And he was gone.

There was no need to set the alarm clock. I lay awake all night.

Before my mom or brother could get up, I dressed and walked to school. The grounds were deserted. The school lay in darkness. On a crumbling concrete bench under an old magnolia, I sat cross-legged, waiting for daylight and people.

Staff and faculty trickled in. Buses arrived. I hunched over, watching the drop-off lane for a silver SUV.

It roared up at ten 'til eight. Kimberley bounded up the sidewalk, brimming with joy. Today, it was not contagious.

I slipped off the bench and joined her as she climbed the front steps.

"Hi," she said. Her smile faded. "You look terrible."

"Thanks."

"What happened?"

I deflected her question with a flick of the wrist.

"Did Grant break up with you?"

Could she read minds too? "It was the other way around." My voice was rough.

"Why?"

"I'm bad for him."

She didn't argue. She didn't ask questions. There was only silence until we arrived at our class. First period. APUSH.

Damn. I'd forgotten about Mr. Jarrett. How could I face ninety minutes of listening to his stupidity? The very thought made me sick. I trudged into the half-empty room behind Kimberley. Mr. Jarrett read *The Washington Post* on his laptop. Flopping into my desk, I sank low in the seat and wished myself anywhere but here.

The bell rang.

"All right, class. Today we'll start the War of 1812, also known as America's most boring war."

My whole body ached. I bowed my head over my desk and traced a finger over its graffiti.

I hated farewells.

In the gray light of an autumn morning, I march on tiptoe in my frilly pink dress and shiny black shoes through America's most boring park. I want to skip, but the adults won't let me.

"The War of 1812 was a huge waste of a war. It did nothing but pile up another stack of dead soldiers."

"Shut up," someone shouted in my voice.

"Excuse me, Lacey," Mr. Jarrett said. "Sit down."

I sit down and look at the bouquets of flowers. They smell too sweet. Nana calls the park a cemetery. I do not like this place.

"Don't you ever, *ever* call them 'another stack of dead soldiers' again."

A tall, handsome Marine kneels before me and holds out a folded flag. I take it and imitate him—one hand on top and one hand on bottom. The flag is heavy and smooth.

On one side, my mother cries. On the other side, my grandparents cry. And they've told me that my father would be here. But they've also told me that he's in heaven. So which is it? And, really, the grateful nation could keep their flag if they'd just let me have my daddy back.

Mr. Jarrett snorted. "Then what should I call them?"

"Heroes—the kind who pay with their lives so that jerks like you can say any stupid thing you want."

Beside me, Kimberley stood and clapped. The person beside her stood and clapped too. One by one, students rose until the entire class was standing and clapping.

I left right then. I picked up my stuff and ran from the room, slamming the door behind me. I could hear my teacher screaming for me, but I didn't stop racing down the empty halls of the high school until I reached the outside.

It was hard to believe they'd applauded. Mr. Jarrett held grudges. Maybe the standing ovation had been my imagination.

I couldn't recall what happened next. My mind checked out and my body took over. It walked and walked. Somehow it managed to get me to my house.

Mom emerged from her bedroom when my foot hit the bottom step of the attic stairwell.

"Why are you home so early?" she asked in a calm voice. "What's wrong?"

My insides were crumbling. I couldn't speak.

"Oh, baby." She drew me into a hug and patted my back awkwardly. I laid my head on her shoulder and felt a few hot tears seep from my squeezed-shut eyes.

"I haven't been able to find Grant today," she said. "Is that what's wrong? Has he left?"

I nodded against her shoulder. A shudder jolted through her body. Slowly, she disentangled our arms, a pinched twist to her lips. "You go on up to bed. I'll check on you later."

I did as she suggested and lay in bed for hours, curled on my side, too numb to think, staring with dry eyes at white walls.

He hadn't really left. Not yet. The music box waited in the studio. All I had to do was walk out there and make another wish. The agony would be over.

No. I have to let him go.

The finality was overwhelming. I wanted him back.

My mom drifted in and out of my attic room. She felt my forehead, muttering. She brought me a mug of her favorite hot sweetened tea and a plate of crackers and then stayed until I consumed them. She asked a thousand times if there was anything else she could do. I answered a thousand times, "I'm fine."

I wasn't fine. I would never be fine again.

There was a loud rap on the door. "What?"

Mom peered in. "I'm walking Henry to practice."

I nodded. It might be too soon for her, but I ached too much to move, and Henry's practice was a commitment.

A couple of minutes passed. There was a second loud rap.

"What now?"

"Hey," Kimberley said. "You still look terrible."

"Thanks." I stayed horizontal.

She came closer. "Standing up to Mr. Jarrett was pretty cool. You're everybody's new best friend."

"Great." I was guaranteed to fail APUSH now, which meant I wouldn't graduate early like I'd hoped. But at least I'd have friends during the spring semester I had planned to skip.

"Do you want to talk about it?"

"No."

"Do you want some company? You could lie there and listen to me talk."

"That would be nice."

"Good." She slid to the floor next to the bed, bringing her face on a level with mine. "My dad came to visit this weekend. He brought his new girlfriend."

"Oh."

"I don't remember her name—it's something fluffy— and she's thirty-one years old. The whole thing is wrong on a lot of levels."

It was like I had a glass bubble around my head. I could see the heat of her anger, but the bubble stopped it from reaching me. I thought I should hurt for her, but I couldn't. I was a bad friend. There was no room left for anyone else's pain.

She talked nonstop for an hour, requiring nothing further from me than my presence, which was good because I had nothing else to give.

Within seconds of Kimberley's departure, the door creaked open. Henry's turn. "Lacey, are you sick?"

"Yes." I didn't want to talk. It hurt to move my mouth.

"Did you catch something at school?"

"No, little man. I'm the only one who has it."

"Do you want me to find Grant? He can fix anything."

Pain rippled through me anew but for a different reason. I had to tell Henry the news, and I didn't want to. "Grant is gone."

He blinked. "Gone gone?"

"Yes."

"For how long?"

I didn't want to think about this. "Forever."

Henry's eyes grew big, round, and watery. "He left without saying goodbye to me?"

I couldn't let Henry believe that Grant would be so callous. "I made him leave."

"Why, Lacey?"

"I can't explain."

He ran from the room and thundered down the steps.

My mother checked on me around supper time, but I pretended to be asleep. She watched for a good five minutes before leaving. She didn't return.

It was a horrible night. I curled around my pillow, wide-eyed, reliving each thought and decision. It wasn't too late. All I had to do was rub my tattoo and he would come right back.

No. I had to stop thinking about it. Our month with Grant was over.

27

A Profound Silence

I awakened at four, having slept enough to be functional, which was good because today was the deadline for Ms. Dewan's essay contest. She believed that my writing skills would do well in a competition. I needed to do this for her. For me.

It would mean writing a draft the old-fashioned way, since all I had was paper and pen, but it didn't seem to matter. The words flowed in such a rush, I could hardly write fast enough.

The Language of Choice
By Lacey Linden
When I turn eighteen, America will recognize me as an adult. I will gain the right to sign contracts, the privilege of serving my country, and the power to vote. Each of these responsibilities requires that I communicate well, making my education in language arts a foundational skill.

How ironic it is that, while America trusts me to be an adult, my public high school does not. After twelve years of encouraging me to think for myself, they do not allow me to choose which English courses will serve me best...

After ninety minutes of drafting, the essay was done.

I threw on some clothes and tiptoed downstairs. The house was dim and quiet at this hour, the only noises the tick of the clock and the hum of the A/C. I'd nearly made it to the door when my mother spoke.

"Morning, baby."

I spun around. "Oh. I didn't mean to disturb you."

She sat on the couch under a navy-blue blanket. Holding up one corner, she beckoned me over. When I flopped down next to her, she tucked the blanket's edges around me.

"Mom, about Grant—"

"Shhh," she interrupted, shaking her head. "I prefer that you don't mention him for a while. Coping with Henry's grief is all I can take. I'm not ready to handle my own."

"Henry's talking to you about Grant?"

She gave a sharp nod. "In his mind, you're the villain."

That hurt. "What do you think?"

"I think it must be one of those things where no one's wrong and everybody loses."

The urge to explain gripped me, but I couldn't. Not now.

We cuddled quietly until the clock struck seven.

"Time for me to go," I said. "I have an essay I need to finish for Ms. Dewan."

"I'll call the school to excuse your absence yesterday."

"Can you excuse my first period class this morning too?"

"Sure, baby."

"Thanks." I kissed her cheek, slid from the couch, and let myself out of the house. I got to school in record time and entered the media center the second the doors were unlocked. After almost an hour of revisions and several frustrated kicks at a jammed printer, I finally got a printed copy of my contest entry. There was no way it would win, but it would give the judges something to think about.

I missed APUSH for the second day in a row, which made me an idiot, but I didn't care. The essay was more important.

Ms. Dewan wasn't in her room at the beginning of second period. I wanted to put the submission directly into her hands, but I didn't want to hang out at her desk. So I went to the back row, slumped in a seat, and stared at my masterpiece. My eyelids drooped. The letters blurred.

"Hey. Are you okay?" Eli's voice seemed to boom next to me.

I jerked upright. "I'm fine."

"You don't sound fine."

"Okay, then. I'm not fine." I picked up a pen and doodled on the cover of my notebook.

"Do you want to talk about it?"

"No." There was a buzzing in my head. Or maybe it was the bell.

"Does it have anything to do with Grant?"

"Yeah." It was incredible how everyone accepted that Grant and I had been a couple. How could it have been so obvious to others when it hadn't been that obvious to me? Maybe I was just slow.

"Did you break up?"

"We did." I shot Eli a quick glance, daring him to ask more.

"Sorry." He nodded and then pointed at my contest entry. "Did you argue against English Lit?"

"Yeah." Safer subject. I shifted the paper so he could see the title.

"'The Language of Choice,'" he said with a half-smile. "I'd guess you aren't choosing to read more Shakespeare."

"Correct. Did you write an essay?"

"I turned mine in yesterday. 'The View Through Shakespeare's Prism.'"

A brief smile trembled on my lips. "Good luck."

"Thanks. You too." His face scrunched into concern. "How's Henry's leg?"

"It's fine. Did he have any problems at practice yesterday?"

"All of the guys seemed a little off. We're planning an extra practice for this afternoon."

"Excuse me, Lacey and Eli?"

Crap. That was Ms. Dewan. We both straightened and faced forward.

"Would you two like to share your conversation with the rest of the class?"

There was a sea of faces staring at us. When had class started? What had we missed? My mind went blank. I couldn't think of a single decent lie.

"We were discussing our favorite Shakespearean sonnets," Eli said.

I looked at him and nodded. Impressive. He nodded back.

"Great. Why don't you tell us your favorite, Lacey?" Ms. Dewan prompted.

She was mad, which happened occasionally but had never before been directed at me. I dropped my gaze and caught sight of my doodle. A music box.

"'Farewell!'" My voice cracked. I stopped, cleared my throat, and tried again, more softly the second time. "'Farewell! Thou art too dear for my possessing...'"

There was silence in the room—a profound silence, as if they were all holding their breath.

"Thank you, Lacey. A lovely choice." Her voice had softened. "Eli?"

I felt his gaze on me but didn't meet it. Couldn't meet it.

"'From fairest creatures we desire increase,'" he quoted, "'that thereby beauty's rose might never die.'"

Utter silence.

"Good save," the teacher said. "We'll cover both of those sonnets in this unit." Her heels clicked on the tile floor as she crossed to her desk. She fished around for a small book, then held it up. "All right, class, get out your copies of *Macbeth*..."

At the end of the period, I walked to her desk and stood until she finished speaking with another student.

Her expression was neutral. "Yes, Lacey?"

I handed her the entry. She took it, puzzled, and flipped through the pages. A smile spread as she skimmed my essay. "You did it," she said, looking up. "I wasn't sure you would."

"I wanted to see if I could."

"You made the right decision. If the first paragraph is anything to go by, I can't wait to read the rest."

The praise felt good. I left the room and lingered in the hallway, glad I'd gone through with it after all.

It was my lunch period, but more than food, I was dying for sleep.

Easy choice. I diverted to the nearest exit.

My mom didn't seem surprised when I arrived home. She didn't ask why I was skipping school or what had happened yesterday. All she said was, "I'm having apple pie for lunch. Want to join me?"

We ate half a pie between us, drank a pot of herbal tea—my mother's new hot beverage obsession—and talked about the garden. It was weird to have a whole conversation that didn't mention Henry, Josh, or Grant.

Afterwards, we quietly washed the dishes and then went our separate ways. She disappeared into her bedroom and I trudged up to mine.

But sleep wouldn't come immediately. I lay on my side, staring into space, wondering what Grant was doing or thinking right now. Would he emerge each day and force me to wish him away? Was he mad? Did he understand yet?

I held up my arm, pushed my copper bracelet aside, and studied the tattoo. It would be so simple to summon Grant and continue with my wishes. Mom needed more from him. We had renovations to complete on the house. I could use his help marketing the shoes. And we hadn't even begun to look for the storage facility.

I needed Grant the BSB. I wanted Grant the guy. All I had to do was call out and I would have both.

No. *No.* I'd made the right decision.

The music box had to go.

When Eli brought Henry home from practice today, I would be waiting.

I hovered in the front yard, peering down the street for the Mustang. When it finally pulled up at the curb, I rushed over to the driver's side of the car. "Can you take me to the flea market?"

"Sure."

I ran to the front porch and picked up the music box. The wood gleamed in the sunlight, rich and dark. I clamped my lips against the pain of what I was about to do. Taking Henry's place in the passenger's seat, I buckled up, clutched the box to my chest, and closed my eyes.

"What do you have?" Eli asked.

"Nothing special."

"I think it *is* special."

The stereotype that portrayed guys as not talking much? That hadn't been my experience, and I wished it was. "Why do you say that?"

"You're crying."

Was I? I lifted a hand to my wet cheek. "It's hard for me to sell this box."

"Family heirloom?"

I shook my head. "Family treasure."

"Are you selling it because you need the money?"

I nodded. His assumption was as safe an answer as any.

Eli didn't say anything else until we reached our destination. "Here we are."

I fixed my gaze on the sign. "Magnolia Grove Flea Market" was painted in peeling black paint on a crooked board warped by weather and neglect.

My legs mutinied, not wanting to participate in my plan. I frowned, willing them to cooperate. The decision was made. There was no use in delaying it.

The muscles twitched reluctantly. Time to move. "I'll be back soon."

"Do you want me to come with you?"

"No. Thanks." I pushed the door open with my foot and slid from the car. My sneakers slapped against the broken asphalt as I wove through the sparsely filled parking lot and turned into the entrance. My journey down the main aisle was slow and measured. Vendors reclined lazily, some reading, others half-dozing, while a thin stream of customers wandered around without buying much. A few nodded at me as I passed.

Four weeks ago, I had arrived, blissfully unsuspecting of what was to come. A different girl. A different world.

Madame Noir was in her spot, her smile dimming when she recognized the object in my hands.

I set it with a *thunk* on her table. "Will you buy this back from me? I've cleaned it up."

"Well, now, there hasn't been too much business lately for music boxes."

"If you pay cash, I'll take whatever is reasonable." It was important for her to complete the transaction quickly, and it might help if she thought I was desperate for the money. At this point, I would've given it to her for free if it wouldn't have raised too many questions.

"Twenty-five?"

One dollar per wish. "Deal."

She bit her lip, surprised at how easily I gave in. She counted out the bills and pushed them toward me.

I opened the lid one last time. I longed to say something to Grant. A speech of gratitude. Of love. I touched the tiny ice skating couple, Norah and Charles. Deep from within the box, four notes of "Silent Night" tinkled. "I already miss you," I said.

Grief rushed up from my gut, threatening to overwhelm me. I couldn't stay there a moment longer. Snatching the money, I crumpled it in a fist as I ran down the aisle. When I reached the refreshments section, I threw down two dollars, grabbed a lemonade, and found an empty wooden bench under a sad pine.

It was there Eli found me.

"Want a sip?" I asked. There was a millimeter of lemonade at the bottom of the cup.

He smiled, shook his head, and dropped onto the bench beside me. Silently, we watched people pass for a few minutes. Moms with strollers. Old men pulling wagons with their newly purchased junk.

"I apologize for taking so long, Eli."

"Not a problem." He picked up a pine needle and twirled it between his fingers. "I'm worried about you."

That got my attention. "Why?"

"Henry told me that you want to go to William & Mary, but you've decided not to apply."

My head ached at the news. "Did he share any theories about the reason?"

"He did." Eli flicked the pine needle onto the dusty path and leaned forward to rest his elbows on his knees. "He knows it's not money. He says your dad left you enough to go to college."

My lips twitched into a half-smile. "Right so far."

"He thinks you're going to Magnolia Community College because you'd be too homesick anywhere else."

Why was my eight-year-old brother worrying about stuff like this? "That's close enough."

Eli pushed off the bench and looked at me, face mildly curious. "You know what I think?"

I frowned. "No."

"I think you're afraid that your family might fall apart without you." He held out a hand and helped me up, but he didn't let go right away. Instead, he pulled me into his arms for a gentle hug. "Your brother is sad that he can't help you more than he does."

I groaned. *No, no, no.* He was just a little boy. He ought to be playing and laughing and leaving crap like this up to the adults. "I don't want him worrying about me," I whispered.

Eli's arms tightened. "Find a way to let him help you. He needs that."

I closed my eyes. Henry was too young. What could he do?

Wait. He was a smart little kid. Really smart. Maybe *he* would know what he could do.

Yeah. I'd try to talk to him tonight, if he'd let me. If he'd stopped viewing me as the villain who banished Grant. Henry would have ideas. This might be good.

28

Unsolicited Praise

*F*or the third time this week, I was going to the flea market, except today I had something to sell. Twenty-three pairs of adorable shoes.

I was keeping my favorite pair. It had a place of honor on my keepsake shelf.

Without Grant around, my confidence sagged. What if I priced them too high? What if I had the wrong sizes?

What if no one liked them?

I came out of the studio with a plastic tub of shoes and my backpack. Mom and Henry stood at the curb, waiting for a ride to the game with the Samms.

Henry ran over and looked in the box. "What're you going to do with all the money?"

I smiled at the top of his head. My confidence bloomed. "Buy a new tire for the car."

"Cool. I get tired of asking for rides."

"Sorry about that, little man. It'll get better. I'm going to buy even more shoes and make even more money."

"Pure economics," he said with the air of a seasoned businessman.

I decided I must not laugh. "The more capital I have, the more I can increase production."

"So true." He nodded wisely. "Will yours be as good as Grant's?"

"Yes, Henry. They will."

"I hope you're right."

The Samms' minivan rolled around the corner and pulled to a stop. Before my family had settled inside, an SUV stopped behind them.

Mrs. Rey waved me into the front. "Kimberley forgot to set her alarm and overslept, so she stayed home."

"That's fine." I set the tub on the backseat and buckled myself in to the front. "Thank you for taking me."

"I don't mind." She gave me a smile as she pulled away. "Did you bring a card table to set up?"

"No. The empty stalls have their own tables."

"Just in case, I threw an old toddler table in the back with a couple of little chairs."

"Thanks, Mrs. Rey."

"Teresa." She reached for my hand and gave it a squeeze.

When we arrived, I discovered that, in planning this business opportunity, there was one detail I'd overlooked— the flea market bureaucracy. They had rules about vendors— the most critical being *Stall Rental.*

The security guard stopped us at the gate. "Fifty bucks a day."

"I don't have fifty bucks."

"So we're done talking here." He slouched on his stool and resumed picking at his beard.

Teresa pulled me aside. "I'll loan you the fifty bucks."

I stared into the tub at the lovely shoes, torn about accepting her offer. The decision didn't take long. I'd learned to hate debt over the past year, and I intended to stay away from it for good. "No, I'll figure something else out. You go on. I appreciate the ride."

She gave me a hug and strode across the asphalt to her car. I watched idly, not thinking, hoping inspiration would spring into the vacuum of my brain.

Customers streamed in steadily. There was a good crowd this morning, and it was a perfect day for shopping. Not too hot. Puffy clouds. No signs of imminent rain.

My gaze fell on a scraggly tree, complete with a picnic table, garbage can, and tiny pool of shade. It was one hundred feet or so from the entrance, and out of view of the security guard but visible to shoppers if they turned their heads.

I'd found my free stall.

After selecting the six shiniest pairs, I turned the tub upside down, set up my display in the shade, posted my sign, and waited.

For the first half hour, people merely glanced my way as they walked by.

In the second half hour, I waved. Shoppers waved back and kept going.

As the morning progressed with not even a glimmer of interest, the knot in my stomach tightened. What had gone wrong? This should've been a slam dunk. I'd invested our entire emergency fund in this project. I hadn't expected such an epic failure.

Another hour had passed when I spotted my brother running in from the parking lot. "Henry!" I called.

He detoured smoothly in my direction, happy and sweaty and full of energy. Eli followed more slowly, his limp almost unnoticeable.

"Lacey, wow. Do you only have six pairs left?" Henry shouted.

My smile wavered. "I have twenty-three pairs left."

He frowned. "You haven't sold *any*?"

"No." It was sickening to admit it.

"It's because you have a bad location, Lacey. You have to go where the customers are. Why aren't you inside?"

I didn't know whether to laugh or cry. "The overhead is too expensive."

Henry flung himself onto the top of the picnic table and posed like *The Thinker*. Eli crossed to my side, fighting a smile.

"Did they win?" I asked.

Eli nodded. "We're undefeated. It was an awesome game."

"Sorry I missed it." Surprising but true. Even though I hadn't learned to love soccer, I did love watching my brother win.

"Hey," Eli said, touching me lightly on the arm, "have you had a break?"

I shook my head.

"Here," he said, pulling a ten-dollar bill from his wallet. "I promised Henry a drink. Why don't you take a quick break and buy us two bottles of Gatorade? We can handle the shoes until you get back."

This was an easy offer to accept. I grabbed the cash and walked into the flea market. First stop, the nasty bathrooms. Second stop, the refreshments stand. As I headed back toward the entrance, I wandered past Madame Noir's table. "Morning."

"Morning, Lacey. How are you?" Madame fanned herself in spite of the mild weather.

"Good." I scanned her tables. There was no sign of the music box. "Hey, what happened—?"

"I sold it. Same day you brought it in." She bared her teeth in a gleeful grin. "Nice profit too."

"Lucky you." I hurried away, so fast she couldn't see the sudden tears blinding me. At the next corner, I whipped behind a brick wall and collapsed against it, falling to my knees, withering under the knowledge. Pain throbbed in my skull and crushed my chest. Why had I asked her?

Somewhere out there, someone had Grant. Were they treating him well? Did he hate me?

What was I doing here, crying behind a wall? I needed to get myself under control.

My month with Grant had been wonderful. Not at first, of course, while we were getting to know each other. Our trust had taken time to build. But once it had, I'd loved it. I'd counted on having someone to lean on and share my problems with. I'd enjoyed his humor, his logic, even his prickly way of standing up for himself. I loved being cared for, not having to remember all the details, believing that everything would work out because he was there. Grant had been my rock until I sent him away. I hadn't stopped falling since.

I reached instinctively for my wrist and felt reassured by the cool links of my copper bracelet. But I didn't look down. This should've been Grant's final day. I didn't wish to see that the tattoo was gone.

Slowly I stood, head swimming. I held onto the wall until the world stopped wobbling. I'd been gone from my makeshift stall long enough. Fortunately, I hadn't bothered with makeup this morning. I dabbed at my face with the hem of my shirt, released my hair from its braid, and walked purposefully to the entrance.

Something major had changed in my absence.

Eli stood with Sara Tucker in the shade, laughing at my brother.

Henry danced around in a circle, pumping his arms and chanting, "I'm the man."

"What happened?" I asked, joining Eli and Sara.

Eli pointed at Henry. "He made your first sale."

"Really?" I gaped at my brother.

He stopped his dance long enough to wave two twenty-dollar bills in my face. "I'm the man."

"I guess you are."

Sara smiled. "You missed it, Lacey. Your brother is an amazing salesman."

I shook my head, trying to clear the dizzy excitement of our first sale. "How did you do it?"

"One word." Henry held up his index finger. "Grandparents."

"Grandparents?" I repeated.

"Yeah. They're our target market." He slapped the twenties onto my palm and gave me a patient look of supremacy. "Grandparents love to spoil their grandkids, and they have plenty of money. It's a perfect match for dorky shoes."

I was speechless, possibly for the first time in my life. I looked from Henry to the other two and could think of nothing to say.

"You should've been here," Eli said. "An older couple walked by with three-year-old twins. Henry ran over to them and dragged them over. He sold a boy pair and a girl pair."

"You're the man," I said.

Henry fist-bumped with me. "I knew that." He launched into his victory dance again.

Dazed, I turned to Eli and Sara. Both were shaking with laughter. It rubbed off on me.

When we calmed down, I smiled at Sara, and she smiled back. That was a good sign. It might be an okay time to show polite interest. "Why are you at the flea market?"

"Buying trip," she said, inclining her head toward the entrance. "I'm on the hunt for items to sell at Mom's consignment shop."

"How's the shop going?"

"Great. Mostly, we have nosy people trying to satisfy their curiosity about my parents, but we don't care as long as they walk out with a shopping bag." She pointed at my display of shoes. "I love this idea. Would you consider featuring some in our shop?"

"Sure." Her request swirled around me like a cleansing breeze. This hardly made us friends again—too much needed to be worked out—but it was movement in the right direction. "How soon and how many?"

"Twenty girl pairs. Ten boy."

"So many for boys?"

"Yeah. You should've seen that little kid's face when he saw the trains on his shoes." She got out her phone and tapped away. "We have our grand-opening celebration in a couple of weeks. Could you be ready then?"

"Sure."

"Good. Are you open to custom orders?"

"Maybe."

She tapped a half-dozen keys and then slipped the phone back into her pocket. "Cool. We'll talk more soon." After a quick wave at Eli and a fistbump with Henry, she merged into the flea-market crowd.

Eli checked his watch. "I've got some errands to run, but I could swing back by here around five if you want a ride."

My mouth opened to refuse the offer. "That would be nice."

He frowned at me in mock surprise. "What just happened? Lacey Linden actually accepted help without arguing?"

I exhaled noisily. That didn't deserve a response.

He stepped closer and lowered his voice. "Can I take you and Henry to The Backyard Grill for dinner?"

"You can." The more I said *yes*, the easier it got.

"Great." He sauntered away and then paused, looking over his shoulder. "Just to be clear. It's my treat."

"So noted."

We sold every pair before Eli returned, and I could've sold more if we'd had them.

Would the idea catch on? I sure hoped so. The money was good, and making them would be fun. And a little scary. There was no way I could duplicate the quality of Grant's work, but I could probably paint well enough to produce shoes that were still cute.

With an "order" of thirty pairs for Mrs. Tucker's shop and then another thirty to make for next Saturday, I needed to make a plan. Later that night, I sat at the kitchen table, with my designs spread around me and half of today's cash to use for supplies. Our emergency fund would get the other half.

The shoes with butterflies had gone first. I'd double up on them. They would do better with glitter than jewels—

"Lacey?"

I looked up. Mom slid onto a chair beside me, a mug of tea in each hand.

"Want some?" she asked.

"Sure." I took a sip. Citrusy with a hint of honey. "Thanks."

She nodded, sipped, nodded again. "Things went well today?"

"Yeah. Great."

"I had a nice day too." She frowned at me. "Kyra Samm has invited me to a survivors' group. They meet monthly at her church."

There were three more weeks until my birthday. Close enough, right? I thought so, but it didn't stop a tornado of fear from spiraling inside me. With an even tone, I said, "That might be good. Will you go?"

She shook her head. "I'm not ready."

A second tornado spiraled, only this one held disappointment. I wanted her to go, to get out there and find ways to feel better, even though it would agitate me until my birthday was safely past. "Okay, Mom. There'll be other chances."

"I'll think about it again. I promise." She wrapped both hands around her mug and stared into her tea. "Why did Grant leave?"

Even though I'd expected her to ask sometime, it surprised me that it had come so soon. After admitting she couldn't accept help from something as low-key as a support group, she wanted to know this, and it would hurt. "I guess you could say I fired him." I watched her steadily. "He was willing to stay with us for as long as we needed him. I thought that was a bad idea."

She frowned into her tea. "Bad for him?"

"Yeah."

"He loves you."

I nodded, my throat aching too much to speak.

"You love him too." Her voice was sad.

I closed my eyes and pressed my lips together, battling the raw pain that threatened to overwhelm me.

The chair creaked as she rose. "We all do." Her shuffling footsteps drew even with me, then stopped. Thin fingers threaded through my hair and pressed my head against her waist. "You did the right thing, Lacey. You always do."

I clung to her, thankful for the first unsolicited hug and unsolicited praise I'd received from my mother in many months.

Production took more effort than I expected. On Sunday, I rode my bike to the flea market and the discount stores, hunting for bargains on toddler shoes, sequins, glitter glue, and jewels. Then I headed to the studio to see if I could duplicate Grant's skill with fabric paint and bling.

I ruined five pairs before I got the hang of it.

Eli showed up in the late afternoon, appearing in the door to the studio, staring with confusion into the garbage can. "What's wrong with those?"

I looked up in surprise. "Why are you here?"

"The Samms asked me to babysit Reynolds. I thought I'd drop by on my way home to see how the production line was going." He pointed at the garbage can. "What's wrong?"

"I messed up the designs."

He grunted and pulled the ten shoes out. "If we smudge some more paint on them and add a little glitter, we'd have Picasso-esque masterpieces."

I nodded to paint and brushes at the other end of the work table. "Have at it."

We worked in silence for an hour. When he was done, I had to agree that they didn't look half-bad.

And, of course, the abstract shoes ended up being a hit. Eli was not the least bit humble about the news.

In fact, we sold out our entire inventory during the grand-opening week. Mrs. Tucker reminded me that Thanksgiving was just around the corner, with all of the Black Friday shoppers hungry for Christmas gifts. "We'd love to feature more of the shoes. They really draw people into the store."

I reveled in the feeling of success, not that I set the bar very high. It would be nice to feel relaxed when I went to the grocery story or to pay bills with confidence. "Thank you, Mrs. Tucker. I can do that."

29

Incredibly Nice and Optimistic

B etween school, my bookstore job, and the shoes, I was so crazy-busy that I didn't notice October twenty-eighth creeping up, but my subconscious knew. I awakened early and lay in bed, pondering the significance of turning eighteen. With all the distractions I'd had lately, my actual birthday felt like an anticlimax. The usual stuff was true. I could vote. I could trade my provisional driver's license for a regular one.

There was also a big personal thing. I didn't have to fear Child Protective Services.

This was already one of the nicest birthdays ever. If I included everything I'd gained recently, it had been a wonderful two months.

I didn't permit myself to think about what I'd lost.

I took extra care getting ready for school, because it was going to be that kind of day.

Mom was ahead of me in the kitchen. It smelled like cinnamon and butter in there. French toast. My favorite.

"Happy birthday, baby," she said from the stove.

"Thanks, Mom." I shoveled it in—yum—and waited for more gushing over me.

She slipped onto the seat across from me with her own plate. We ate as silently as was possible with such an amazing breakfast. Five minutes passed with no gushing and no *eighteen years ago today* stories about my birth.

I left for school, a little disappointed. It wasn't as if Mom had forgotten what day it was, but it hurt that she hadn't done or said more.

Sara caught me at my locker before first period. "Here," she said and shoved a tiny gift bag into my hands.

It was a beaded hairclip I'd admired in the consignment shop last week. "Thanks for remembering." Being nice to me again was an even better present, but I wouldn't thank her for that. Sara had always had a hard time apologizing to people. I learned long ago that she did things to say she was sorry. Selling the toddler shoes at her mom's store had thrown us together a lot lately, and she'd been polite with me each time. Maybe—just maybe—we could put last autumn's nasty fight behind us for good.

When I looked up to smile at her, I saw something sad and lonely flicker in her eyes.

"Be sure and tell people where you got it," she said with a shrug. "It's good advertising."

I watched her walk away and wondered what she was hiding behind all that brittle perkiness. One day, I would ask—but not yet.

Kimberley had something for me too. I'd barely taken my seat in APUSH before she handed it over.

The attached card explained the gift, although I wasn't sure whether she'd included the details for me or her. I read aloud, "Here is a prepaid phone. One thousand minutes of usage and unlimited texts. Love, Kimberley and Teresa Rey."

I looked up. "This is great."

"That's what we thought. You need one for your new business."

"Ladies," Mr. Jarrett said, rapping on his desk. "May I start class now?"

"Certainly." Kimberley inclined her head regally.

I muffled a laugh. Mr. Jarrett had finally connected Kimberley with her important grandfather. The difference in Mr. Jarrett's attitude was great, not just for her, but for me. And since Mom had excused away all of my absences, I didn't have to worry about passing his class anymore. Which meant I'd graduate early as planned.

By late afternoon, the only person I cared about who hadn't wished me a happy birthday was Henry. Even though I made myself available to him, my brother stayed oddly quiet. He didn't mention my special day. He didn't hint about any presents. He just walked around, not meeting my eyes, acting overly nonchalant.

That raised my suspicions. Add that to the banging in the kitchen and I was pretty sure something had to be up. I went to find my mother.

She met me at the threshold, blocking my way. "Can you do me a favor?"

I tried to look over her shoulder. She shifted.

"Yeah, sure, Mom. What do you need?"

"Frozen green beans."

I made a face. "I hate green beans."

"They're not for you."

Behind me, there was a giggly little-boy snort.

"Can the green beans wait?"

"We want them tonight. Don't we, Henry?"

"Yes." He nodded repeatedly.

"Fine." I headed out the front door.

Fifteen minutes later, I was back with the package and a scowl. The lady in front of me in the express lane had cheated. Eight cans of tomato paste did not count as one item.

I could hear Henry whispering in the kitchen, or his version of whispering, which was pretty loud but not clear enough to make out the words. I stomped in there. "Listen—" I stopped.

"Surprise," Henry said, jumping up and down.

The kitchen had been draped with streamers. Balloons had been tied to my chair. Each plate had a piece of steak and a baked potato. In the middle of the table, there were cards, a vase of mums, and a large glass dish of my absolute favorite dessert, banana pudding.

"Thank you, guys." I slid onto the chair and refused—completely refused—to speculate on how much my mom had spent on the steak. Or where she got the money. "This is wonderful."

Henry hopped from foot to foot. "Open my card first. I made it myself."

"The very best kind." His card was silly and charming and definitely earned a kiss on the top of his shampoo-fresh head. The other cards were from my mother and my Linden grandparents (with a twenty-dollar bill tucked inside, which I might actually spend on myself for a change).

It was way nicer than I'd hoped for.

Mom sat beside me, eating tiny bites and listening to me and Henry talk. It was hard to know what was going on inside her head, but she hadn't seemed as depressed lately. Whether from the switch to tea or from hanging out with the incredibly nice and optimistic Mrs. Samm or from the volunteer work she was doing at a local thrift store, my mother's moods weren't quite so alarming anymore.

My brother finished his meal in a couple of gulps and then rested his chin on his forearms while he waited impatiently for me to finish mine. As I put the last forkful in my mouth, he said, "Are you ready for us to sing?"

The doorbell rang.

I pointed at my full mouth and then toward the front of the house. He blew out a noisy sigh and nodded his understanding.

Chewing quickly, I hurried to the front door and pulled it open. Eli stood there, shades on and hands behind his back.

I gave him a tentative smile. "Hey."

"Happy birthday." He held out an envelope. "I have something for you."

"How'd you know?"

"Henry. He's reminded me five times in the past week."

Heat rose in my face. "I'm sorry."

"It's okay. Really."

I stepped onto the porch, let the door swing shut behind me, and took the envelope. Inside was a heavy note card with fancy printing. A gift certificate to Rima's House of Henna.

He tapped it with his forefinger. "You used to have this tattoo on your wrist, and it was really...pretty. I thought you might like another one."

The gift was unexpected and so very thoughtful. Of course, I had Grant's bracelet on my wrist, and I never took it off. But I could try a tattoo somewhere else, like on my ankle. Or the palm of my hand. I smiled up at him. "This is incredibly nice. Thank you."

"Yeah. Well, see you." He turned to go.

"Wait, Eli." Things were changing between us. Even though we'd known each other since our freshman year, the past two months had been particularly intense. It felt like we'd really become friends. I opened the door wide. "Want to come in? We're about to have banana pudding."

He hesitated, his reaction hidden by the sunglasses. "Are you sure your family won't mind?"

"Positive."

He removed his shades. "Does the banana pudding have whipped cream or meringue?"

"Whipped cream. Of course."

He smiled. "Then I accept."

I was glad, really glad, that he was there. As I showed him to the kitchen, I couldn't help thinking that this birthday, which could've been so bad, had turned out perfect.

30

Top Of the List

The mystery about Josh's storage unit was finally solved on Halloween.

I'd been so busy that I'd forgotten about the key and the puzzle it represented. So when I pulled the letter from the mailbox, I thought at first that it was junk. But the company name tickled my brain until I gave it another glance. Westside Storage.

I ripped into the envelope, drew out the letter, and hastily skimmed it.

Dear Mr. Jones,

This is your final notice.

The lease on Storage Unit #142 expires on October 31. Please remove your possessions before November 15. After that date, the items will either be auctioned off or taken to the landfill. Your deposit will be forfeited...

"Mom," I shouted as I ran into the house, "where are you?"

"Kitchen."

I skidded to a stop. She and Henry were wrapping crispy rice bars in orange plastic wrap.

"Do you recognize a business called Westside Storage?"

She shrugged.

"Have we received any letters addressed to Josh recently?"

"If we did, I would've thrown them away."

I bit back a sigh. "Westside Storage was where Josh stored his stuff."

Mom looked up, a crease between her eyebrows. "How do you know?"

"Westside Storage has been sending us letters. They're going to throw his things out if we don't pick them up by November fifteenth."

"That's too fast." Her hand crept up to her mouth and plucked at her lips. She backed up a couple of steps and sat down hard on a chair. "I haven't had time to prepare. I can't look at his things yet." She plucked harder at her lips.

"I can do it. You don't have to come with me." I crossed the kitchen and knelt by her chair. "I'll bring the stuff home and store it in the studio. You don't have to look at a thing until you're ready."

The plucking slowed. "How soon?"

"Tonight."

Her hand dropped into her lap. "Do you think I can handle trick-or-treaters by myself?"

My brother looked first at my mother, then at me. She watched me steadily, eyes worried.

We'd passed the big hurdle of letting her take care of Henry again. I'd had no choice. Without Grant around, it had either been trust her or quit my job at The Reading Corner.

She'd done fine with Henry, but this would be another big step. I wasn't concerned, since she wouldn't really be alone. The neighbors would be around. Henry would be roaming the nearby streets with Reynolds, Mr. Samm, Mr. Taylor, and his three kids.

"Yes. I know you can do it." I nodded confidently, stood, and grabbed the car keys. "I don't know how long I'll be gone."

It took me fifteen minutes to get there. The guard barely looked my way as I drove through the gate. Unit #142 was near the front.

The key stuck a little. With effort, though, it turned and the lock slid open. I paused nervously, mind racing, scared and excited about what awaited me.

The door protested as I rolled it out of the way. I flicked on the lone light bulb and stepped into the space.

My first response was a sense of disappointment. I wasn't sure what I had expected, but the jumble of musty boxes, old lamps, and battered furniture had not been it.

I walked farther into the unit, caught between wanting to laugh and cry. There were no hidden treasures here. It was ordinary stuff.

Should I look through the cartons, or haul what I could home? I glanced at my watch. I had time. It wouldn't hurt to peek.

The first two boxes held grubby rags for staining wood. Weird. I pushed them to the side. They could go to the landfill.

The next box had antique carving tools. I'd forgotten about them. Josh had been psyched when he discovered the set at an estate sale. No way could I sell them. I carried them out to the car.

Cartons of papers and books followed. A crate held a dozen wooden candlesticks in various shapes and styles. We could sell these for a nice profit, if my mother could bear to part with them.

I pushed more boxes of junk to the side, all candidates for the landfill. Then I hesitated. There was a rocking chair at the back, one I'd never seen before. I approached it curiously, almost fearfully. The style was simple—but, oh, the wood! The grain was gorgeous and polished into a cherry red. A tag dangled from one arm. I flipped it over and found my stepfather's scrawl.

Merry Christmas, Crys
Love forever, Josh

He'd died two weeks before Thanksgiving, but he'd already made her Christmas present—and it was this beautiful rocking chair. When had Josh begun to experiment with making furniture?

Christmas had been horribly sad last year. We didn't put up a tree or decorations. Mom hadn't even emerged from her room most of the day. Santa came, of course, but he'd been unusually frugal. I'd already discovered our dire straits by then.

Had Santa left the real presents here?

Frantically, I pushed aside an old carpet and a pair of lampshades, desperately searching for other presents, but there were just more boxes of junk—until I reached the farthest corner. Under a beach towel, I caught a glint of something red and shiny. I surged toward it.

Josh had left two packages, wrapped in glossy red paper with big green bows and tags with our names on them. Henry's gift was huge and rattled slightly. I would definitely want to be there when he opened it.

Mine was smaller, yet surprisingly heavy for its size.

I couldn't wait to see it, but not in this dark cave of a room. Carefully, I carried the package to the car, set it on the passenger seat, and loosened the lid. My heartbeat ramped into overdrive and I backed away. As much as I wanted to see it, I was terrified too.

Okay. Deep breath. I lifted the lid. Whatever object was inside had been obscured by a wad of tissue paper. A note rested on top.

Lovely Lacey,
I'll bet you didn't expect to get a Mustang for Christmas this year.
Hope you enjoy this one.
Your adoring Josh

I tore the tissue paper aside. Nestled beneath it lay a small jewelry box of dark wood. Carved into its lid was a horse with its head thrown back and one hoof pawing the ground. Its rippling mane and tail had been inlaid with blond oak.

Josh had made me a mustang, not like the toy car my dad gave me, but Josh's own special kind.

When I'd answered the door last November and found a sheriff's deputy waiting for us—hat in hand—I didn't cry. When my mother collapsed screaming in the hospital as they shut off her husband's life support, I didn't cry. I survived the visitation, the funeral, and the sad-faced well-wishers swarming our house afterwards—all without tears.

I cried now.

Our Thanksgiving meal was simple this year. We'd made enough money on the shoes at the consignment shop that we were able to buy a turkey breast and a few trimmings, which was a good thing since I really did like leftover turkey.

Mom offered to do all of the cooking. There was no argument from me.

Eli volunteered to show up midafternoon, ready to help me with a last-minute batch of shoes. Sara's mom thought we might sell out during Black Friday sales, which was why I now sat on a stool in the studio, gazing wearily at fifty pairs of tiny shoes. "We'll never get done."

"We will," Eli said, brandishing the hot glue gun, "but we have to get going. When are we supposed to deliver them?"

"Seven o'clock tonight." I needed to move. The sneakers weren't going to decorate themselves. "Mrs. Tucker thinks half should have jewels, and the rest should have sequins and glitter paint for this extra batch." I looked to Eli for confirmation. "I think we'll do my half of the table in jewels."

"Whatever you say."

I picked up a mint-green pair. "What about silver crystals on these?"

"I am a guy. I have no opinion regarding the shoes worn by toddler girls." He made a manly grunt. "That is why I am holding the gun."

"Excellent. I prefer to be in charge anyway." I lined up six lavender sneakers. "Fire away."

Over the past month, we'd learned to function smoothly as a team. Eli had helped whenever he could. At first, he would only do assistant-type things—sweeping, stacking, cleaning. Recently, though, he'd graduated to creative participation on the production line. The glue gun was his specialty, a task I'd been glad to pass along.

For the next hour, we moved from pair to pair, doodling, gluing, glitter-painting. We worked so hard that we didn't even hear my mother until she cleared her throat. "Hi, guys."

Eli and I looked up, blinking our way back to reality.

"What is it, Mom?"

"Do you want some pumpkin pie? Henry and I are about to have a slice."

"Not yet." I rolled my head, trying to ease the knots in my neck. "Give us fifteen minutes." I smiled.

She smiled back, a little hesitantly. She'd made an effort today to look good, and she'd succeeded.

"Lacey?" Again, that catch in her voice. Was it fear? Resignation?

"Yeah, Mom?"

She held out a plastic grocery bag. "Here. I made these for you." She waited until I had it securely in my hands, then took off.

"What's in there?" Eli asked, stepping closer.

"I don't know." The bag contained blobs of fabric. No, make that lace. Little strands of lace. I pulled one out. "They're shoestrings."

With a snap of the wrist, I dumped the bag's contents onto the center of the table, excitement burning through me. There were hundreds of shoestrings of different lengths and widths. Most were white, but she'd included a few colors—blue, pink, orange, and yellow.

I glanced at Eli. Clearly, the delight of lace shoestrings eluded him.

"Little girls like this kind of stuff?" he asked.

"Oh, yes. Very much." I selected a pair of bejeweled sneakers that were already dry, threaded in my mother's creation, tied them into bows, and stepped back to admire. "It's absolutely adorable. Grandmas will go wild." I smiled up at him. "Isn't this wonderful? They're perfect, and *she* made them."

"If you say so."

"Trust me. It's true." This was a good sign. Small but good. I felt gratitude swelling inside me. "Thank you," I said as I gave Eli a quick hug.

"For what?"

"For being here. For helping. For…everything."

He nodded, his eyes studying my face. "It's been fun. Lacey?"

"Hi, everybody," Kimberley said from behind me.

Eli and I swung around to find Kimberley and Sean standing in the door.

"Hey," I said. "Come in." The two of them together was a surprise and likely very recent. Kimberley wouldn't have forgotten to mention something as important as hanging out with Sean. She'd been trying to get his attention for too long.

They came closer and studied the shoes.

"Can we help?" Kimberley asked as she picked up one of the lacy strings. "Shoelaces?"

"Yeah. Aren't they great?"

"They're perfect."

The guys exchanged glances. Eli held up the glue gun. "I like my job better."

Sean nodded. "I can see why."

"Come on. Let me show you…" Eli and Sean went to the opposite end of the table and bent over an unadorned pair of red shoes.

I tapped her arm. "What's up with that?"

"Sean?"

"Yeah."

"I asked him to spend the afternoon with me, and he said yes."

"Like dating?"

"I don't think so." She smiled with resignation. "He's being really sweet and friendly. Nothing more."

"I'm sorry." I watched him down the length of the table. He looked tired but happy.

"It's fine," she said. "Okay, tell me what I can do."

Before I could respond, though, my brother appeared in the door. "I'm ready for pie, but Mom says we can't get started until you and Eli come in."

I smiled. "Tell her we'll be right there, and we have two more guests."

"Will they want pie too?"

"Probably." Thank God that we had enough to share.

"Okay." He stomped away.

As I led my three friends to the house, I felt this surge of joy welling up within me. We hadn't celebrated last Thanksgiving at all, and even two months ago we couldn't afford a decent meal. There was so much that I was thankful for this year.

At the top of the list was Grant.

31

Best Gift Ever

On December twenty-first, Mr. and Dr. Harper left for a cruise around the Hawaiian Islands. Since Eli didn't want to go with them, Mom had invited him to spend Christmas with us.

Henry was ecstatic when he heard the news. Over the past month, he'd grown used to having his favorite coach around most afternoons. They usually kicked the ball in the backyard while I worked in the shoe factory. Eli claimed that my brother gave him a good workout, which he needed to build the strength back up in his knee.

I planned every detail to make this a wonderful Christmas Day. Food. Music. Presents. With Eli scheduled to arrive by seven, I'd set the alarm for six-thirty.

But it turned out to be unnecessary. I awakened five minutes early, instantly wired by excitement. After dressing, I crept down the stairs and stood in the hallway, listening hard. My mom and brother still slept.

I went first to the kitchen. There was a can of cinnamon rolls in the fridge awaiting their fate.

Next came the Christmas tree, silent and dark in the bay window of the living room. I flipped a switch and drank in the beauty of the ornaments and multicolored lights for the gazillionth time.

There weren't many presents under the tree. Santa had visited, of course, but he had to be smart again this year, since there wasn't too much spare money to go around. But at least there had been some. Cash flow wasn't quite as bad as I would've predicted a few months ago, for which I had the Tuckers to thank. They'd featured my sparkly toddler shoes in their consignment shop since October. Sales had been brisk. Word of mouth was a beautiful thing.

My mother got some of the credit too. Her fabulous shoelaces became the perfect signature for *Crystal & Lace Shoes*.

Mom was showing signs of progress, baby steps but in the right direction. She'd finally agreed to attend the survivors' support group that Mrs. Samm told her about, and had returned from her first visit a little more peaceful.

Our financial crisis wasn't over. I still worked at the bookstore. After I graduated in January, I'd be able to double production on the shoes, but it would be a while before we'd be as safe as I wanted us to be. Yet the family income now had sufficient funds to cover the bills and eat better. I had even worked out a reasonable payment plan with the hospital to cover Henry's emergency room visit. Success was the best gift ever.

I put on a pot of coffee for me and Eli and a teakettle of water for Mom. Then I peeked into the dining room to check the table settings. Everything was ready.

A quick glance at the clock let me know that Eli could be here any second. I grabbed a blanket and a small present and then unlocked the front door. A cold wind gusted, whipping a loose strand of hair across my face and rattling the leaves on the lawn. I sat on the top step and stared through the darkness at the stop sign near the end of the street, willing a black Mustang to appear.

As the sun made its first rosy streaks across the horizon, the faint hum of a car broke the silence. Moments later, Eli pulled into the driveway and got out, a smile on his face.

He set a stack of presents on the porch behind us and joined me on the top step. "Merry Christmas," I said.

"Merry Christmas to you too."

"Are those for us?"

"Yes."

"You got something for Henry?"

"Yes. And your mom."

"What a good boy you've been this year. I have something for you too." I handed over a small box. "Open it." I quivered with nerves.

He rested it on his lap as his face settled into a serious expression. "So, I have a question for you first."

"Okay."

He took a deep breath. "One of the guys on the varsity soccer team is throwing a New Year's Eve party, and I was wondering if you'd like to go with me."

Wow. I had begun to sense that his feelings were changing. It started a couple of weeks ago when he let me drive his Mustang. That was a big deal for him. It had made me wonder if he wanted more. Even now, I could see the hope warring with worry on his face, and I wanted him to be happy, especially on this day. But…this felt weird and nice and too soon. "As your date or as your friend?"

He looked away. "Your call."

It had been three months. Our friendship was important to me. Maybe it was time to see if I was ready. Eli was making it easy. No pressure. I leaned closer and kissed his cheek. "Yes, I'll go with you."

His eyes sought mine, shining with joy. "Great. That's… great. Yeah." Reaching behind him, he pushed the largest gift box forward. "This is yours. Go ahead and open it."

I pointed at the present on his lap. "You first."

"No, I insist. Ladies first."

"It is better to give than to receive."

"Okay. You win." He took the package, ripped off the comic-strip paper, and pulled out a hand-crocheted scarf in caramel brown.

"I made it myself," I said. "It's supposed to match your eyes."

He looped it around his neck. "Thank you."

"You don't have to wear it if you don't like it. I mean, I'm not very good yet and I understand you can do better—"

"It's amazing, Lacey," he interrupted. "No one's ever made me a gift before."

I leaned back to check his expression, which was gratifying and genuine. It was stupid to feel so pleased. "Really? You like it?"

"Yes, really. Now open yours."

The package seemed heavy for its size. "What do you have in here? Rocks?"

He smiled. "You'll see."

With an excited laugh, I slowly peeled the tape away from the paper. It was beautiful, expensive wrapping paper, metallic embossed gold, which I could reuse on other occasions for smaller gifts—an idea which had, no doubt, occurred to Eli.

The paper was forgotten when I realized what it hid. The music box. *My* music box. Grant's music box.

I stared in stunned silence, unable to believe my eyes.

Eli twisted the key. "I bought it, the same day you sold it." He lifted the lid.

Silent night, Holy night. All is calm, All is bright...

I put the lid down and laid my hands on the polished wood. I could feel a pulse. Grant was inside, perhaps listening to us. Emotions welled up within me, threatening to burst the dam I'd placed around my feelings for him.

How ironic. Eli returned Grant to me.

"Lacey?" There was uncertainty in Eli's voice.

"This is wonderful." Which was completely true. Somewhere inside here, Grant waited. With a single word, I could summon him. Be with him. Hold him.

How could something that I wanted so badly make me want to cry?

I'd released him all those months ago, so that he could continue with the life he was meant to live. And instead, he'd been waiting at Eli's house for me.

There was only one option available to me—find him a new assignment. He deserved his promotion, and the world deserved him. I knew plenty of people with problems to solve. The Tuckers, the Reys, Mrs. Williford, some of the folks in Mom's support group. I would find him the right place to be.

"Thank you." I put the music box down and smiled into Eli's anxious face. "I absolutely love that you got this music box for me. I can't even begin to tell you how much."

From within the house, pounding feet charged down the hallway. The door banged open as Henry shouted, "Lacey, when does Eli get here?"

We laughed.

"I'm here now," Eli said.

"Cool." Henry nodded before turning to me. "Lacey, have you seen the tree?"

"Yes."

"Have you seen what's under the tree?"

I shared a smile with Eli. "I don't know what you're talking about."

"Come and see." The door slammed shut and then squawked again. "Lacey, the oven is beeping."

"Oh, yeah. The cinnamon rolls."

Eli helped me up and then bent over to pick up the stack of gifts. "Come on. Let's go in."

"Can you help Henry check the rolls? I'd like to take the music box to my room."

"Sure."

We walked into the house together. Eli went straight into the living room while I continued to the attic stairwell.

"Henry, I'll need an oven mitt..." Eli's voice faded.

I reached my room, closed the door with my foot, and placed the music box in the center of my desk. Backing up, I perched on the edge of the bed and stared at my gift.

My feelings began to liquefy, oozing like warm syrup through my limbs. I longed for the sight of Grant, and I feared it. Would he be angry at his confinement? Would he be happy to see me? How much had he heard?

The clock ticked downstairs. Henry would be up here after me soon. It was time. "Grant?"

The tornado swirled and cleared. He stood before me, alert and wary, hands behind his back in his subservient stance.

"Hey." I stood too.

"Yes, Mistress?"

He was hurting. His eyes seemed to be glazed with pain.

I was hurting too. For months, I'd thought he was lost to me forever. Seeing him now was beautiful and agonizing. It was all I could do to keep from grabbing him and never letting go. "I'm not your mistress anymore."

"As long as I owe you wishes, you are."

That was unexpected, since he'd been out of my reach since September. "What about Eli? Doesn't he get wishes?"

"My boss doesn't activate a new assignment until he is sure the possessor intends to keep the box. In Eli's case, it was clear from the beginning that he intended to give it away."

"So you've had a break?"

"Yes. I've stayed busy with meetings and my studies."

We were being too polite. Too impersonal. Why did it have to be this way? Why couldn't I have fallen in love with someone who could love me back, free and clear? I took a step closer, aching to touch him, to be held. "How are you?"

"Well." His gaze dropped to the copper bracelet on my wrist and then flicked back up. "Have you replaced me with Eli?"

I shook my head. "I can't replace you, Grant. *Ever.*"

"But you have moved on."

"No, I haven't. Not yet."

He breathed in sharply and then exhaled through his mouth. A lonely sound.

Okay, that was enough. I wanted to touch him, and I would. If he rejected me, it would be worth it. Reaching for him, I slid my arms about his waist and pressed my face to his chest. Beneath my cheek, his heart quickened its pace. I braced myself to be pushed away.

"Lacey," he said in a strangled voice. There was a moment's hesitation, and then his arms enclosed me in a light embrace. "What are we doing?"

"I've missed you," I murmured.

"I've missed you too." He shuddered. "I didn't want this."

"Please try to understand."

"I do."

"Really?"

He nodded against my hair. "I didn't when we parted, but I understand now."

That wasn't quite forgiveness, but I'd take it. "Have you learned more about being chosen?" I looked up into his face.

"Yes."

"Was I a blemish?"

"No. You are perfect." He smiled sadly. "However, the leave of absence would have been a blemish."

A tight ball of sorrow eased within me. Here was confirmation that my decision hadn't been a waste. "So being chosen is still a possibility for you?"

"As far as I know, yes." His hand cupped my face. "Thank you."

This time, my smile was wide and hopeful. He smiled back, the sadness fading.

"Okay, then." I stepped away from him and squared my shoulders in my most businesslike manner. "It's time for you to be promoted to principal. May I suggest a friend for your next assignment?"

"You may."

"Would your boss approve of Kimberley?"

"Kimberley?" Grant's brow creased. "Because of the cancer?"

"How do you know about that?"

"My boss and I have discussed all of your friends."

All of them? How many had they included?

Never mind. Did not want to know.

I would take it as a good sign that Grant already knew about Kimberley. Maybe this meant she was pre-approved. "Then you know that she had leukemia at age seven and that the chemo affected her brain."

"Yes, I do." He sounded professional, competent, as if talking about his job felt good. "She will present unusual difficulties, but I am certain we can help her."

Okay, here came the hard part. The thing that we both had to acknowledge and get through. "We would see each other sometimes."

He nodded, his calm expression firmly in place. "Will you keep the music box?"

"I would like to." I loved it. The music box brought me and Grant together. I didn't want to give it up.

He inclined his head. "When should I be ready?"

"Probably this week, as soon as I find you a nice place to live." There were several possibilities. A Christmas ornament shaped like a house. A snow globe with a castle. An old Barbie dollhouse—although that one might be especially hard to slide past Teresa Rey without a lot of explanation.

"I shall be waiting."

I clasped both of his hands with mine, reluctant to let go. Knowing that I must.

He leaned forward and kissed my brow. I closed my eyes and memorized the feel of it.

"Hey, Lacey," my brother yelled up the stairwell. "What's taking you so long?"

"Be right there," I called. After one final squeeze, I released Grant's hands. "I've got to go."

"Lacey." He looked away, took a deep breath, and then met my gaze again. "Would you like a final wish?"

My last wish. I walked slowly to the door and paused. I could hear Eli, Henry, and Mom in the kitchen, preparing breakfast. Someone had turned on a Christmas CD. It was exactly right. There was nothing else I wanted, at least not for me.

I smiled at Grant. "I wish you well."

Acknowledgements

This was the little book that could. It was my first fully realized novel. It took six years and dozens of rewrites to go from concept to publication. It's hard to count the number of people who helped, but I'll try. Thank you to all of the contest judges who critiqued this book. Your feedback—kind or not—made the story stronger. To Laura Steckbeck, Laura Ownbey, Anna Masrud, Anna Rodriguez, Hannah Brodie, and Sabrina, your comments were invaluable; it won't take much effort to see your suggestions throughout. To Tia, Tom, and Mark, thanks for extraordinary patience in the face of my curiosity. To my writing buddies in RomVets, RWA, Rubies, HCRW, Capital Eyes, and Retreaters, thank you for having my back. To Jessica, Rich, and Spencer Hill Press, I am so glad to be in a publishing family that takes such good care of its authors. To my amazing agent, Kevan Lyon, I'm grateful that you didn't give up on this one! But mostly, to Amy, Julianna, and Rick—it took love, faith, and understanding to give me the freedom to write. There are no words.

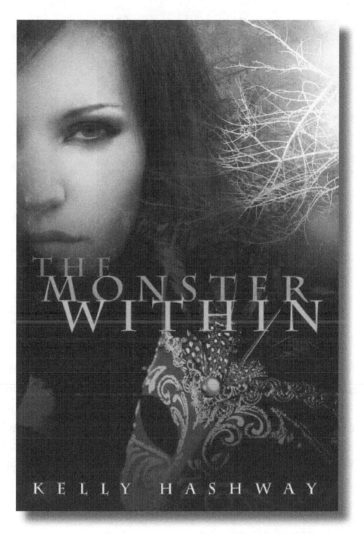

The moment seventeen-year-old Samantha Thompson
crawls out of her grave, her second chance at life
begins... Only Sam came back wrong.

SPENCER HILL PRESS · spencerhillpress.com

About the Author

Photo by Liza Lucas

Elizabeth lives in North Carolina (midway between the beaches and the mountains) with two daughters, one husband, and too many computers. When she's not writing software or stories, Elizabeth loves to travel, watch dance reality shows, and argue with her family over which restaurant to visit next. She is also the author of the *Whisper Falls* series; *I Wish* is the first book in her new series.

CPSIA information can be obtained at www.ICGtesting.com
Printed in the USA
LVOW05s2344011114

411631LV00004B/5/P